I0831496

**Her only hope for justice is the man she will never trust...**

Sarah Thomas has sworn to avenge her mother's fate at the the hands of a corrupt legal system. When she gets her chance to go up against Haley National Bank in a quest to save her clients' homes, she finds the fight she has been looking for her entire life.

Nathan Haley grew up helping his father rebuild a broken town one paycheck, one investor and one mortgage at a time. But his father leaves the bank to Gavin Neilson, the last man Nathan could ever imagine his father trusting.

She's out for justice. He's fighting to save his family's legacy. But he is the kind of man she will never trust. And if he can't convince her to see beyond her own past, they'll never find the only thing that can save them both - each other.

Also by Michael J Lawrence

Novels:

*Firestorm*
*Broken Wing*
*Protocol Zero*
*The Terran Mandate*
*Unchosen*
*Two Before Me*
*Breaking Silence*

Short fiction:

*Box in Snow*
*Helot*
*A Sudden Change*
*The War was Far Away*
*I remember the First Time I Saw Her*
*And All Our Yesterdays*
*We Went Too Far*
*Dark Winds*
*Marsha's Last Stand*
*War Widow*
*48 Hours*
*RST*
*The Last Architect*

MICHAEL J LAWRENCE

# THE PRICE WE PAY

Copyright © 2025 Michael J Lawrence
All rights reserved

ISBN-13 979-8-9928748-0-8

No part of this book may be reproduced, or stored in a retrieval system, or transmitted in any form or by any means, electronic, mechanical, photocopying, recording or otherwise, without express written permission of the author.

Transfer or copying of any part of this work to any digital medium, computer or data processing system for the purposes of AI training or machine learning is explicitly prohibited.

The characters and events portrayed in this book are fictitious. Any similarity to real persons, living or dead, is coincidental and not intended by the author.

Cover art:
Portrait by Enrique Meseguer
Statue by Skycinema

Edited by Amy Davis

For my mother, who never lost a case and enjoys a good Nurse Jane book. You are my hero.

And for my friend Elisa, who stood upon the rampart to hand me sword and shield even as defeat was all but certain.

# *PROLOG*

When she was twelve years old, Sarah Thomas sat by her grandmother's kitchen window and watched a sky full of snow, dreaming of the better world that had to be hidden behind its icy curtains.

She wrapped the hand-knitted shawl tighter around her shoulders and basked in the warmth wafting in from the fireplace in the living room. It was a real fireplace where they burned oak and cedar so you could hear the wood pop and crackle and smell its scent filling the room.

This was why Sarah loved winter so much. The smell of cookies and cedar while she was safely ensconced in a warm house looking out at an icy world where the slate had been wiped clean and anything was possible.

It wasn't that she felt like an orphan. It was more like she felt she was trapped in a life that would somehow be better some day. She lived with her mother, a woman who worked two jobs to support them and, as Sarah would later learn, to save for Sarah's education.

On days like this when her mother was working two shifts, Sarah stayed with her grandmother. The single-wide that she and her mother lived in had thin walls that let the cold seep in and snow whistle through the cracks of the outside door even when it was closed. The whole thing would shake and shimmy when the wind blew hard enough. She loved her mother, but the trailer was just a place where they lived. It wasn't a place Sarah could call home.

But her grandmother's house was sturdy and old, withstood the wind and kept out the cold so she could stare at the sky full of snow instead of hide away from it.

Soon enough her mother would come by to pick her up and take her back to the trailer and do her best to cook her dinner with cheap groceries from the only market still open when she got off work. Fish sticks and canned green beans.

Nothing like the hand-made chicken pot pie with a thick crumbly crust her grandmother made. Or the same crust covering a home-made peach cobbler like a blanket. Sarah always giggled when she tore the crust away to see steam wafting from the sliced peaches and sauce inside.

Sarah would have loved to call her grandmother's house her home. But she knew she couldn't. It wasn't where she lived. It wasn't where she curled up under that same hand-knit shawl and a thin blanket to ward off the cold seeping through her bedroom walls. She and her mother were a team and she knew they were doing the best they could. And that some day, Sarah would find a world for them both. A world where her mother didn't have to work two shifts. A world where they had their own house with a fireplace and cedar firewood.

A place hidden away by the white icy fairies drifting through the sky. A place they could call home.

Caught up in her reverie, Sarah flinched when somebody knocked at the door. She threw the shawl off her shoulders, leapt to her feet and ran for the door.

As always, her grandmother hobbled over and pulled her away. "Let me get that dear."

Sarah peeked around her grandmother, anxious to see her mother's face when the door opened.

Instead she saw black pants and a wooden stick. As her gaze drifted upwards, Sarah saw a blue shirt with a gold badge and then a stern face with eyes hidden behind mirrored sunglasses. All topped by a brown, wide-brimmed hat.

"Oh my goodness, Sheriff Rosley," her grandmother said. She stepped back, opened the door wider and said, "Come in out of that cold. Don't they give you a coat to wear in this weather?"

The man stepped inside, a flurry of snow following him in to scurry across the front entrance. He tipped his hat, looked at Sarah, then took off his sunglasses.

Turning back to Sarah's grandmother, he said, "Something's come up." He gestured towards the living room.

"Oh," her grandmother said. "Of course." Sarah started to follow them into the living room when the Sheriff glanced down at Sarah. Her grandmother stopped and said, "Why don't you go wait in the kitchen, sweetie. We won't be long." Sarah recognized the smile her grandmother showed her - the one that tried to hide something.

Sarah leaned towards the living room as the sheriff and her grandmother walked to her grandfather's chair on the other side of the room. He grabbed his cane and pulled himself out of the chair. The three of them huddled together while the sheriff spoke in a low voice and gently weaved the air with his hand. Her grandfather looked at Sarah for a moment, then turned his eyes away.

Then they stopped talking and all three of them looked at Sarah as her grandmother hobbled back across the living room towards her.

Her grandmother stopped in front of her and let out a sigh. She didn't smile this time.

"Sweetie, I'm afraid we have some bad news."

## *THE SHADOW*

It turned out that making money the easy way wasn't as easy as Gavin Neilsen had thought it would be.

Left high and dry during the CDO market crash in 2008, Gavin had sworn he would never again be left holding the bag while everyone else drove off into the sunset with what should have been his money. Especially when they drove off with his wife, too.

How many of those people who had smiled at him and shaken his hand were now lounging in the Caribbean instead of rotting in a prison as they deserved?

Not a one. Crime, it seemed, did pay, and Gavin was not about to be left out.

The problem was the cash flow statement sitting on his desk. Not only did he owe, but he owed to the wrong kind of person. The people he had watched flee New York might be basking in the sun, but they weren't killers.

He was pretty sure Olivia Banishaw was. He had never met the woman, but the sound of her cool husky voice reverberated in his memory. *You need to make sure I get my money. Everything else is excuses*. She hadn't said anything for a long moment after that. He had remembered watching the seconds tick by on his computer's clock. *And I don't like excuses.*

And now he watched a drop of sweat splash against the cash flow report sitting on his desk. Leaning his forehead against the palm of his hand, he could not will the numbers to line up the way they needed to.

It should have been easy enough. Place the cash. Co-mingle it with legitimate holdings of the bank and take a cut. Olivia had staked him for all that, but it wasn't working out. Bitcoin. Casinos on every corner in America. These were the ways in which criminal enterprises were laundering money these days. Some people still preferred the old-fashioned way where they could talk to somebody and see their money on a clean bank statement. There just weren't enough of them.

And now the numbers weren't lining up.

Gavin leaned back in his leather chair, picked up the half glass of Seagram's sitting next to the paperwork and slugged it back, focusing on the burn as it trickled down his throat. He wondered for a moment if that's how it would feel if somebody put a knife to it.

He shook his head and lay his palm on a different stack of papers. He patted them gently, as if they were an old friend. He wished he had thought of it sooner. Writing mortgages was a natural act for a bank. And selling them was an everyday occurrence that nobody would notice.

As long as Nathan didn't get wind of what he was doing. That kid was a pain in his ass, but his old man had written it into the contract when he sold the bank to Gavin: his son would stay on as Vice President. A corporate officer who could make decisions for the bank. Somebody who could get in the way. And there was no question about it - Nathan was the kind of soft-hearted sap who would get in the way if he had known what Gavin was up to.

He clenched his jaw and gently tapped the desk with his fist when he felt a flutter of remorse about the hundred or so families he was going to have to put on the street to make it happen.

But they were like Nathan and anything else that got between him and paying off Olivia. They were excuses.

# *THE LAWYER*

Sarah Thomas walked into the Emmerson Community Legal Clinic and stopped dead in her tracks. She knew that public service law was austere, but her new surroundings were a shock, even to her.

Linoleum tiles curled at the edges in the small waiting area where a few plastic chairs lined the meager wall space. A wooden clapboard on squeaky hinges was closed over a small gap between two half-walls guarding the entrance into the clinic.

Sarah raised the clapboard, stepped through and let it slap back down. There were only three people in the office and none of them seemed to notice.

Two young men - boys, really - sat at scratched and dented tank desks from World War II, tapping away at their laptops and scribbling on yellow legal pads. She knew they would be gone in six months, after they had added a bullet for community service to their resumés. After that, they would never see another public service case except for a rotation on pro bono work for whatever glitzy law firm they landed at. Sarah would still be at the clinic after they were gone. And after the next batch was gone.

She surveyed the worn blue carpet with more runs than carpet. She could make out the vague streaks where somebody had run a vacuum cleaner. The walls were dingy with gouges and scratches in paint that had to be older than she was, but they were clean.

No, Sarah would still be here in six months. And probably in six years. This was why she had become a lawyer. She took a deep breath and smiled. This was where she belonged. This was where people who had nowhere else to turn would come for help. She was home.

A slender black woman stood up from her desk sitting next to the far wall. Her softly curled black hair cascaded to her shoulders and she wore black-rimmed glasses. She picked up a file from her desk, came at Sarah in a brisk lanky stride, smiled and stuck out her hand.

"You must be our new girl."

"Or lawyer," Sarah said.

The woman's smile faded and her eyes glazed over. "Right." They shook hands and she said, "Welcome to Emmerson. Your desk is right over there. Sarah looked over her shoulder to see an empty tank desk with a stack of papers abandoned in a small wooden box and a laptop. The chair was upholstered in dark green plastic with a crack running right down the middle.

Looking back at the woman, Sarah said, "OK."

"Maureen," the woman said. "Maureen Henderson. I'm the Chief Legal Assistant."

Sarah looked around, confirming that there were only the two lawyers in the room besides them.

"Where's the staff?" she asked.

"We're a little short-handed right now." Maureen handed Sarah the file. "And this is your first case."

"Oh," Sarah said. "Um, OK." She took the file and said, "I was kind of expecting some kind of orientation."

"Yeah." Maureen gestured behind Sarah. "Like I said, that's your desk over there." She turned her hand towards the back wall and a small table with a coffee maker, instant coffee, plastic cups and condiments. "Over there is the coffee." She then pointed at a windowless corner office with a steel door that was closed. "And that's Stanley's office." She didn't say anything more, as if Sarah was supposed to know who Stanley was.

"Who is -"

"Stanley is Chief Counsel."

Sarah stood in silence for a moment, waiting for Maureen to say something more. Instead the woman raised a brow impatiently.

"Anything else?" Sarah asked.

"Yeah. Your first case. There's your desk. Go."

Sarah scanned the room. There wasn't a single bookcase to be found. "Statutes?"

"Lexis. Password is taped on the bottom of your laptop."

"I prefer the books," Sarah said.

"There's a legal library downtown."

Sarah stood in silence again, waiting for Maureen to say something more. "I guess I'll head down there, then."

Maureen took a step forward, smiled disarmingly and said, "I'm not sure you understand. You need to go to your desk - " She again pointed at the empty desk behind Sarah. -" that one over there, sit down and get ready for your hearing."

"I think I could get more done at the library."

Just then, a young woman with paper-white skin and freckles with a two-year-old on her hip walked in the door.

"That would be nice," Maureen said. "But right now you don't have time." She gestured towards the woman. "Because your client has just arrived."

"Oh," Sarah said. "I guess I better -"

"Hold on a sec," Maureen said, waving the woman over.

"Sarah Thomas, your client Angela Ferguson." Sarah looked briefly at the girl's tired eyes and then her son, who looked around the room with blissful curiosity, not knowing what his mother was going through.

"Um, OK," Sarah said, turning towards her desk. She laid down her purse, looked around for a chair and seeing none, said, "I guess just stand here Ms. Ferguson, and we'll get started."

Angela looked at her watch and readjusted her son's perch on her hip. "Do we really have time for that?"

Sarah shot a glance at Maureen. "When's the hearing?"

"An hour," Maureen said. "You need to go now." The smirk on Maureen's face sparked a thin sizzle along Sarah's forearm. Sarah had met her kind before. Somebody with an axe to grind who stroked her ego by putting people in their place. Except Sarah Thomas didn't belong in any place that she didn't choose for herself.

"I haven't even looked at this case."

"Yeah, because you didn't go to your desk when I told you to."

At this, Sarah held up her index finger. "Hold on for just a minute, Ms. Ferguson." She approached Maureen. "Can we talk over here for a minute?" She headed for the coffee table and waited for Maureen.

"What are you doing?" she asked.

"Trying to get you to do your job," Maureen said.

"You can't treat me like this. If I'm going to do my job properly, I need time and resources. I know this is community service, but surely we can scrape together a law library from eBay or something." She paused, took a breath and said, "and I am a lawyer. I don't need a parade or anything, but I am due simple courtesy."

Maureen laughed. "Oh, you think you're a lawyer do you?"

"Yes."

"You passed the bar, right?"

"Yes."

"Good for you. How many times have you been in front of a judge in a real courtroom?"

"Just because I don't have experience -"

Maureen put up her hand. She stepped over to her desk and picked up a thick stack of papers. "You know what these are?"

Sarah saw Angela check her watch again. Sarah felt the sizzle again. "How is it that I don't have time to prepare my case, but we have time for whatever that is?" Sarah pointed at the stack of papers in Maureen's hand.

"You brought us back here, counselor. And these are applications for your job. Young eager lawyers just like you who want to do their six-month tour at a legal clinic." She slapped the papers down on her desk. "You're not entitled to special treatment, Ms. Thomas. There's the door. I can have your replacement here in an hour."

"That's why your recruiter called me six times then?"

"You don't know what you're doing yet," Maureen said a little too loudly. The two lawyer-boys briefly looked up, smirked and went back to their work. "And you don't have time to stand here and argue with me. Your client is waiting. And so is the judge."

"How am I supposed to represent her if I can't even prepare my case?"

"Do you see any other lawyers around here without something else to do? You do like the rest. You prepare in the backseat of an Uber."

Sarah let out an exasperated sigh. "You're kidding."

"Have I given you the impression of being somebody with a sense of humor?" Maureen adjusted her glasses while she glared at Sarah. "Are you going to help or not?"

"No, you do not." Sarah shook her head, grabbed her purse and headed for the door. "Come with me, Ms. Ferguson."

## *THE BANKER*

Nathan Haley was just starting to settle into his morning routing when the wide oak door to his office opened and Devorah Harlow strode the fifteen feet from the door to his rosewood desk. Keeping his head down, Nathan tried not to notice.

Devorah stopped just a foot short of his desk. “Nathan.”

Wishing he could just ignore her, Nathan looked up to see her beaming at him. Devorah was a tall woman with a lean hard body and none of the curves in any of the right places. He never understood why so many men were vulnerable to her wiles. Probably because of the black skirt cut just above her knees that hugged her slender hips and the blouse that perpetually revealed just enough lace on her bra to invite a glance. Her hair was jet black and fell straight down to just between her shoulder blades with bangs covering her forehead. Her makeup always looked like she had just gotten a makeover. Overall, she looked like the picture on a box of hair dye.

Uninvited, she sat down on the corner of his desk, flipped her hair behind her shoulder and smiled. “What say we get a drink tonight?” she asked.

Nathan grabbed a pen and started scribbling on a pad just to look busy. “We’ve been over this. I don’t date the help.”

Devorah’s smile faded. “The help?” She leaned closer. “Is that what you really think of me? The Director of Financial Services, just ‘the help’?”

“You know what I mean. Company ink.”

“It’s just a drink, Nathan. Geez.”

“I’m a VP. You’re a Director. You know how it works.”

“And how long do you think you’ll be a VP if you’re not willing to be friends, Nathan? The only reason you’re still a VP is because of me.”

This again. Nathan looked up, leaned back in his chair and said, “The only reason I’m still a VP is because it’s in the contract.”

"There are ways around that. You're not bullet proof."

"I don't have to be bullet proof. I just have to be honest and useful. And don't ask - my shares aren't for sale."

Devorah slowly weaved her head back and forth. "Oh come on, don't be like that. I didn't come in here for a fight. Just come have a drink with me. It's not like you have anything better to do."

"Yeah, I do."

"What?"

"Work. Something you should look into."

"Now you're just being rude. I work plenty."

"Then where are those applications I asked for two days ago?"

Devorah sighed, her eyes darting to the side for a moment. "You don't need to worry about those, Nathan. I looked them over. They're fine. You have more important things to worry about, I'm sure." She shifted even closer. "All work and no play -" She smiled and ran a finger across her chin.

"God, you really are shameless, aren't you?"

Devorah pulled her head back and sniffed. "You know, I do have feelings. And I'm not sure hurting them would be in your best interest."

"As much fun as this is, Ms. Harlow, I really do have some work to do. So unless you've brought me something useful, you should probably go now."

She stood up, smoothed down her skirt and tapped her foot. "You know," she said, "one of these days you're going to look back and realize you had the chance to be my friend. That opportunity won't last forever."

Weary of the game, Nathan asked, "What did Gavin send you in here for?"

Devorah's gaze narrowed for a moment. She didn't like being called out. "Just to let you know that the applications are in good order and that you don't need to worry about them."

Nathan knew this to mean that they didn't want him to see them and that he should mind his own business.

But Haley National was his business. Even if Gavin had bought his father out, his family's name still adorned the front door. And he wasn't about to trust that legacy to one Devorah Harlow.

"That's fine. Tell Gavin thanks."

"What about our drink?"

Nathan went back to scribbling on his pad. "Good morning, Ms. Harlow. That will be all."

She stood up, stared at him for a moment and when he didn't say anything more, she gave up, turned and strutted towards the door.

At the door, she stopped, turned and said, “Oh, and one other thing.”

Nathan looked up to see her tilt her head coyly. She wrapped the strap of the security badge hanging from her neck around her index finger. “You have a new security badge. Maggie has it when you’re ready.”

“Why do I need a new security badge?”

“See, that’s just the sort of thing you would know if you and I could have a drink.” She slipped through the door, closing it quietly behind her.

## *NO DEAL*

The papers fell out of the file and spilled onto the seat between Sarah and Angela when their Uber driver swerved to avoid a stray pedestrian. Sarah shuffled them back into the file and continued reading.

For all her bluster, Maureen had done a fine job organizing the file. The complaint was simple enough - her client wanted her heating fixed because it was starting to get cold out. The appropriate statutes, along with pertinent case law, were printed out and clipped to the complaint. There were no instructions on what to do, but it was a simple tenant dispute that Sarah would have no problem arguing. She sighed and closed the file.

Noticing that Angela was staring out the window with a worried look on her face, Sarah reached across her son sitting between them and took Angela's hand. "Don't worry. This is a very simple case. Everything will be fine."

Angela turned towards her, looking dejected and Sarah realized that the woman didn't trust her. "Will it?"

With Angela and her son in tow, Sarah worked her way down the crowded corridor of the courthouse. She glanced at the file again: room 14K. Was that room 14 or something on the 14th floor? She didn't know and was hoping to find a directory of some kind when a man in a blue polyester suit and mismatched striped tie stepped up to her.

He took out a handkerchief and mopped his brow. "Sarah Thomas?"

Sarah stopped and studied him briefly. "Who's asking?"

The man stuck out his chubby hand. "Robert Calhoun. But most folks just call me Calhoun."

Without taking his hand, she asked, "And you are?"

"Opposing counsel. For your hearing this morning? Something about a furnace."

"Alright." Sarah studied the man for a moment. He looked like he was trying to sell her something. "Pleased to meet you." She briefly shook his hand then looked around and bit her lip, cursing the fact that she was going to have to ask him. "It's my first day. Could you tell me where this courtroom is?"

Calhoun casually waved his hand. "Oh, hell, don't worry about that. We won't need any of that."

"What do you mean?"

"Well," Calhoun said, smiling, "this is really just a simple misunderstanding."

"Her furnace is broken and your client won't fix it."

"Oh, that's not true." Calhoun's smile broadened. "He's just waiting on parts. Look, he'll credit her a full month's rent if she can hold on for just two more weeks."

At this, Angela perked up and said, "Yes, a rent credit sounds good."

For the first time since meeting her, Sarah noticed a hopeful look in the woman's eyes. "Hold on."

Turning to Calhoun, she asked, "And what does your client want in return?"

"Just a withdrawal of the complaint. See, it looks bad to the PHA and he really doesn't need that kind of trouble." Smiling at Angela, he said, "Ms. Ferguson here can save a little money and my client can get on with the business of helping people in need. What do you say?"

Sarah scoffed. "I say this. If I withdraw the complaint and your guy doesn't come through, then we're right back to square one."

"I'm sure the judge will sign off on it," Calhoun said, "If you're worried about making it formal and all."

Angela tugged on Sarah's sleeve. "A month's rent sounds good to me. We have blankets. I think we should make the deal."

Sarah frowned. "Wait here." She pulled Calhoun aside and said, "I may be new around here, but I know a song and dance when I see one. Your client just doesn't want to get in front of the judge."

"No doubt about that," Calhoun said.

"Then he should have thought about that before neglecting due diligence to make sure my client's apartment is in proper working order."

"Look," Calhoun said. "The judge has a full docket. He really doesn't like to take up his time with something you and I can work out here in the hallway. He would prefer that we handle it out here. Trust me."

"And why should I do that?"

"You never know when you're going to need the judge to pay attention in a real case. He remembers this sort of thing. He runs a tight ship and frankly we don't need him to listen to me make this offer in court just so he can say yes."

"No, Mr. Calhoun. This is how it's going to work. Your client is in statutory violation. That means fines, penalties and a report. That's just the sort of thing that seems to me to be a deterrent against him ignoring people like my client in the future. He has a duty. He failed to meet it. He needs to face the consequences, not get some two week pass for a few bucks under the table. That's called justice."

Amused, Calhoun's smile thinned. "Wow, you must have been something else in moot court. Look. This isn't the Nuremberg trials. Cut the guy a break. He cuts you a break. Trust me, it's better than what you're going to get from the judge."

Sarah considered him carefully, nodding slowly. "Yeah, trust you. Just what I've heard all my life. Trust somebody doing the wrong thing to take care of the people suffering because of it. No deal. We're going to court."

Sarah turned on her heel, grabbed Angela and continued down the hall in search of room 14K.

"I really think we should take the deal, Ms. Thomas," Angela said.

"Don't worry about it. Everything is fine."

## *JUDGEMENT*

The courtroom was small and awash in the constant din of chatter from the gallery. The judge was shuffling papers and talking to his legal aid. With Angela in tow, Sarah worked her way into the center aisle and walked towards the bar.

Once they reached the bar, she stopped and looked at it for a moment. The bar exam was literally a test to allow her to walk past this physical barrier between the court well and the rest of the world. With some solemnity, she placed her hand on the wooden banister and swung it open. For the first time in her life, Sarah Thomas, Esquire, was breaching the sanctuary of the well as she exercised her privilege of walking past the bar. She couldn't help smiling, knowing that she would remember this moment for the rest of her life.

As she looked around, nobody seemed to notice. The gallery continued squawking. The judge continued his conversation with his legal aid. The bailiff came in from a side door and took up his position next to the bench.

Sarah pointed at a seat behind the plaintiff's table. "Sit here," she whispered to Angela, who took the seat and let her son sit on her lap.

Sarah sat down next to her, placed her purse and the file on the table and folded her hands. She glanced at Calhoun as he settled in behind the defendant's table. He nodded and gave her a quick salute. She couldn't help feeling that he was laughing at her.

The judge dismissed his legal aid and turned his attention to the well. He motioned towards the bailiff, who handed him the docket file. The judge skimmed over it, then looked at Sarah over the rims of his glasses.

Without so much as an introduction, he asked, "What do we have here?" Sarah looked around, not knowing who he was talking to. "You there, counselor," he said, pointing at Sarah, "what do we have here?"

Sarah cleared her throat stood up, and started to walk towards the podium. The judge waved his hand and said, "You're fine right there. I can hear you from there."

The lack of decorum threw her off balance for a moment as the judge stared at her blankly. When he arched a brow, Sarah cleared her throat again and said, "Your honor, what we have here is a statutory violation regarding landlord's responsibility to maintain a habitable residence for my client."

The judge looked at the file. "Says here that the furnace is broken."

"That's right, your honor. And it's getting cold out."

"So why are we here?"

Sarah studied the man for a moment, at a loss of how to respond. She was used to citing statutes and case law in support of a legal theory, not explaining to a judge what his job was.

"To compel the defendant to meet his statutory responsibilities and fix the furnace." She paused, unable to keep from scrunching up her forehead as she looked at him. "Your honor."

For his part, the judge looked at her with a blank expression, as if he were confused. His gaze still fixed on Sarah, he said, "Mr. Calhoun?"

Calhoun stood up. "Your honor, we're waiting for parts. We'll have the furnace fixed in two weeks. If Ms. Thomas is willing to withdraw the complaint, my client is prepared to give the plaintiff a full month's rent in rebate."

The judge set down the file. "Well, there we go." Sarah watched transfixed as he picked up his gavel.

Just as he was about to hit the strike plate, she said, "No sir."

The judge stopped short and glared at her over the rims of his glasses. "What was that?"

"No sir. That is a settlement offer and we're not willing accept it. I want summary judgment on this matter."

The judge laid the gavel down and leaned back in his chair. "I don't understand Ms. Thomas. The defendant is willing to comply with your request and give your client a break on the rent, which he is not required to do by law. Not to mention how much money it will save the tax payers if we forego a judgment. Why would you refuse the deal?"

Unprepared for such an absurd question, Sarah could only tell him the truth. "Because I don't want him to get away with it, sir. He needs to know, through the force of law, that he can't just ignore his tenants. He has a responsibility here."

"It seems to me that he's offered to meet that responsibility."

Sarah felt the sizzle along her forearm and gently bit her tongue. She knew she had to control her anger. She also knew that she was right. "Begging your pardon, your honor, but do you have an interest in this matter, sir?"

The judge spoke in a low, fatherly tone. "Watch yourself counselor. I understand you have your Irish up, but you are an officer in my court, not the other way around."

"You're making an argument for the settlement. You're testifying."

"That's enough, Ms. Thomas. You want your pound of flesh, is that it?"

"Yes sir. I want justice done."

The judge looked at Calhoun, who shrugged and sat back down.

"Alright," the judge said, "Here's the deal. In accordance with the law. Mr. Calhoun, your client has thirty days to cure his breach of due care for his tenancy. By such date, I expect a report from him and confirmation from Ms. Thomas here that the furnace has been repaired and is in proper working order."

Sarah's jaw dropped. "Your honor."

The judge slammed his gavel down and bellowed, "So ordered." Then, in a calmer voice, he said, "You just won, counselor. I have rendered summary judgment in accordance with the law. If you find that I have not fulfilled *my* duty under the law, you are free to appeal my decision. Next case."

Sarah traipsed down the corridor, Angela trailing by several steps. Then she heard her client say, "Wait a minute."

Sarah turned to face her. "Yes?"

"What am I supposed to do for thirty days while I wait for my heat to come back on?"

"I'm sorry. I - " Sarah looked at her shoes. Then she forced herself to look her client straight in the eye. "I - " But Sarah didn't know what to tell her client. All she could see was Angela and her son huddled under blankets in a cold apartment, looking back at her, wondering why Sarah hadn't saved them.

"You should have taken the deal," Angela said.

She pushed past Sarah and walked out of the courthouse shaking her head.

"I tried to tell you." Sarah whirled around to see Calhoun looking down at her. He wasn't smiling. His voice was gentle. "My client didn't like the deal, either. But I talked him into it because it would spare him a problem with the housing authority."

"So now he gets away with it."

"Not really. This goes on his record. And he's not going to like it. Which means this isn't going to go the way you think it is."

"What do you mean? Are you threatening me?"

Calhoun sighed. "You'll see."

## *COFFEE JUSTICE WARRIOR*

Sarah left the court building and stood on the sidewalk in front of its concrete steps, not knowing what she was supposed to do.

She had lost her first case. Technically, a win, but she, and everyone else in the courtroom, knew she had lost.

It wasn't supposed to go like this. She was supposed to be a champion of the unprotected. She was at least supposed to win a statutory slam dunk against a landlord. About the only thing she did right was show up at the courthouse.

Dumbfounded, Sarah watched cars meander down the street between buildings standing sentinel over a world that did not notice and did not care. That was fair. That was why she had a job. She noticed. She cared.

But when she looked into the faces of the people wandering down the sidewalks, they all seemed to look at her with one thought: *You lost.*

The green of a Starbucks sign caught her eye. The sight of that beacon in a gray sea of indifference perked her up a bit as Sarah imagined the simple sensation of a triple shot white mocha trickling down her throat.

The thought that she should go back to the office intruded on her small reverie, but Sarah decided that the other disasters awaiting her there could wait a little longer. She needed a minute to lick her wounds.

As she always did when she felt unsure of herself, Sarah tugged at the belt of her size 16 skirt. Once again, she reminded herself that she needed to get to a gym and do something about that. This ritual had begun when she had arrived at size 12.

Sarah frowned, lamenting the fact that she was gaining weight. Little did she know that not only was her assumption historically inaccurate, but also, not everybody saw it that way.

Standing six deep in the line at Starbucks, Sarah fumed at the man in front of her. He wore a London Fog trench coat and stood at an angle where she could see an expensive-looking suit that included a peach-colored shirt. It had taken Sarah a minute to settle on peach. It wasn't pink or mauve or fuchsia. It was peach. What kind of man wore a peach-colored shirt anyway? His six feet and two inches to her five feet and four inches meant she had to look up to complete her survey. His black hair flecked with gray was cut short on the sides and wafted up into a gentle wave on top. The man's face wasn't the sort of thing Greeks chiseled in marble. He had a long angular face and a receding chin. Handsome wasn't the word that came to Sarah's mind. But he had a rugged perseverance about him. If he weren't wearing a suit, she would have said he looked like somebody you could count on.

Just as Sarah was imagining going to battle with him over a workers' rights complaint, the barista held up a drink and said, "Hey, this one didn't work out. Anybody want it?"

The man standing in front of Sarah stepped up to the counter and said, "I'll take it."

That did it.

Sarah stepped between him and the counter and said, "Excuse me, but did it occur to you that the four people in front of you might want it?"

The man look perplexed then amused. Was he laughing at her? The man held up the cardboard cup and asked, "Does anybody mind if I take this?"

A couple people shook their heads. The other two didn't seem to hear. Nobody cared. Whatever.

The man waved the cup in salute and started to take a drink. But before he could, Sarah grabbed the cup from his hand. Addressing the rest of the line, she said, "Hold on a minute." She read the label and asked, "Nobody wants a caramel latte no-whip no-foam with soy?" Her own immediate mental response was, *not really*.

"It's fine," one of them said, rolling his eyes.

This was why men like Peach Shirt won, Sarah thought. Nobody was willing to fight. It was like the guy who goes all in with 72 on the river, knowing everybody will fold. Take what you want because chances are nobody will fight back.

Sarah shoved the cup back into his hand. Just as her hand thumped against his chest, the lid popped off and hot caramel latte no-whip no-foam with soy sloshed onto his peach shirt and matching tie. Sarah looked up, expecting to see an angry man looking back down at her. Instead, he looked worried.

Nathan felt the hot coffee seeping through his shirt. It started to burn a little, but he didn't care. He didn't know if it was the softly-curled red hair that waved in a waterfall down her back, the freckles perched around her prim nose or just those delicious green eyes.

She looked angry, but what Nathan saw beneath that was anguish. The coffee justice warrior glaring up at him was wounded. It had happened a long time ago and it drove everything she did. He could tell that much.

"It'll be alright," he said. She probably thought he was talking about the shirt.

He couldn't help notice her buxom chest restrained behind a blouse buttoned to the collar and all the right curves blossoming beneath her skirt. He couldn't remember ever seeing a woman so voluptuous. But that was just a pleasant distraction. The pain that lingered in her gaze was like an electrified fence. He knew not to touch it, but he wanted to reach out and grab it with both hands and make it stop.

It wasn't that he had only met her just a moment before and thus such a thought was ludicrous. As ridiculous as the thought was, it was intensely real. But that wasn't it, either. It was that he had never felt this way about a woman in his life. Ever.

As he was pondering how she would respond if he just reached out and brushed his hand against her cheek, she gasped in horror at what she had done.

She took his hand and gently placed the cup against his palm. "Here, take this," she said. The feel of her fingertips against the back of his hand sent a tingle up his arm. Smiling in fascination, he stared into her eyes, wondering exactly what was happening to him.

She looked away, dug through her purse and pulled out a tissue. "Sorry, it's all I have." She started to dab at his shirt, which sent a soft sizzle through his body. She sighed and shook her head because she knew it wasn't going to do much to clean his shirt. "Sorry." She looked up at him for a moment, waiting for him to say something that would make it easier to hate him. Instead, he repeated himself. "It will be alright."

Then she turned on her heel and headed for the door.

Once she was outside, he stepped out of line and walked through the door to watch her walk away. It wasn't even a thought - more of an instinct. He stood transfixed at the luscious parade of womanhood that was walking away from him. His skin still tingling from her touch, he wondered how she would feel if he touched her the same way. He wanted her to feel that. He wanted her to stop hurting. He wanted.

It never occurred to him to call after her as she turned the corner and disappeared from his life.

## *DUTY TO SERVE*

Maureen was driving the red Ford Fiesta while Sarah sat in the passenger seat, fuming because Maureen, the Lead Legal Assistant, would not tell her, Sarah Thomas, Attorney at Law, where they were going.

The tone of the neighborhoods deteriorated with each passing block. Sarah hadn't been in town for even a week, but she could tell they were descending into the wrong part of town. She sat up straighter and started scanning her surroundings.

With a smirk, Maureen asked, "Worried about something?"

"A little."

"I grew up around here," Maureen said.

Sarah wasn't sure what to do with that. "OK."

"It used to be worse."

Maureen turned onto a side street and parked.

The sidewalks were broken, light poles leaned and the tenement buildings looked like they hadn't been re-sided since 1952.

Nervously, Sarah asked, "Why are we parked here?"

Maureen pointed through the windshield. "Because of her."

Peering through the windshield, Sarah saw a woman locking the door of her second-story apartment. When she noticed the red hair, Sarah leaned forward and squinted. When the woman turned around with the toddler on her hip and a rollerbag in one hand, Sarah gasped.

"Angela?" she whispered.

The woman worked her way down the wooden staircase, the rollerbag thumping each step as she descended. Once at the bottom, she flipped her hair over her shoulder and shuffled down one of those broken sidewalks.

"Wait." Sarah turned to Maureen. "What is this?"

"Eviction."

Sarah knit her brow. “No. No no no.” She reached for the door handle but Maureen grabbed her arm and pulled her back.

“They can’t do this,” Sarah said. “You cannot evict a tenant when there is a defect in the residence. That’s retaliation.”

She reached again for the car door and once again, Maureen pulled her back.

“Let me go, dammit.”

“Stop.” Sarah could see a brutal past lingering behind Maureen’s eyes that now reached out and told Sarah she had to listen. “Did you read the file?”

“Of course. And I did see the note about the eviction, but I know you can’t evict during a breach.”

“Except,” Maureen said, ”that this eviction was filed a month ago and the furnace broke down two weeks ago.”

Puzzled, Sarah said, “So?”

“So a tenancy defect does not negate a prior breach.” Sarah felt her shoulders sag as it sunk in. “Or didn’t they teach you that in law school?”

“Then why did they offer the deal?

“Because he didn’t want trouble with the housing authority, so he was willing to give her a break on the rent, which would have given her an extra month to come up with the rest. It’s called a settlement.”

“And that’s not right.”

Raising her voice, Maureen said, “Enough about right. She wouldn’t be out on the street if you had been her lawyer instead of a damn crusader.”

Sarah ran out of words as she watched the logic of Maureen’s argument walk down a broken sidewalk with whatever possessions she could cram into a rollerbag and her son on her hip.

“She tried to tell me,” Sarah said.

“That’s right,” Maureen said. “She wanted to take the deal.” Maureen reached into her purse, pulled out a yellow sheet of paper and held it out to Sarah.

“What’s this?”

“It’s a complaint for negligent counsel.”

Sarah grabbed the sheet and read it. “What the hell is this? I won. Well, technically.”

“It’s common,” Maureen said. “But Stanley wouldn’t like it.”

Sarah turned her gaze on Maureen. “Wouldn’t?”

“He doesn’t need to see it,” Maureen said. “You’ll have to go to a hearing and tell the board your story. They can’t disbar you for requesting summary judgment under the law. But this sort of thing gets around.”

“What do you mean it gets around?”

"You said you wanted to make a career of public service law?"

"That's right."

"Good. Because that's all you'll be able to get for a while."

Sarah shook her head and started to hand the sheet back to Maureen.

"No, you keep that. That's your copy. Read it. You might learn something."

The two fell silent for a moment, but Sarah knew there was more. "What did you want to say to me?" she asked.

Maureen breathed uneasily and her gaze wandered, refusing to settle on Sarah. "Are you listening?"

"Yes."

"Why are you here? And don't tell me what you put on your application or your law school essay. You tell me the truth, the real truth, or so help me God, I will leave you standing here to find your way out of this God-forsaken cesspool and back to civilization."

Regret was still heavy on Maureen's brow, but Sarah knew she wasn't going to hear about whatever memory from Maureen's past was tightening her jaw. There was a deeper reason for Maureen's question. It had been a while since somebody had tried to teach Sarah. She took a deep breath and decided to tell the truth.

"I'm here because of my mother. She needed help at one time and instead, the system protected her abusers because they had the power and she didn't."

"Abusers?"

Sarah clenched her jaw. She really didn't want to talk about this. "Sexual abuse at work. Not harassment. Abuse. There's a difference."

Maureen slowly nodded. "I can appreciate that. I can. But now, listen to me."

Sarah nodded. "Go ahead."

"Contrary to popular belief, we're not on a crusade. Our job is to provide legal representation to people who have gotten into a situation they do not understand. Sometimes, we find a fight. Mostly, we usher them through an unfamiliar process that can't be changed much." Maureen paused and looked through the windshield, then back at Sarah. "Your job isn't to punish those who corrupt the law to their advantage. Your job is to protect your client's best interests. Those are two very distinct and different things. Do you understand?"

Angela was out of view now, but Sarah knew the image of that woman walking down the sidewalk wouldn't fade for a long time. She hated to admit it, but she knew there was an important lesson in that image. A lesson that had put her client on the street. She asked, "Did I do this?"

"Did you put Angela on the street? No. She did that to herself when she played her last five hundred dollars on the slots after the father of her child left her in the cold."

Sarah knew that wasn't meant to let her off the hook. If it were, it wasn't getting the job done. "But?"

"But you took a month away from her. A month where she could have found a job to scrape together enough rent to keep from being evicted. And that's where you failed -"

"-to look after my client's best interests."

"Which were?"

"Stay in her apartment."

Maureen smacked the steering wheel and nodded once. "There you go."

"I'm sorry," Sarah said, knowing it was a lame stab at assuaging her own guilt.

"Don't apologize to me. I'm going home to my apartment tonight."

Sarah reached for the car door again. "Maybe I can -"

Maureen grabbed her arm, harder this time. "No." Resenting the tears brimming in her eyes, Sarah looked at Maureen's hand gripping her arm. "That relationship is done," Maureen said. "You're not her friend. Her mother. Her sister. Her social worker. You were her lawyer. And you blew it." Sarah looked up to see Maureen wince at whatever memory was torturing her. "And you don't get to take it back."

Sarah let go of the door handle and slumped in her seat. Staring at the empty space where her client had walked into the unknown, Sarah asked, "What am I supposed to do?"

Maureen let go of Sarah's arm and pulled back onto the street. She drove a full block before she answered. "Better."

## *SECOND CHANCE*

Sarah stood before the book shelf she had put in front of her desk, a bookshelf now filled with bound copies of state statutes, rules of evidence and case summaries. While the debacle with Angela was still steeping in the back of her mind, she couldn't help but feel a sense of newfound hope at the sight of her law library now standing guard over her desk.

She glanced at the fluorescent light hanging over her desk, still buzzing intermittently so she could never forget it was there. She took this as a penance of sorts. Maureen had said nothing more on the matter after their Angela trip.

She was alone in the office as she had stayed late to research tenancy statutes when she heard a faint voice from the waiting room - "Hello?"

Sarah turned to see an old man standing next to the clapboard with an envelope in his hand. "The door was open," he said.

Sarah walked over to the man and asked, "What can I do for you?" The old man handed her the envelope.

Sarah fished out the papers inside and laid them out on the clapboard. The words were like a slap in the face: *Notice of Foreclosure.*

Sarah glanced at the man. "Have you been keeping up on your payments?"

"Mostly."

Sarah's mind raced. With Angela, there had been a tit-for-tat angle that probably didn't work in this case. The relationship between homeowners and the bank was different and generally gave homeowners considerable leeway before it came to a foreclosure.

"How far behind are you?" she asked.

The old man shrugged. "A couple months?"

Sarah eyed the man carefully. "Just two months? Are you sure?"

"That's right."

"What did they offer for abatement?"

"For what?"

Sarah studied the man again. Something wasn't adding up, but she couldn't tell if it was the client or the bank. One way or the other, she wasn't getting the whole story.

"Did they send you something that talked about a payment arrangement or any kind of relief under special circumstances?"

"No, nothing like that. This is the first thing I've gotten from the bank. Honestly, it kind of surprised me. I would have thought they'd give us more time. But this is it, just out of the blue."

"Uh-huh." Sarah thumbed through the paperwork. The address was complete. The payment history was included, showing the last two months delinquent. The payment history was also short - the loan was less than a year old. The formal notice that they had filed a complaint with the court was included last.

"Did they serve you?"

"Come again?"

"Did somebody come to your house and hand you some legal papers?"

"No, nothing like that."

"Are your name and address correct here?"

"Yes ma'am."

Sarah smiled. "It's Sarah."

The man smiled and tilted his head in deference.

"Do you have any money you can make a payment with? Anything you can sell?"

"Just my old Mustang, but I really don't want to give that up."

"If it comes down to a choice between your house and your Mustang?"

The man let out a slow breath and scratched his cheek. "That's not as obvious an answer as you might think."

"Can you live in your Mustang?"

The man smiled. "I see your point."

Sarah folded the paperwork and stuffed it back in the envelope. "Well, everything here looks in order, but I do have a few questions for the bank. Let me make some phone calls and get back to you. Meanwhile, the best thing you can do is make a payment. Or at least offer one. Banks generally don't like to short sell. We'll try to work something out."

The man covered his mouth and stared at the clapboard. "Thank you."

Sarah held her hand up. "Look, we're not out of the woods yet and if they serve you, this is a process that is very hard to stop. You need to make some decisions. You need to offer them something. Tomorrow."

The man's shoulders slumped. "Oh."

"I'll be in touch." Sarah nodded once to let him know the conversation was over.

The man let out a sigh and lightly slapped the clapboard once. "OK then." He glanced at Sarah one last time before he turned and shuffled back into the hallway.

Sarah sat down at her desk. She grabbed a Post-It and pasted it to the top page. Just as she started writing, the light over her desk started buzzing again.

Her first instinct, of course, was to go after the bank. They hadn't offered him an abatement. They hadn't served him. Yet. They were playing hardball and she wanted to know why.

She scribbled a note. *No complaint served.*

Then she thought of Angela.

Frowning, she grabbed another Post-It and scribbled another note. *Client interest: keep house.* After a moment, she added: *Wants to keep Mustang.*

Then she remembered something that had caught her eye while talking to the old man. She took the papers back out and shuffled through them again until she found his credit report. She set the other papers aside and laid the report in the center of her desk. Leaning her forehead against her palm, she studied it carefully.

The question burned through her mind and she couldn't think of an answer. *Why would a bank loan out a mortgage to somebody with a 501 credit score?*

# *ATONEMENT*

Sarah had done everything she could think of to keep it quiet. She had made all the calls on her personal phone. She had scraped together nearly every penny of her savings into a cashier's check. She had made the trip to Tropical Cadence apartments under the guise of going to the courthouse. She had driven in her used Honda Civic instead of taking an Uber, so there wasn't a record of the trip.

Because she knew Maureen wouldn't approve. In fact, Sarah was fairly certain she would be fired.

But atonement was the only way she could set it behind her and move on.

She still had one fingertip on the cashiers check but the man behind the desk wouldn't look at it.

"This covers six months, right?" she asked.

"Sure," he said. "But we typically do this on a lease."

Sarah cast her gaze down to the check, her finger still holding it tightly in place.

"Alright," he said. "What's the name?"

"Angela Ferguson."

"Alright Ms. Ferguson, and are you employed?"

Sarah again cast her eyes down at the check, but the man looked straight ahead, his eyes fixed on her. "Do you have a job?"

Sarah let out a sigh. "Me. Sure. But this isn't for me."

"What's your name?"

"Does that really matter?"

His back still ram-rod straight in his chair, the man crossed his arms and leaned back a few inches. "It might. Look, this place may not look like much, but it's respectable. We don't cater to people who camp for cash so they can peddle meth. We run a clean joint."

Sarah's stomach tightened and she felt her knuckle ache as she pushed on the check harder, willing him to look at it. Instead, he turned his head to look out the window next to his desk

"Look," she said. "Between you and me, my name is Sarah Thomas. I am an attorney with the Emmerson Foundation. I am an officer of the court who is just starting her legal career." She nudged the check forward. "And I promise you I have no interest in engaging in any illegal activity of any kind."

Still looking out the window, he said, "That's nice. What about this Ms. Ferguson person?"

"She works at the bowling alley. She has a two-year-old son. The father abandoned her and she really needs a break."

The man looked back at Sarah with a narrowed gaze. "What is she to you?"

Sarah tapped the check with two fingers, almost wishing she were in court facing the judge instead of the man sitting across from her. "She's a client."

"Emmerson is handing out apartments now?"

"Not exactly. This is my own initiative." She grimaced and thought hard for a moment before saying, "Like I said, this is just between you and me."

"And what guarantee do I have that she won't be a deadbeat that brings the police every Friday night? I'm serious. I have good people living here. People who deserve peace and quiet when they come home, not blue and red lights flashing against their living room wall."

"She's clean. She has a two-year-old to look after. She has no interest in the kind of people you're talking about." Sarah didn't know if that were actually true, but based on their conversation in the courthouse and the fact that she would rather hit the street than succumb to hooking to keep her last apartment, Sarah made a gut call. "And if I'm wrong, I'll call the police myself."

"Yeah, and you'll be out the rest of the rent. Are you sure you're willing to put this kind of bet on her?"

Sarah hadn't thought of it that way. Maybe Maureen was right. Maybe Angela had just been a client and Sarah would have to accept that she was wandering the streets because of her. Maybe it was her penance to have to face that and not be able to do anything about it.

Or maybe her penance was to put her own reputation on the line for a woman she didn't know. A woman who lost her home because of Sarah. A woman who deserved at least a second chance. Sarah owed her that much.

"I am."

The man leaned back in his chair, glanced around the room and then looked back out the window. Sarah sat as still as she could, as if she were watching a deer in the forest, afraid that any sound might send it bolting. She kept her index finger firmly planted on the check. After several moments where Sarah wondered if she was going to have to see Angela walking down the street in her mind's eye for the rest of her days, the man finally looked at the check.

"Like I said, this is typically a lease deal. You're six months short."

Sarah let out a sigh as she realized that he was now negotiating. He wasn't saying 'no'. He was just saying 'more'. But she had no money left and wasn't willing to open the door to bartering. It was one thing for a man to say he was loathe to nefarious deeds. It was quite another to prove the point. She made the only move she had left.

Sarah slowly pulled the check back. "I'm sorry we couldn't do business today."

The man reached out and placed his hand on the check. "Now hold on. Don't be hasty. All I'm saying is that with a month-to-month, if she doesn't have month 7, she'll get a three-day notice and an escort from the sheriff's office. And if there is a hint of anything that would affect our reputation, I'll make sure she lands in jail. And you won't see a dime of this money back."

Sarah knew she couldn't bargain for anything better. She didn't like the idea of him making some kind of excuse to evict Angela and pocket the money. But he did know she was a lawyer so he probably knew there would have to be a legitimate reason. She lifted her finger and he pulled the check across the desk.

He spent a few moments filling out the application and then said, "She'll have to sign to get the key."

Sarah picked up the rental agreement and read it over, if for no other reason than to look like a lawyer.

As she laid the agreement back on his desk, she said, "I'll be by from time to time to check on her."

"That's fine. I'm sure it will all work out the way you're hoping." But he looked at her with a flat expression. She could tell he thought she was fool.

"You don't think it will?"

"It could. But I've clearly been a landlord a lot longer than you've been a lawyer."

Sarah stood up and offered her hand. When he accepted it, she made sure to grip his hand the way she thought a man would. When he winced, she realized she had overdone it, but she didn't back off. "Like I said, I'll be by to make sure she's moved in."

## *THE FULLER GLASS*

The place was called Bernards. No apostrophe. Brass railing lined the carpeted steps that led down to a hard-wood floor polished to a sheen with a maître d' behind a solid-wood podium guarding it all.

Sarah found Elaine sitting on a high leather-backed stool in front of a granite-topped bar with brass railing to match the front entrance. The bartender wore a vest and bow tie. The top-shelf liquor was displayed in front of a backing mirror that ran the entire length of the bar.

Sarah's first impression was that she was glad Elaine was buying. She sat down next to her law school friend who leaned over and gave Sarah a hug.

Elaine had dressed modestly in law school because, like most everyone else, she didn't have any money in those days. But now she wore a Max Mara long coat over a Milly blouse and Prada skirt. Her Coach bag was slung over the back of the bar stool.

Sarah hoped her friend didn't notice she was still wearing the same outfit she had worn for moot court.

"God, it's been forever," Elaine said.

Sarah waited for the hugging to stop and said, "It's been a week." That's how long it had been since Elaine had stood waiting for Sarah next to the luggage carousel.

"Well, it seems longer," Elaine said. "What'll you have?"

Sarah started to say, "I'll have a Bud-" but then noticed the labels on the taps. None of them were commonplace and she ordered the only one she recognized. "-er, make that a Sierra Nevada."

"You look like you need something stronger," Elaine said.

Sarah smiled sheepishly and glanced at the rocks glass in front of Elaine half-filled with what she was sure was Grey Goose over ice. "I could, actually, but I have a lot going on. The last thing I need is a hangover." Not to mention that she felt uncomfortable spending $20 on a drink, even if she wasn't paying for it. The meager mug of beer that the bartender brought her cost ten. Before Sarah could reach into her purse, Elaine twirled her finger once and the bartender smiled. *On the tab*. He smiled at Sarah and tapped the bar once before turning away.

"Thanks," Sarah said. The charity made her uncomfortable somehow but she couldn't put her finger on why.

As Sarah took a drink, Elaine spun her seat around to face Sarah, clasped her hands in her lap and asked, "So, what's going on with you Pipsqueak?"

It had been her nickname all through law school, and she knew Elaine said it with affection, but seeing her friend decked out in Sak's Fifth Avenue while Sarah wore whatever she had found on the discount rack at Ross six months before, she couldn't help but feel a little barb in Elaine's tone.

"It's been an interesting week," Sarah said, which was about as positive a spin as she could put on the ordeal that had been her first week at Emmerson.

"So I've heard," Elaine said, running her hand across Sarah's back and then resting it on her shoulder.

Sarah couldn't help feeling embarrassed. She was surprised to feel a touch of resentment at the person who had shared blood sweat and tears with her during law school. They had been as inseparable as soul mates, but now Elaine seemed to be a different person. In law school, she had been a pit bull, but now she just seemed comfortable.

"Yeah, well, you seem to be doing pretty good."

Elaine smiled and then shook her head. She swept her hands down her side and said, "Never mind all this. You're doing what you said you were going to do. You're fighting the hard fight that nobody else wants to." She re-clasped her hands. "Your mother would be proud."

"I'm not so sure," Sarah said, and took another drink. "I don't seem to be making much of a difference."

"Well sure. No resources, no assistant, no mentor. You're totally on your own over there." Elaine leaned forward and cocked her head. "Just the way you wanted, right?"

Sarah took a third drink and looked at the empty mug in disgust. It couldn't have been more than six ounces. "You got something besides the sampler?" she asked the bartender. Elaine looked down with an embarrassed smile at the barb. Sarah knew it was uncouth in such a swanky place where everyone was supposed to pretend that money held little meaning. But she couldn't see it that way.

"Of course," the bartender said as he picked up the empty muglette.

"I do have a mentor," Sarah said. "Of sorts. Kind of hard-nosed, but she makes her point."

"Maureen Henderson?" Elaine asked, her eyebrows arching.

"That's right. Do you know her?"

"I know of her," Elaine said. She picked up her glass and daintily sipped a minuscule bit of vodka. "Everybody's heard of her."

"What, a lead assistant of a public law clinic is famous?"

"She wasn't always a legal assistant."

Sarah could only guess. A reformed streetwalker. Or worse. It didn't matter. She worked hard and she meant well. Sarah decided she didn't want to inquire further into the infamy of Maureen.

Instead, she said, "I don't know. It's been tough. Not what I expected."

The bartender arrived with a real grown-up mug of beer and Elaine once again twirled her finger. Sarah wanted to ask her how much, but after draining her savings for Angela, she really couldn't afford it. She would catch up to her friend next time.

"How so?" Elaine asked.

"You know, when I wrote my essay, I said I wanted to make a difference."

"Everybody writes that in their essay."

"But I meant it. I really believe that there is this vacuum of legal counsel for people who can't afford justice-for-hire."

"That's true."

"I think I'm beginning to understand why."

"Don't say that. You know that what you're trying to do is important."

"Is it? Nobody else seems to think so and so far all I've been able to do is show up so people can say, 'yes, I have a lawyer.' I'd like to do more than just stand there. And so far, it seems like I would have been doing a better job if I *had* just stood there." Sarah reached for the mug and took a long drink, resisting the urge to check the belt of her skirt.

"I told you it was going to be like that."

Sarah shot Elaine a hard glance.

Elaine put a hand on Sarah's shoulder. "I didn't mean it like that. I meant that I told you it was going to be tough fighting a rigged system. You said you knew that. I told you that they didn't want you to fight and win. You said you knew that too. But you were determined anyway. Remember?"

Sarah sighed. "Yeah, I remember." But in that moment, her words seemed empty. "Seems like you were right."

Elaine puckered her lips in disapproval. "You've been at it for a whole week. Give it a minute."

Sarah laughed. "I'm just so, you know, pissed off."

"Well, yeah. You're a crusader. You're supposed to be pissed off."

"They don't tell you the part where you can make a difference. The kind of difference where your client is worse off than before. Even if you do your job."

"Yeah, I know. You just need to find your tactical line. Every lawyer has a groove - something they're good at and a particular way of approaching a legal problem. More importantly, they find the kind of legal problems they're good at solving. With your line of work, there's not much of a playbook except lances and windmills." Elaine paused for a moment, mulling over her next words. "And toeing the line."

Sarah winced at that. "What line?"

Elaine let out a sigh. Sarah was beginning to resent her friend for knowing things that were obvious to her but utterly incomprehensible to herself. It had been like that in law school, too. Probably because Elaine was 45 and coming off a corporate human resources career. There was a hard-won edge in her outlook. But Sarah wasn't always sure they were on the same side.

"Look," Elaine said. "Emmerson is a write-off for its contributors. Mostly. And also a public relations arm. They can lay claim to helping the community while doing what corporate does."

"Which is what?"

"Well, mostly pissing you off." They both laughed at this. "You can't expect them to send in helicopters and special forces to cover you every time you go four-wheeling off in the weeds. It doesn't work like that."

Sarah took another drink and set the mug down a little too firmly, betraying her frustration. "Then how does it work, Elaine? Tell me." She knew she wouldn't hear anything new, but maybe she would finally understand it after her first week at Emmerson.

"Well, for one thing, you need to make the foundation look good. Your job is to feed the PR machine and keep the money rolling in."

"I thought my job was to look after my client's best interests."

Elaine smiled at Sarah as if she were talking to a pre-teen daughter. "Well, of course you look after your client's best interest. That's a given."

"So on top of that, I'm supposed to be a photo op?"

"Pretty much."

"And what if those two don't align with each other?"

Elaine drained the rest of her drink and set down her empty glass, the ice clinking against its side.

"Then," she said, "You remember rule number one."

Sarah could guess, but she wanted to hear Elaine say the words. "Which is?"

"Never bite the hand that feeds you."

Sarah locked her gaze on Elaine. He friend was smiling softly, as if she were trying to ease the pain of a hard truth that everybody but Sarah understood. Or maybe Elaine just hoped she was right because she wasn't willing to stand up for what she knew was right. Mostly, she looked like somebody Sarah didn't really know anymore.

"Maybe that's how it works in your world." Sarah shook her head, finished her beer and stood up. "But not mine. I gotta' go."

"I'm sorry Pipsqueak. I know you don't like it, but I'm just trying to help."

"I know."

Sarah leaned over to give her friend a hug. As she pulled back, Elaine said, "And one more thing. Like I said, Maureen hasn't always been a legal assistant. But she knows more about the law then you and I will forget in the next ten years."

## *HIDE AND SEEK*

Nathan stood in the conference room, waiting for Calhoun to arrive. He glanced at his watch. The man was already five minutes late. His father's lawyer, a personal family friend, had never failed to be fifteen minutes early. Now, dealing with megafirm Foley, Crane and Who Cares - where lawyers kept him waiting - was yet another benefit of his father selling out the family business to Gavin.

An associate, a quiet and helpful looking woman that Nathan had never met before stood next to the door. "Would you like to take a seat, Mr. Haley?" She gestured at the chair at the head of the table and smiled.

Nathan smiled back and said, "No, I prefer to pace, thanks." It was true. He traipsed up and down along the side of the table, noting the stray thoughts that came and went through his mind. Sitting and staring at the wall was just not something he did.

Standing sentry at the door, the woman asked, "Can I bring you something?"

Nathan checked his watch again. Still pacing, he asked, "When does Calhoun get here?"

She smiled and said, "I'm sure he'll be along shortly." As best as Nathan could tell, she was all style and no function. She wore some ensemble that looked more expensive than his Armani, but she didn't actually seem to do anything except stand around and ask pointless questions.

Nathan Haley really hated waiting.

For a moment, the forlorn gaze of the woman at Starbucks flashed through his mind. He had no doubt she would not stand around asking stupid questions. He actually stopped pacing and looked out one of the wide pane windows as he imagined her striding down the hall to find Calhoun and drag him to the conference room. Imagining her body in motion sent a shiver through his body. He really should have gotten her number.

Just as Nathan was about to leave and reschedule, Calhoun stumbled into the room. His powder-blue suit was rumpled and his collar was unbuttoned even though he wore a tie. He pulled out a handkerchief to mop his brow and glanced at the woman standing guard. "That will be all, Elaine. Thank you." The woman nodded and slipped out of the room.

Calhoun turned to Nathan and stuck out his hand.

"Robert Calhoun."

With some hesitation, Nathan took his hand. "Nathan Haley."

Calhoun plopped into a chair and asked, "What's up?"

Still standing up, Nathan took the envelope out of his jacket pocket and slid it across the table towards Calhoun.

"I got a call about this yesterday. What do you know about it?"

Calhoun opened the envelope and glanced through the paperwork. "Looks like a standard foreclosure to me."

Nathan pulled another envelope from his suit jacked and smacked it down on the table in front of Calhoun. "Take a look at the application."

"What about it?"

"Anything there seem unusual to you?"

"I'm not a banker, Mr. Haley. I just go to court and make deals."

Nathan felt like slapping the man across the forehead, but he didn't want to get his hand wet. "Take a look at the credit score."

Calhoun set aside the foreclosure paperwork and thumbed through the application. "Yeah. 501."

"Doesn't that seem a little low to you?"

"I see your signature here."

"Yeah. I'm looking into that. That's a copy, not the original. I'm pretty sure I wouldn't sign off on a loan for somebody with a 501 credit score."

Calhoun laid the papers down. "Mr. Haley, do you have a legal question for me?"

"Wouldn't something like this constitute predatory lending? Cutting a check to somebody who clearly can't pay it back and then kicking them out less than a year later?"

Calhoun weaved his head side to side, studied Nathan for a moment and then said, "Well, I wouldn't worry about it too much. Predatory lending laws are pretty lightweight and they have to show a pattern before it's really a problem."

"I didn't ask you if we could get away with it. I asked what you knew about it."

"Nothing until now." Calhoun picked up the application and tapped his finger against the bottom edge. "And it says here you signed this."

"Who do you work for, Mr. Calhoun?"

Calhoun smiled and shrugged. “I work for your bank, then Mr. Gavin. Then you. In that order. And you are a distant third in that equation.”

Nathan placed both palms flat on the table and leaned forward, glaring at Calhoun. “Your name is not on the front of the building. Gavin’s name is not on the front of the building.” He jabbed his chest with his thumb. “My name is on the front of the building. Haley National. And I don’t sign out loans to people who can’t repay them. So I’m going to ask you again, what do you know about this?”

Unfazed, Calhoun ignored the bulk of Nathan’s tirade and asked, “Where did you get this foreclosure paperwork?”

“Emmerson.”

Calhoun’s eyes widened with surprise. “The clinic?”

Nathan pulled out his smart phone to look up the note he had jotted down. “Yeah, the clinic. Sarah Thomas.”

Calhoun let out a laugh. “Oh her. Well, you really don’t have anything to worry about. We can handle her.”

“You’re not hearing me, Mr. Calhoun. I’m not interested in handling anybody. I want to know who handed out that loan.”

“Well, like I said, this application says you did.” Changing the subject, Calhoun asked, “Hey, did you know that she paid up six months rent for one of her clients?”

Exasperated, Nathan asked, “What? What are you talking about?”

“Thomas. She paid up six months of rent for one of her clients after she blundered their case. Real bleeding heart type. Like I said, we’ll have no problem dealing with her.”

Nathan had no idea who Sarah Thomas was, but in that moment he wished she were his lawyer instead of the corporate lackey sweating in front of him.

Nathan stretched out his hand. “Gimme those.”

Calhoun carefully folded the paperwork, slid it back into the first envelope and handed it to Nathan.

“And when you go back to your office to report to Gavin that ‘Haley’s kid’ was over here stirring up trouble, you tell him I’m going to get to the bottom of this.”

“Look, Nathan, there’s no need to get worked up here. My advice to you is to keep quiet and see what happens. One foreclosure isn’t going to make much of a splash. I will talk to Gavin about this. I do have a concern about possible predatory lending here, but my personal advice to you is to settle down and let me sort this out.” He stood up and straightened his tie. “But if there are more of these, you may need to get your own lawyer.”

“If there are more of these, then somebody has just pissed all over my family’s name. And God help the man who did that.”

“That sounds a little bit like a threat, Nathan. Careful with that.”

“It’s not a threat. It’s a goddamn promise.”

## *SHUTOUT*

Nathan stormed out of the law offices of Foley Crane and - he had to look up at the sign to remember the third name - Winkler, and headed straight for Haley National. It would have been faster to grab an Uber, but he was fuming and needed the walk and the time to cool off so he could think things through.

He had fully expected Calhoun to defer to his authority, not to mention his family's legacy, and tell him what was going on. If there was one thing he understood about lawyers, it was that they always knew. And he had no doubt that Calhoun knew. But the man was in Gavin's pocket, so Nathan was on his own.

His first priority was damage control. He instinctively knew that whatever was going on had the potential to topple the legacy that he and his father had sacrificed their lives to build.

But Calhoun was right - the signature at the bottom was Nathan's. Which meant he was being set up as the scapegoat if whatever this thing was went sideways.

Nathan knew Gavin was a snake. He knew that it was a mistake for his father to sell the bank to such a man. But he never imagined that he would try something like this. And with Nathan's name.

The truth was, he wasn't used to dealing with these kinds of people. He was out of his element and he knew it.

*Think. You can't fight this from a prison cell. Think.*

Then he realized what he had to do. It hit him like a freight train and he picked up the pace as he pulled his smart phone from his jacket pocket and texted Maggie: *Meet me at the vault. Bring the card.*

Maggie did not work for Gavin. She didn't even really work for Haley National. For the past fifteen years, Maggie had worked for Nathan. Before that, she had worked for his father, both at the bank and often as Nathan's nanny. He never had figured out when she had found time to sleep. So he had to believe that he could still trust her. His instincts told him he could. That he had to. But the meeting with Calhoun had shown him just how insidious Gavin could be. Men were willing to betray their conscience for him. What if he had gotten to Maggie?

Nathan tried to push the thought away. *You're being paranoid. Good people don't change colors overnight.* It was all he had - a gut feeling. There was no other play.

Once inside the bank headquarters, Nathan headed straight for the elevator and, for the first time, wished the camera staring down at him from the corner were out of service. It was a bank. He understood that. But just then, he didn't want anybody watching him. He inserted his access key, pressed "B" and let out a slow breath. He had hoped the brisk walk would give him a chance to pull himself together, but his mind was racing and he could do nothing to stop it. All he could do was listen and try to filter the useful information from the noise.

The elevator chimed. He stepped out and headed straight for the floor-to-ceiling door of the vault, where he found Maggie standing by with his access badge in her hand.

She handed him the card. "Did anybody see you come down here?" he asked.

"I'm old Nathan, not senile." He smiled at her, thankful for the one person he knew he could count on.

He slid the card through the reader, waiting for it to beep and flash green. After a moment, nothing happened. He slid it again. This time, he was greeted with an unfamiliar buzz and then a red light flashed.

Nathan's heart stopped.

He slid the card through the reader again. The reader buzzed and flashed red again.

Under his breath, Nathan said, "Oh man, this fucking guy."

"Language, Nathan." It was then that he knew he could trust Maggie with his life if it came to that. She still saw him as the eight-year-old that she used to take care of when his father was working late building their community one home loan at a time.

He smiled sheepishly. "Sorry."

"Let me try mine," she said. She fished her card out of her bra, but as she moved her hand towards the reader, Nathan grabbed her wrist.

"No. They don't need to see your name on the report."

"But what if it works?"

"Then you'll be in as much trouble as I am."

"I'm going into the vault. How much trouble could that mean?"

Still gripping her wrist, he said, "No, Maggie, I'm not going to let that happen. I don't know everything yet, but I know we're dealing with the kind of people who will toss you and your twenty years of loyal service right out the front door." He lifted a brow and she put the card back in her bra.

"Well, aren't you sweet?" she said, and then smiled at him, the same smile from when he was eight years old.

"I'm serious."

"I can come down later," she said.

He took a step closer, towering over her. "No, Maggie. You need to promise me you won't. I will not see your life turned upside down because of me."

"It's mine to turn upside down."

Damn the woman. "OK, then. I need you free to move on the side. If you get caught up in this, then where will I be? For me, OK? Promise me you won't get yourself in trouble."

"Alright Nathan. For you. I'll stay out of it." Then she winced and blinked a few times. "But I'm as much a part of this family as you."

"I know that. And that's why they'll be watching you, too. That's why you need to keep your nose clean."

Maggie nodded somberly. "What are you looking for?"

"What do you know about Sunfield Farms?"

Maggie smiled and said, "There's talk of a buyer."

Nathan blinked in disbelief. "They're selling the paper?"

"That's what it looks like."

Nathan glanced around the room, thinking. "Can you find the buyer?"

"I'll see what I can do." Maggie knit her brow and absently rubbed her elbow. "What are you doing to do?"

Nathan twisted one hand around his wrist. "I need to find a way into this damn vault."

## *CAT'S PAW*

It was the most obvious thing to do, but Nathan wasn't sure if it was the smartest. And he didn't have time to figure out the difference.

Gavin's office was actually less opulent than Nathan's. The floor was carpeted and his desk was some ensemble from Ikea. There wasn't a single sheet of paper in sight, but the man had no fewer than three computers, each feeding multiple monitors. Gavin Neilsen wasn't a banker. He was a speculator.

He stepped out from behind his desk, smiled warmly and stuck out his hand. Gavin was unremarkable in appearance. A balding head, round face and glasses with round frames. He looked dopey, but Nathan knew better.

Nathan winced as Gavin shook his hand. "How are you doing, Nathan?" It wasn't a greeting, it was a sincere question, as if he were Nathan's analyst and not his boss. It was one of the many disarming mannerisms Nathan knew he had to watch out for. So he lied.

"Fine, sir. How are you?"

"Oh, well, you know, can't complain." Gavin sat back down behind his desk. "What can I do for the Vice President of Haley National?"

Nathan stood there for a moment, trying to size Gavin up, trying to find an angle he hadn't thought of before.

Gavin must have noticed because his expression tightened and he started quietly tapping his fingers against his desk. Nathan realized the man was reading him like a book. And there was nothing he could do about it.

Gavin gestured towards a chair. "Sit down, then. Tell me what's going on."

Eying Gavin, Nathan pulled the envelope from his suit pocket and handed it to his boss. "It's about this foreclosure situation, sir."

Gavin took the envelope and held it in one hand without opening it. "What situation is that?"

For a moment Nathan thought he caught a glimpse of a man who looked like he had been caught when Gavin's posture stiffened.

"Well, take a look and you'll see."

Gavin studied him for a moment, his eyes narrowing. He still held the unopened envelope in his hand. "Just tell me."

"It's the credit score, sir. We wrote a loan for somebody who can't pay it back. I'm concerned that -" Nathan stopped short, considering his options for a moment. He decided to test his boss, just to confirm his suspicion. "-I'm concerned that we should be more careful about putting our clients at risk. Dad always said, 'Show me a hard-working family man and I'll give him a loan.'"

Gavin stared straight into Nathan's eyes. "Yeah, I know. He never loaned money to deadbeats."

"I wouldn't call them deadbeats -"

"No, you wouldn't, would you?" Gavin dropped the envelope on his desk. "Deadbeats. And there's more where this came from." He tapped the envelope.

Nathan felt his mouth fall agape and tried to will it closed, but he couldn't get past the frigid audacity in Gavin's voice. He knew the man was sleazy, but listening to Gavin dismiss real people he seemed willing to toss into the street as just 'deadbeats' sent a shiver down Nathan's spine. Then he felt a bead of sweat trickle down the side of his face.

"What do you mean there are more?"

Gavin turned one of his monitors around and tapped a flashing red line. "Says here you tried to get in the vault earlier."

"That's right. I'm the Vice President. I have a legal right to be in there."

Gavin chuckled. "Well, of course you do. Did Devorah give you your new badge?"

Nathan slumped. The man had been a step ahead of him from the beginning. "She mentioned something about it. She said Maggie had it." Still standing, Nathan leaned forward slightly, staring down at Gavin. "My old badge got me into the vault. Why doesn't my new badge do the same?"

Staring at Nathan flatly, Gavin said, "I'll look into it." Gavin clasped his hands on his desk. "In the meantime, the thing you need to focus on is that your signature is at the bottom of every single one of those applications."

Nathan's breath caught in his throat. He studied Gavin carefully, trying to remember when he had mentioned his concern about his signature. He was almost certain he hadn't said anything about it as a second bead of sweat crept along the side of his face.

"I did not sign that," Nathan said, pointing at the envelope. "There is no way I would write a loan to somebody with a 501."

"Oh, I know that." Still staring blankly at Nathan, Gavin tilted his head, as if he were waiting for Nathan to catch up. "Look, even if you did, it's not that big of a problem. Predatory lending is a minor civil liability that goes against the bank. I mean, you'd probably lose your position as Vice President." Gavin's mouth curled into an impish smile of mock sympathy. "We can't very well sponsor corporate officers who go around signing up deadbeats. But you'd still have a job. If it gets to that point, which it won't."

Nathan slowly raised his head and his throat tightened as he realized what had happened. "I didn't sign paperwork that said 501." He looked back down at Gavin, seeing the man as if this were the first time he had met him. He would never underestimate the man again. "I signed paperwork that said something else."

"Well now, that's an entirely different matter. See, fraud is a criminal liability and one that would fall on you personally." Gavin grimaced with mock sternness. The man seemed to enjoy the game a little too much, like a cat batting a dead mouse across the floor. "If anybody managed to ever see the originals."

"Which are currently locked away in the vault."

"That's right. Where nobody can get at them."

"Including me." Nathan clenched his jaw and took a step closer to Gavin's desk. Jabbing his thumb into his chest, he said, "I have a right to access that vault."

"Yes, yes, I know. Like I said, I'll look into what happened with your new badge. Meanwhile, you don't need to worry about it. The originals are safely locked away. Where nobody can get at them." Gavin steadied his gaze on Nathan and leaned forward. "Unless, for some reason, we're compelled to reveal them to the authorities." Then he smiled. *Friends*?

Nathan felt nauseous and couldn't stop another bead of sweat from trickling down the side of his face. "What about the discrepancy between the credit scores with this application?"

Gavin waved dismissively. "Oh that. Calhoun will take care of it. It's a one-time thing. Nothing to worry about." He stood up and walked over to Nathan, putting his hand on his shoulder and edging him towards the door. "Thanks for coming in today. I'm glad we were able to sort things out."

At the door, Nathan turned to face him as Gavin stuck out his hand again. *Seriously, friends*?

Nathan reluctantly took the man's hand. Watching Gavin's smug grin, Nathan wanted to slug the man. But that wouldn't bring him any closer to finding his way into the vault.

## *FRIENDS WITH BENEFITS*

Devorah propped her head up with two pillows as she lay stark naked on a bed strewn with rumpled sheets. Somewhere along the way, the bedspread had wound up on the floor. She flipped through the channels while steam wafted from the bathroom.

When it had cleared, she saw Gavin standing in front of the sink with a towel around his waist, shaving. His balding head was round. His belly was round. His arms were bulbous and round. Everything about him was round. And yet she had taken him into her bed.

It wasn't that she found him attractive. Who would? Except for the lure of power that she suspected most women secretly found arousing. But that wasn't it, either.

She and Gavin found a natural attraction to each other because they had learned an obvious ideology the hard way: good guys finish last. The daring and the audacious win. Rules were obstacles that were either violated, avoided or obviated. Pursuers were purchased or otherwise persuaded to abandon their efforts. The most amazing discovery she had made was that when you break the rules, people often don't notice or care. The world lets you get away with it. Once she understood that, she was baffled by people who voluntarily restrained their progress with good behavior.

Men like Nathan Haley, for example. How much more could he have done with his life if he had understood what she and Gavin took to be natural law? He would never admit it because he thought he was modest, but Nathan's pride got in his way. Pride in being the good guy. As if anybody really cared about that.

But, Devorah had to admit, she was eager to find out what he was like tangled in the sheets with her.

For Gavin, it was a matter of comfort and reassurance. She knew he found solace in her arms. And with the pressure he was getting from Olivia, his need for that solace had grown. She hoped they could resolve that pressure soon because, if she was honest with herself, she was growing weary of the frequent trysts that Gavin had come to demand.

Gavin's voice floated out from the steam. "We need to keep an eye on Nathan."

Devorah rolled her eyes. He was setting up yet another problem where he would need to seek her comfort. A line had to be drawn.

"We already know that."

Gavin talked with a muffled tone as he stroked has face with a safety razor. "Nah. Not like this. He's looking."

Devorah let out an exasperated sigh. "Of course he's looking. He's Nathan."

Gavin grunted, but said nothing more. He finished shaving and stepped out of the bathroom. He opened the closet door and stood behind it while he got dressed. Devorah was thankful for him seeming to understand that while she was happy to entertain him, she didn't much care for looking at him afterwards.

After putting on a button up shirt and slacks, he dragged a chair next to the bed and sat down.

"He found one of the loans." Devorah arched a brow at this and sat up. "And he came to me about it."

"How did he find out?"

"Some do-gooder at Emmerson representing a deadbeat who got a foreclosure. Too early, I might add. We're not to that point, yet."

"Yeah, Maia got ahold of it and processed it as a matter of routine."

"Does she know what's going on?"

"No, she was just doing her job."

"You sure?"

"Yeah."

"She sent the borrower the copy with the original credit score. It's going to be a problem if that sees the light of day before we're ready." Running his hand along his tie, he said, "If the buyer finds out, we're dead in the water. What are we doing about that?"

"I already fired her. I gave her a generous severance and a referral. I plugged that leak."

Gavin nodded pensively, studying her, deliberately keeping his eyes focused on hers without letting his gaze stray to the rest of her body.

"Alright then." He took a deep breath and leaned forward. "I need you to get him under control."

Devorah scoffed. "I've tried. He has zero interest. Honestly, I wonder if he's gay. Have you ever seen him with a woman?"

"You're making excuses."

Devorah swung around, crossing her legs and leaned her chin on clasped hands. "I changed his badge. I can have our infosec people keep an eye on him. I can monitor his e-mail. And I can let you know if something comes up. But, I'm telling you, Nathan Haley has no interest in the luscious lady sitting before you."

Gavin didn't blink. His mouth was set in a thin line and he kept his gaze steady as he stared straight into her eyes. "I heard from Olivia."

"Oh?" Devorah wanted to avert her eyes, but she knew he wouldn't appreciate that. Gavin demanded rigid attention when he was being serious.

"This can't go wrong. We're out of time."

Devorah felt a shiver run down her spine. "Oh."

"You are a smart, resourceful and audacious woman. And I need you to put Nathan right in your pocket."

Devorah watched Gavin closely as he stood up and dragged the chair back to a small round table in the front part of the suite. The light was off and he looked back at her from the half-darkness.

"Olivia doesn't know about you. I've made sure of that."

Devorah gulped. "I appreciate that."

They were both silent for an uncomfortable moment. Then, he said, "I'd like to keep it that way."

## *MOUSE'S TAIL*

Standing in the hallway outside Devorah's office door, Nathan shook his hands loosely and took a deep breath. He straightened his tie. He ran his fingers through his hair. He rubbed his face, feeling the light grit of his afternoon beard.

He wasn't ready for this. And he knew he never would be.

He opened the door and stepped inside to see Devorah hunched over her desk, her eyes flitting between two monitors.

At first, she actually didn't notice him. He leaned against the door jamb, crossed one foot over the other and cleared his throat.

Devorah jerked with surprise. He caught her face set in a rigid expression, her mouth half open and her forehead creased. An instant later, her face lit up with a smile.

"Nathan. Well, hello there."

Nathan looked at her, a sheepish smile on his face. And he froze because he didn't know what to do next. He hadn't chased a girl since college. It hit him in that moment. There had been nobody in his life since he started working for his father's bank. They were too busy building a community from the ruins of what had once been a thriving industrial town. Now, it thrived on service and technology industries. He and his father had done that. There had never been time for anything else. Standing in Devorah's door, wondering how to entice her to go have that drink, he realized what he had given up. He had never thought about it before, but somewhere along the way, he had given up the idea of sharing his life with somebody. Suddenly, his mind was paralyzed by a vision of the woman from Starbucks looking up at him with those haunting green eyes revealing her wounded soul to a man she had never met. He knew she hadn't meant for him to see that. But he had seen it. And he would never forget. He blinked and looked away for a moment when he realized he would never want to forget.

Somewhere on a distant day, he would close his eyes for the last time and his last memory would be those haunting eyes.

Nathan shook the vision away. He didn't know how long he had been standing there, but Devorah was still looking at him, smiling, waiting for him to say - something.

He flashed what he hoped was a disarming smile and said, "About that drink."

Still smiling, Devorah stepped out from behind her desk, smoothed down her skirt, flicked her hair behind her shoulder and actually walked across her office floor as if she were modeling some new fashion from Paris on a runway.

It pained Nathan to watch as he fought to keep his smile pasted on his face. It wasn't that the walk did nothing to salvage the mantis-like slenderness of her body or the hard angles that supplanted what should have been soft curves. Some men found that sort of thing attractive, he knew that. No, it was that Devorah Harlow genuinely believed in her sirenesque power to summon any man to her will. Nathan would rather have had a grilled cheese at The Diner, where Devorah would never think to find him. Cheddar and provolone on thick Canadian bread. Nathan's mouth started to water just thinking about it.

Devorah must have noticed, because she stopped in front of him, fingered his tie and let out a sultry "ooooh." Running her other hand up his lapel and around his neck, she said, "I knew you would come around. You'll like it better this way. Trust me."

Nathan shook his head, cleared his throat and tried to resist the tingling from her fingertips. He had to admit, it felt nice. To remind him of the price, his nausea returned at the same time.

"I'm sure I will," he said.

They stood next to the small table in the same type of suite that she had occupied with Gavin just the night before. Nathan eyed her purse lying on the table while she fumbled with his tie.

Then she put a finger to his lips and said, "hold on a moment while I go freshen up." She turned and strutted towards the bathroom, looking over her shoulder with a smile, the tip of her tongue protruding through her teeth.

It took every ounce of will for Nathan to not roll his eyes. He stood still, trying to look transfixed.

As soon as the door closed, Nathan descended on her purse and rummaged through it like a hungry bear rummaging through a picnic basket. He tried to be careful to leave things more or less in the same position he found them - some women noticed details like that.

He glanced at the bathroom door, clueless as to what he would say if she stepped out and caught him rummaging through her purse. Then his hand found her wallet. He yanked it out and snapped it open. There, through the clear plastic window, he saw it. *Bingo*.

He jammed her badge into his inside jacket pocket, snapped the wallet shut and placed it back in her purse, hoping it was in the same place as before.

He started to zip her purse back up, but the zipper stuck. He tried to brute force it closed, but it wouldn't budge.

He saw the handle on the bathroom door move. He was out of time. Nathan bolted for the door and ran down the hallway towards the elevator.

Devorah stepped out from the bathroom, unfurled her arms over her head, cocked her hip and with a beaming smile, said, "Ta-dah."

Dressed in lacy action-ready black bra and panties, she looked around. The bed was still made. The TV was off. She peered into the semi-darkness of the suite's living room. A sliver of light danced across the carpet as the door slowly closed against the compressed air of its piston.

As the door latch closed, she called out quietly, "Nathan?" She walked slowly through the suite and into the living area. "Did you go for a drink or something?"

She didn't want to come off looking needy, but she couldn't let him go after getting this close. So she decided to call him. But when she went to unzip her purse, it was already open.

She stood there, holding her already-open purse, trying to remember when she had forgotten to close it. And why. She never forgot. Ever. She looked at the door, then she gently probed the contents of her purse.

She laid her purse down and carefully opened her wallet. Then she saw the blank plastic window where her badge should have been.

"Oh, fuck."

# *ALL IN*

Nathan stepped from the elevator and ran for the main lobby door. He had already put in his Uber order and held his phone in his hand, painstakingly watching the display update with the car's position. It told him he would have to wait four minutes.

Standing in front of the hotel, he nodded at the doorman, hoping he didn't see that Nathan was now a fugitive on the run with stolen property. "Four minutes," he said, waving his smart phone. The doorman smiled politely and looked away. Nathan grunted as he though of all the strange goings-on such a man must have seen and heard throughout the day. Things he probably never paid attention to. Hopefully.

Nathan ran the numbers through his head. It would take her a minute, two at the most, to figure out what had happened. Another minute to get dressed. Another minute to the lobby. That was four minutes at the most. By the time his ride arrived, she could be right behind him.

He glared at his smart phone, the display painfully slow with its updates. "Come on come on."

When the Uber pulled up, Nathan had been waiting three minutes and thirty-eight seconds. *Close enough.*

He opened the door. As he was sitting down, the driver asked him, "Who are you?"

"Nathan."

The driver checked the smart phone mounted on his dashboard. "Alright," he said, and pulled gently out of the curved driveway and back onto the street.

The guy was professional, careful and smooth. Which meant he was slow. Nathan fished a $100 bill from his wallet and waved it in front of the driver's face. "Go as fast as you can."

The driver glanced at the money and said, "I'm sorry sir, I can't."

Nathan grumbled and pulled another bill from his wallet, waving both in front of the driver's face.

The driver tapped the phone and said, "I can't. They track us and I'll get a warning or suspension. I can't afford either."

Nathan grunted, stuffed the bills in his suit jacket pocket and glanced at his phone. They were ten minutes away. Devorah would have to wait at least as long as he did for her Uber. Longer if she decided to call the bank for a ride. Unless she -.

The car stopped at a red light and Nathan jumped out.

The driver called after him, "Hey!" Nathan hit the sidewalk at a dead run and barely heard the driver yell, "You're gonna' get charged anyway."

The thick soles of Nathan's Murray Reserve cap-toes clopped against the sidewalk. He unbuttoned his suit jacket and let it flap behind him. His tie fluttered up over his shoulder. Nathan felt his heart beating at a rapid but steady pace. He may not have had time for a relationship, but he had adamantly refused to give up his fitness routine at the gym. Sometimes that kind of decision comes to a head in a single moment and he was grateful that he could outrun Devorah if nothing else.

Gulping air as he glanced at his family's name declare itself in glass and steel, he pushed his way through the revolving door and bolted across the lobby to the elevator. Heads turned to watch him. He was going to be seen. There was nothing he could do about that. It didn't matter. It had to be done.

Once in the basement, Nathan ran to the vault, whipped out Devorah's badge and stared at the reader.

What if it didn't work? What if she had called ahead and told them to disable her badge? What if she had reported that he had stolen it? What would happen when her name flashed red across some screen and the camera staring down at him from the ceiling recorded him at the same time?

Then it would be over, he realized. But, in that moment, there was nothing he could do about it. What absolutely had to work either would or would not. If it didn't, he would be put out on the street for violating however many corporate policies they could drum up to skewer him. He would never work in a bank again. His name would be ruined. His family's name would be ruined. He could already see Gavin standing behind a small forest of microphones at the press conference: *Well, you know, this is the sort of thing that happens for some people who can't adapt to progress. The world has to move forward but some people would rather keep it standing still. We wish Mr. Haley the best of luck. And I can assure you this will have no impact on our commitment to build our great community into the great city it deserves to be.*

Would it be so bad? He could give up now. No harm, no foul. Assure Devorah and Gavin that he understood. People who should have been smart enough not to sign in the first place would get what they probably deserved. It wasn't his job to save the world. Was he really supposed to risk his career, everything he had spent his life building, just because his father sold the bank to the wrong man? What if he could find a way to fix it later? Couldn't he do more good from the inside? He couldn't do much if he were kicked out on the street.

Nathan was shaken from his reverie by the sound of a beep. He looked at the steady green light on the reader and then the badge in his hand, which had decided on its own to run the badge through.

That was it, then. He ran the numbers on the combination lock, turned the handle and opened the vault door.

The cash vault was locked behind another door which required two keys to open, neither of which he had in his possession. His breath hitched when he realized they could have stashed the applications in there.

The front room housed the filing cabinets and some smaller vaults for various treasures like paintings, jewels and other collateral that the bank actually collected for larger loans.

He looked around and decided to open the closest filing cabinet first. It was locked with a simple key lock. He had that key.

He was working on the third cabinet and still nobody had come storming into the vault to stop him. Then he realized why. They were waiting for him to come out with stolen documents. Documents with his signature, but documents recovered with a stolen badge. Again, that put him on the street, even if he would eventually prevail in court. By then, it wouldn't matter. Whatever they had planned would be done and over.

So he slowed down, took his time and found what he was looking for in the fourth cabinet. An assortment of about 100 files sitting behind a cardboard partition marked "Sunfield Farms." It was one of the first tract of houses his father had funded. Starter homes for young families or late bloomers. Decent homes, but far from opulent. They were the beginning. Ground zero of over two decade's worth of building up a thriving community.

That was why his hand had run the badge. Somewhere deep inside he knew he couldn't forsake the sacred ground where his family's legacy had been born.

He laid the files out on a long steel table sitting between the filing cabinets. A locker against the far wall yielded a large money bag. He piled the folders into the bag, zipped it up and slung it over his shoulder.

When he stepped out of the vault, the hallway was still empty. He pushed the door shut, heard the latches clang and confirmed the reader was dormant. He glanced at the cameras in the ceiling. They had to know he was coming out.

He called the elevator, half expecting security guards to come storming out. But it was empty. Once inside, he thought about it for a moment and instead of pushing the button for the lobby, he went to the fourteenth floor.

He stepped out and walked over to a long balcony and the gallery window looking down on the lobby. Fourteen floors below, he saw two security guards hovering around the elevator. Another two were stationed at the revolving door.

He knew he could outrun the two guarding the elevator. They got paid to stand around. Nathan could run. But getting past the two at the door meant he was going to have to knock at least one of them down.

Now he was looking at assault. And he wouldn't be able to get through them both. He adjusted the bag on his shoulder as he studied the scene.

Resigned to going down with a fight, Nathan took out his smart phone and started to order an Uber when it chimed with a message from Maggie. There were only two words: *out back.*

Nathan ran back into the elevator, rode down to the second floor, stepped out as casually as he could and walked around to the stairwell. He sucked in a breath and pushed against the metal bar that declared he was using a fire exit. Just as he opened the door, an alarm repeated a down-sweeping tone and then every fire alarm in the building flashed white.

Nathan ran down to the lobby level and through the outer door that led into the employee parking lot where he found Maggie waiting for him in an early-model Corolla. She looked around and then waved to him.

Nathan heaved the bag into the backseat and then jumped into the front passenger seat. Eying the two security guards that burst from the door and into the parking lot, Maggie pulled a shawl from the backseat and said, "Here, cover up with this." Nathan hooded his head with the shawl and hunkered down while Maggie waved and smiled at the guards who were now running towards her.

She eased onto the street and casually accelerated. In her rear-view mirror, she saw the guards speaking frantically into their radios.

"Where to boss?"

"Gallery."

## *SANCTUARY*

The Knife and Palette art gallery was almost big enough to be an art museum and Nathan owned every square inch of it, so when he stepped into the lobby, he knew he was beyond Gavin's reach.

He had run the last six blocks after Maggie had dropped him off at a subway station. He didn't think Gavin actually had the wherewithal to put a tail on him, but Maggie reminded him not to underestimate his enemy.

Still panting, Gavin stepped into the cavernous room where a myriad of original oils and folios hung, most from unknown artists. Nathan had a curator who often threw her hands up in exasperation at his choices, but he believed in showing work that would likely not find a home anywhere else. Most of it wasn't quite good enough to actually sell, but some of his finds where downright stunning. Commissions were scarce and the gallery had never made money, but he kept it going with his mandatory share of quarterly profits from the bank. But it was known well enough to attract buyers and occasionally article-writers from the likes of American Art Collector. His father had been against it, knowing that it would be a losing proposition. But Nathan won him over with the remark that a community was more than houses and grocery stores.

Nathan strode through the gallery with the money bag slung over his shoulder, smiling as he was blanketed by the warm contentment of watching people peruse paintings. The quiet soul-searching that came from looking at an artist's heart-felt vision of the world reminded him that there was still more to the world than the heartache that was Haley National.

He quietly unlocked a door on the far side of the gallery and stepped into his studio, closing the door behind him. He dropped the bag to the floor and leaned with his back against the door. He let the darkness envelop him, hiding him from the world as he waited for his breath to subside.

After a few moments, he flicked on the lights. Unlike his office at the bank, Nathan's studio was a maelstrom of managed chaos. Blank canvases, oils, knives and palettes filled a shelf against the wall. A few paintings hung on the wall, but most of them were stacked against it at random intervals. Only one person besides himself had ever seen any of them and none of them hung in the gallery. Nor would they. He just wasn't that good and he knew it. While some artists rendered works that could inspire others with the same spiritual yearning that drove them to paint, Nathan recognized that art was more often a process than a result. Still, he smiled absently as he recalled what that one person had said. *Art unseen is a conspiracy against the human soul.* Maybe so, but Nathan wasn't willing to worship spiritual cleansing at the alter of humiliation. If the art didn't connect with the viewer, Nathan didn't see the point in showing it.

He laid the bag on the floor next to the wall, unzipped it and took out a few files. He opened one of the files and placed the application against the blank canvas sitting on his easel. Credit score: 751. He placed another one on the easel. 802. Then, another. 703. 749. 721. He went back to the bag to find the application corresponding to the one the Emmerson lawyer had sent him. There, in a simple box above his original signature that read *credit score,* he saw the number: 738. He distinctly remembered the copy she had sent him saying 501. It could have been a clerical error, but somebody with a 738 simply did not miss their mortgage payments. More importantly, he would have never signed a mortgage for somebody with a 501.

Nathan closed the files and dropped them into the bag. He zipped it up and stacked a few paintings in front of it. It wasn't hidden, but it wasn't obvious. He had the only key to the room and the only other person he would ever bring into his studio wouldn't notice. Or care.

The ordeal done, Nathan felt the fatigue from the day wash over him. His mind was racing, filled with the events of the day and countless next steps and contingencies. He needed to clear all that away.

He unfolded the note Maggie had given him once they were clear of the bank. On it, she had written the word *buyer*, followed by a name. Nathan studied the note, nodding slowly as he realized what he had to do next.

But that would come later. Nathan folded the note, tucked it into his suit jacket pocket and eyed the coffee-stained shirt draped over a wire hanger hooked into a hole in the shelf rail. He smiled, stripped off his suit jacket, shirt and tie and pulled the coffee-stained shirt from the hangar. He put it on and left it unbuttoned, the sensation of a faux intimacy wrapping him like a blanket.

Sitting down at his easel, Nathan picked up the palette sitting on a rickety wooden table next to him and rummaged through the tubes of oil sitting in the easel's tray. He mixed a few, starting with green.

Next, he picked up a clean number 1 round brush. He studied it for a moment, twirling it in his fingertips to check for stray hairs. He stared at the canvas for a moment and then lightly dipped the brush in the mixture of oils he had concocted.

He was doing it wrong. He was supposed to start with the broader strokes first. But Nathan didn't care. He started with the thing he remembered most clearly. The essence that cleansed his soul and induced an unfamiliar yearning ache in his heart.

Art was a process.

## *UPON THIS HILL*

After painting for an hour, Nathan heard a soft knock at the door. He tilted his head to the side, confirming the pattern. He smiled and nodded. He put down his palette and brush and draped a cloth over the painting. He never showed a painting in progress. And to most people, he never showed his work at all.

He stood up and opened the door to see his friend Jerry Westland standing at the threshold massaging his forehead.

Nathan grunted. "Maggie?"

"Yeah, she called. Said you were in a pickle."

Nathan stepped back to his easel. "Close the door behind you." He stood behind his easel, but did not remove the covering. He studied it anyway, evaluating how the painting looked so far in his mind.

"If it's money -"

Nathan put up his hand. "I know. But the gallery still isn't for sale."

"It's not the gallery, it's your curator. Why is she still here?"

"I don't know, but she thinks your obsession with Monet is pedantic."

"Snob."

Smiling, Nathan said, "So the bid is withdrawn?"

"No. Still stands."

"Noted."

Jerry came around to stand next to Nathan and stared at the covering. He pointed at the shirt. "What happened there?"

"Oh, that." Nathan tugged at the shirt and looked at the coffee stain. "I met a girl."

Jerry's eyes widened in surprise. "Really?"

Nathan studied the stain for a moment. "Well, sort of."

Jerry smiled at his friend's embarrassment. Then he asked, "So, what's up?"

"Maggie's right. I got myself into a real jam."

Jerry waited for the silence to grow uncomfortable until he said, "Well, what's the story?"

Nathan took a deep breath and shook his head. "I don't know if I should say anything."

Jerry let the silence grow between them. Still looking at the covering, he said, "You know that anything you say here stays here."

Nathan looked at his friend. "Even if you're sitting in a courtroom under oath?"

Jerry looked somber. Nathan knew he wanted to help, but he didn't want to drag his friend into whatever nightmare he had stirred from its deep slumber.

"Especially if I'm under oath."

"That's easy to say."

Jerry waited for a moment before saying, "No, it's not."

Nathan took a deep breath and said, "Alright then. But remember, you asked for this."

To this Jerry said, "I won't remember a thing sir."

Nathan smiled and grunted. "I've got a situation on my hands where I may be up against fraud charges."

Jerry turned his head all the way this time. "That does sound serious."

"It is. It's not something I did on purpose." Nathan wasn't sure he wanted to say the next part because it sounded dubious, even in his own mind. "I think I might have been set up."

"He's connected, you know."

"Who?"

"Gavin. Everybody knows. He's no good."

"Well, I can't disagree with you on that."

Jerry waited a moment and then placed a hand on Nathan's shoulder. "So, ditch it"

"What? Ditch what?"

"All of it. Take my money and move somewhere far away from all this and start over."

"I can't. I have to look after the bank."

"The bank? Are you serious? God rest his soul, but the bank was doomed the moment your dad shook Gavin's hand. The bank is gone. Has been for a long time."

Nathan shot his friend a glance. He had to know that one hurt.

"Look," Jerry said, "all I'm saying is that it's not your fault and it might be better to get away from all of this before it blows up in your face."

Nathan shook his head, his mouth set in a hard thin line. "And let him win?"

"Jesus Christ. Winning. Losing. It's not about all that. You're one guy. He's an army of CDO washouts from Wall Street. All they want is their money back and they don't care how they get it."

Nathan knew the man was telling him the truth. He just didn't see the rest of it.

"You're saying I can't win."

"I'm saying you've already lost. Just get out while you can. There's no shame in dodging something you can't stop."

"You know I can't do that."

Jerry looked at the floor. His voice was tight and his words came out in clipped stabs. "I know. But somebody has to tell you these things. The world that you and your dad lived in is long gone."

Nathan stared at his friend. Couldn't he see the obvious? "No it's not," he said, jabbing a thumb into his chest. "It lives right here."

"So take it with you. Plant it somewhere it has a chance to grow."

Nathan looked at the ceiling, his eyes welling up. "It doesn't work like that. This dream lives or dies here. Now."

"Why? Dude, you can be a good man anywhere. There are still places where that matters. Just not here. Not anymore."

"Because this is where my father and I built this dream. It's the only one he and I will ever have. I may wind up living in a cardboard box under an overpass, but Gavin is going to have to go through me to bring it down." He looked at his friend and sniffed back the tears. "It's all I've got."

## *CAT BAIT*

By the eighteenth hole, Nathan had established a comfortable rapport with the man who would usher him across a line he never thought he would cross. He had caught Gavin off guard and now he had to knock him down at least once to let him know that Nathan could defend himself. That he was willing to get down in the gutter alongside him, even if he wasn't as experienced at that sort of thing.

He had to push away the image of Maggie and the people who trudged to the bank every day so they could pay rent, buy groceries and keep a roof over their heads. That image had weighed on him for the seventeen holes he had spent listening to the buyer talk about his yacht, his art collection and a pandering nod to Nathan's "little gallery." He hadn't meant that as an insult and sincerely admired Nathan's curation. He was just the kind of man who saw the world as slightly beneath him, a social casualty of a lifetime of wealth.

People like Maggie didn't have a yacht. He knew that the first response to a lag in revenue was to cut a company's greatest expense - payroll. Who would sit at home wondering what had happened, wondering what they had done wrong, because of what he was about to tell this man?

It would come to that eventually anyway, wouldn't it? Gavin was already driving the bank into the ground, wasn't he?

But Nathan couldn't unshoulder responsibility that easily. People were going to lose their jobs and it was going to be his fault. He honestly didn't know if he could live with that. But he knew for certain than he couldn't live with Gavin destroying his family's legacy without paying a price.

After uncoiling with perfect form to send the ball 150 yards down the fairway, the buyer bent over, picked up his tee and turned to Nathan with a smile. Nathan checked to make there wasn't anybody on the seventeenth. He needed a minute.

They were both fit and had agreed to the challenge of walking the course instead of taking a cart. If the buyer's shoulder hurt as Nanthan's did and if he were aching from fatigue as Nathan was, he didn't show it as he picked up his bag and slung it over his shoulder. Nathan's plan had been to wear the buyer down so he would be less resistant to what Nathan had to tell him. Now, he wondered if it hadn't worked out the other way around.

The buyer watched Nathan, waiting for him to take his turn at the tee. The buyer tilted his head and squinted when Nathan put his driver back in the bag and said, "Listen, there's something we need to discuss for a moment."

Still squinting, the buyer said, "Oh no you don't. I'm up by one stroke here and you're not going to put me off my game with fake shop talk."

"It's about the paper you're buying."

The buyer let out a sigh and shook his head. "What about it?"

Nathan unzipped a pouch in his bag and pulled out an envelope. He tapped it lightly in his hand, wondering one last time if it was worth the risk of letting the man see a document that could not only ruin his reputation but could lead to a prison cell.

He stood up and held the envelope out to the man. "You need to see this."

Eying Nathan carefully, the man took the envelope. Cradling it in his hand for a moment, he asked, "What is this?"

"Something you need to see for yourself."

The man scratched his chin, pursed his lips and then opened the envelope. Thumbing through the pages, he asked, "What am I looking at?"

"One of the applications."

The man thumbed through the pages again, then stopped and flipped to the credit report in the back, staring at it for a moment. Then he flipped to the other credit report. "Which one is right?" he asked.

"The last one. You can check the rest for yourself, but you'll see the same thing."

The buyer turned his gaze on Nathan and said, "What, did you get cold feet?" Then his face went tight and Nathan could see the vein in his neck starting to swell. "You come at me with a bullshit stunt like this and wait until I'm just about to sign to change your mind?" He stared at Nathan, fuming. "I will end you."

"It's not like that," Nathan said.

"Then what is it like?"

"It's not me."

The man shook the papers in Nathan's face. "Your signature, right here."

"I know." Nathan fell silent, hoping the man's curiosity would get the better of him.

The buyer let out a sigh and asked, "What do you mean it's not you?"

Nathan took a small step closer, closing the distance between them. He spoke in a low tone so the man had to focus on his words. "Those applications were brought to me with the altered credit reports attached to them. I didn't give it a second thought and signed off on them."

The buyer scoffed. "What, you're saying you were set up? Come on."

"I don't think anybody was supposed to find out. Least of all, you."

"I've already made commitments based on this deal. Commitments that cost me money."

"And now you have a due diligence problem. If it comes out you knew about this, you'll be liable, just like me."

The man's eyes widened. Poking Nathan in the chest, he said, "Blackmail? Seriously? Me?"

Forcing himself to remain calm, Nathan said, "I'm just pointing out that you are now obligated to walk on the deal. It's tainted. You have to walk away."

Seething, the buyer asked, "Why? Because you grew a conscience? Well good for you. There is real money on the line here."

"Real money that you will never see. Like I said, check for yourself. They're all the same. None of them can pay. That's why you have to walk away. To protect your money."

The man looked to the side, working his jaw as he thought it through. Nathan could tell the man was angry, but his logic was undeniable. The buyer just had to realize it.

"Don't think I'm going to let you off the hook just because you're coming clean. This is going to cost you. I'm going to the DA."

Nathan nodded somberly. "With a copy."

"What?"

"You'll be going to the DA with a copy. He'll need the originals to do anything."

The buyer smiled dismissively. "Fine, I'll get them from Gavin."

"No you won't."

"Look, Nathan, I respect you for what you and your father did for this town, but I'm not going to play this game with you. I will get what I need from Gavin and then it's all over. I hate to see this happen to you, but it's business and I can't have people thinking they can come at me like this. I have to send a message."

"He can't give you the originals."

Nathan could see it in the man's eyes - he had already dismissed Nathan as somebody who was grasping at straws.

"OK, why not?"

Nathan took another step forward. "Because he doesn't know where they are."

## *NO BUSINESS*

The buyer was standing in front of the receptionist's desk. He leaned down with both palms and said, "I don't care where he is or what he's doing. He needs to talk to me right now. Give him my name and tell him I'm not happy."

Two minutes later, he was standing in Gavin's office. Gavin stepped out from behind his desk, smiled and offered his hand. The buyer responded by shoving the envelope in Gavin's hand.

"What's this?" Gavin asked.

"You tell me."

Gavin held the envelope in his hand without moving for several moments. The buyer could see the wheels spinning as Gavin searched for a way to put him off. But he wasn't going to let Gavin off the hook this time.

When he opened the envelope and saw the paperwork, Gavin groaned. "This again?" Folding the paper work and stuffing it back into the envelope, he asked, "Where did you get this?" He tossed the envelope on his desk, as if it were a trivial inconvenience.

But the buyer knew it was more than that. Much more. "I want to see the originals."

"The what?"

"The originals, Gavin. I'm not signing one more goddamn piece of paper until I see original ink applications."

"OK, OK, don't get so riled up." After a moment, he smiled disarmingly and asked, "You know why he's doing this, don't you?"

"Who?"

"Nathan."

"Who said anything about Nathan?"

"Look, you know how it is. He works his ass off his entire life expecting to inherit the bank and his father sells it to somebody else instead. Hell, I don't blame him. I'd be pissed off, too."

"Then why do you keep him around?"

Gavin grunted. "Trust me, it's not my decision." He let out a helpless huff. Holding his hands out, he said, "It's in the contract. The bank came with Nathan, cut and dried." Gavin looked down and let out a thoughtful sigh. "He keeps doing this. I don't think he's ever going to get over the fact that his father didn't let him have the bank."

"Uh-huh." The buyer narrowed his eyes. He was on the brink of killing the deal of a lifetime and Gavin was trying to distract him with family drama. He knew it then. He had been taken for a ride. He sucked in a quick breath when he realized how close he had come to actually getting caught up in whatever scam Gavin had in store. He realized now that Nathan had just saved him a fortune. "Well, like I said, without the originals, this deal isn't going anywhere."

Gavin's eyes fluttered as he looked to one side and then the other. He licked his lips and then settled his gaze on the buyer. "Those are archived. I'll look into it and get back to you."

The buyer watched Gavin stroke his hand with his thumb, leaving a white trail from pressing down so hard. "Show me now."

"What, drop everything and head to the vault right now? I wish I could. There's a process."

"What do you mean process? You're the owner."

"There are still rules I have to follow." Gavin started to put his hand on the buyer's shoulder, thought better of it when the buyer glared at him. Instead, Gavin stepped past him and opened the door. "Look, we're both busy men. I understand what you're asking for. I just can't get to it right at this moment. I'll be in touch." He gestured at the door. "Soon. We'll get this sorted. But I need a little time to get things organized, OK?"

The buyer shook his head, turned and walked out of Gavin's office. As the door closed behind him, he made a decision. Whatever was going on between Gavin and Nathan wasn't his problem. He had learned something a long time before that had saved him millions and probably would again this time. No business was better than bad business. And dealing with Haley National was bad business.

The buyer walked away and never looked back.

## *MOUSE TRAP*

Gavin sat back down behind his desk, picked up his phone and dialed. After it picked up on the other end, he said, "Find Nathan and tell him to get his ass up here." He listened for a moment while Maggie made excuses. "You tell him if he's not here in five minutes, I will fire his ass, contract or no. He's stepped over the line this time."

Three and a half minutes later, Nathan was standing in front of Gavin's desk. He started to sit down when Gavin, standing behind his desk said, "Stand up. Stand up there in front of me and shut up."

Nathan couldn't stifle a smile at Gavin's theatrics and deliberately let his eyelids droop and his face go slack as he tried to looked bored.

Gavin picked up the envelope and threw it at Nathan. "What the hell is this?"

Nathan let the envelope hit his chest and fall to the floor. His chest swelled a little because for the first time since his father had sold the bank, Nathan had put Gavin on the defensive. And he didn't seem to be handling it well.

"We've been over that, Gavin. You said Calhoun would take care of it."

"And how did the buyer get ahold of it?"

"What buyer?"

Seething, Gavin held up a finger. "Don't. You know goddamn well what I'm talking about. We're selling the paper for Sunfield Farms."

Nathan forced a shocked look onto his face. "Well, thanks for telling me. How long has this been going on?"

Pursing his lips, Gavin leaned back and folded his hands on his chest. "OK, if you want to play it that way. But if this gets out, it's your ass on the line. Are you looking forward to spending time in prison?"

"If this gets out, the bank will go down. I might go to prison, but you'll lose the bank to receivership. Are you looking forward to working at Taco Bell?"

"Would you really let that happen, Nathan? Are you telling me that you're actually willing to watch the legacy that your father spent his lifetime building go down the tubes? No, I don't think so. You're too sentimental."

Nathan clenched his jaw. "I don't see how I can stop it while you're over there driving it into the ground."

"Don't presume you know what it's like to sit in this chair, Nathan. You have no idea what it takes to run a bank. That's why your father sold it to me instead of leaving it in your hands." Gavin showed a wicked smile when he saw he had struck a nerve. "He knew you couldn't handle it."

Nathan's mouth fell open. While he was dumbstruck by Gavin's cruelty, he was shocked even more by the idea that he might be right. Did his father really not trust him to run the family business? He had told Nathan that he was almost ready. To watch Gavin carefully and learn what he had to until the time came for him to take the helm. The only problem was that time was never going to come. Because his father had not included it in the contract. Nathan's heart sank as he realized that his father could very well have duped him into believing the bank would be in his hands one day. But why?

"And he didn't know what kind of man you are."

Shifting gears, Gavin said, "The only reason I haven't fired you is Calhoun says you're entitled to bank documents as its Vice President."

"Would you have given them to me if I had just asked?"

Gavin grunted and shook his head. "That smart-ass mouth of yours is going to be your undoing." Gavin sat down behind his desk. "I need those originals. I'm entitled to them, as well. So what say we quit playing this stupid game and get back to the business of running the bank?"

"Well, here's my smart-ass response to that." Nathan took a step closer to the desk. "I don't trust you, Gavin. Those originals stay right where they are. If you want 'em, you can go to court, in which case they become public record and take all of us down."

"And what makes you think I won't do exactly that?"

"Because, while I'm fighting for my father's legacy, you're fighting for just one thing: yourself. You won't risk losing the only shot you have left just because I'm in your way."

Gavin smiled coldly. "Try me."

"I already have."

## *PLAN B*

Gavin clenched his fist when he heard the knock at his office door. *Now what*?

He started to get up but froze in place when the door opened and Ingrid stepped inside, flashing him a smile, a gleaming white fissure that split the barren landscape of a hard face that had seen too much of the world.

Gavin could feel his heart beating faster and beads of sweat seeping out of his bald scalp. He didn't think Olivia would send Ingrid until things got much worse. He had less time than he thought.

Dressed in cargo pants and a chambray shirt with a black shoulder bag slung at her side, Ingrid stood calmly in the doorway, watching his reaction as if she were watching a wounded animal limp across her lawn. "Relax, darling. Sit down." Most mistook her light accent as Russian when she was actually from Azerbaijan.

Gavin knew the last thing Ingrid wanted was for him to relax. He also knew that she wasn't asking him to sit down - she was telling him. That's because he also knew that somewhere inside that shoulder bag was a Smith & Wesson Military and Police 9 M2.0 pistol fitted with a silencer and a 17-round magazine.

Gavin slowly sat down, keeping his gaze locked on hers. He needed her to know that he was listening. She settled into one of the leather chairs in front of his desk, resting one hand on an armrest, the other on her shoulder bag. "What does she want now?" he asked.

"Oh, darling, do I really need to go through all that?"

"I think that would be best. I don't want there to be any misunderstanding."

Ingrid's eyes lit up and she showed a wicked smile. "Oh, I know. Let's play a game. Why don't you tell me what you think she wants and we'll see if you get it right."

Gavin's chest felt even tighter and he could no longer ignore the sweat dripping from his brow. "And if I get it wrong?"

Ingrid smiled coyly and tapped the pistol resting inside her shoulder bag.

"Come on, gimme a break. Just tell me. I promise you, I'm listening."

Ingrid's smile disappeared. "Break time over. Getting it right time has started."

"She wants her money," he said. Ingrid stared blankly at Gavin, looking through him, really. He stared at her hand resting on her shoulder bag, inches away from the weapon stashed inside. "Look, just tell her that something's come up. A snag. Surely, she understands that. She must know what it's like to hit an unplanned obstacle. Tell her that - I've hit an unplanned obstacle."

"Nobody's asking you, Gavin. Please, go on with what you think she wants."

"Look, the laundering thing isn't working out quite as good as we'd hoped."

"She knows this."

"And this latest plan has, like I said, hit an unexpected challenge."

"She knows this too."

Starting to doubt he had any chances left after enumerating his own failures, he asked, "How does she know?"

"Darling, is this a question you seriously want to ask?"

"OK, then she knows Nathan is behind it. Is there anything you can do about it?"

Ingrid narrowed her gaze, a coy smile playing at the corners of her mouth. "Are you asking me to perform a service that only my employer can ask me to perform?"

Licking his lips, Gavin gulped and said, "No no. Of course not. I'm asking if that's something she might be interested in. It could help me."

"Nathan does not owe her money. You owe her money. How you manage your own people is your problem." She looked down to pick a piece of lint from her collar. "You're not doing a good job explaining what she wants."

Gavin let out a sigh, clasped his hands together and stared down at his desk. "She wants her money. She wants it on time. She wants me to keep a lid on whatever is attracting attention because that could lead back to her."

Now a broad smile embraced her weathered face once again. "See, easy to say."

"You gotta' cut me some slack here. I need time."

Ingrid shook her head. "No darling. Time I cannot give you."

"Alright, then I'm open to suggestions."

Ingrid giggled and looked around the room. “You could rob bank.”

Non-plussed, Gavin said, “I’m not going to prison for her.”

Ingrid’s expression went stone cold. “You may wish you had.”

“Tell her I’m going to Plan B.”

Ingrid reared back and sucked in a slow breath. “She’s not going to like that.”

“I know. But it’s all I’ve got if she wants this to move fast. Look, she’s going to make a killing on the back end.”

“Olivia does not like complicated. She likes money.”

“Just tell her, alright. Let’s see what she thinks.”

Ingrid studied him for a moment. Gavin flinched when she leapt to her feet and said, “Alright darling. But I don’t think she will like this.”

She turned for the door. As her hand went to the handle, Gavin said, “Thank you.”

Ingrid’s hand came back to her side and she turned to face Gavin, giving him her full attention. “For what darling?” When he didn’t answer, she smiled softly, turned and left his office.

*For not shooting me.*

## *LANCE AND MILL*

Sarah opened the stairwell door to enter the hallway to the clinic and stopped short when she saw the throng of people spilling out from the clinic and into the hallway.

Working her way through the sea of somber-faced clients with "Excuse me," "Pardon me," and "Coming through," Sarah elbowed her way into the office.

Maureen was sitting at her desk talking to somebody on the phone and waved Sarah over. Without stopping at her own desk to drop off her courier bag, Sarah walked straight over to Maureen as she finished up the call. "Yeah. OK. Yep. Understood. Got it. Thanks again. OK, bye now." She hung up, let out a long breath, looked at Sarah and shook her head.

"What's up?" Sarah asked.

"How did it go?"

Looking at the crowd, Sarah asked, "How did what go?"

"Your hearing."

"Yeah, fine. Got the restraining order. She's with social services now." Looking back at Maureen, she said, "Now tell me what's going on."

"Haley National has declared war on Sunfield Farms, that's what."

Sarah raised her hands and shook her head.

Maureen waved at the crowd dismissively. "Foreclosures. Each and every one of them."

"What? That makes no sense."

"Yeah, I know. I just got off the phone with their loan officer to confirm. She says it's the real thing. They're 'realigning their portfolio.'"

Sarah stared at Maureen, blinking as she ran her hand through her hair. "Realigning their what?" She jutted her arm out, pointing at the crowd. "This is predatory."

"How did you get there?"

"When was the last time you saw a bank walk out on an entire subdivision?"

"I dunno" Maureen pinched her nose. "Look, we need to verify each and every one of these. Maybe we can find something wrong with a couple of them. At any rate, let's check them all just so we can say we did." Sarah was looking at the crowd, only half listening to Maureen. "Sarah, did you hear what I said?"

Sarah turned to look at Maureen and said, "Yeah. Check the paper work." Looking back at the crowd she said, "Unless they couldn't find a buyer. But why?"

Standing up, Maureen asked, "What? What are you talking about?"

Without answering, Sarah walked to the clapboard separating the waiting area from the office. The closer she got, the louder the clamoring became.

She held up her hand. "Quiet please. I need your attention for a moment. Quiet please." But the clamoring only became louder. Just as she was about to try again, Maureen sidled up next to her and boomed out in a voice that came straight from her childhood neighborhood, "Alright now, that's enough. Listen up."

Stunned by Maureen's dead-on impersonation of a drill sergeant, the crowd settled down. Maureen waved a hand at Sarah and took a step back. "Your show."

"Right." Sarah cleared her throat. "Alright, when I point to you, I just need you to tell me how much money you have right now that you can pay towards your mortgage. It doesn't have to be the full amount or even a full payment. Anything you got."

The first three people just shook their heads but then a young woman with round eyes spoke up and said, "I got a few hundred. Maybe."

"Good." Sarah held out her hand. "Here, give me your paperwork." She fished a pen out of her skirt pocket and wrote down *300* on the front page.

"You sir. How much?" This was an older man, much like the one who came to her just the week before about his foreclosure. He let out a sigh. "I can do 500."

"Great."

Sarah took his paperwork and wrote down *500*. She worked her way through the entire crowd this way. Most of them could spare a partial payment. A few had more. A few couldn't spare anything at all. An hour later, she had a stack of foreclosure notices on her desk with numbers scribbled on the front adding up to $38,000.

"Now," she said, "go home and get it."

They all looked at her blankly. "Get what?" one of them asked.

"The money. Go home, get it and bring it back here."

They looked at her, then at each other, several of them shaking their heads.

"Look," she said, "We're going to have to work together on this. If we go to the bank with a class payment, we might be able to work something out. So, if you want to keep your home, I'm telling you, go home, gather up as much money as you can and bring it back here."

"Well, what if we just go to the bank directly?" a younger man asked. "I mean, why are we trusting you to handle it?"

"Because," she said, surveying the crowd, "You have just spent the past hour standing around in front of my legal clinic. And who do you think the bank is going to listen to? You or your lawyer?"

They looked at each other again. Some of them shrugged. A low murmur welled up and they slowly shuffled out the door.

As the last of them stepped into the hallway, Sarah turned to Maureen. "Sorry. I know that was kind of hard-nosed on my part."

Maureen smiled and put a hand on her shoulder. "Don't apologize. Sometimes client's best interest means tough love."

Sarah smiled. "Thanks."

Maureen dropped her hand and gazed out the door. "But I don't know if it's going to work. By the time it gets to this point, they're several months behind."

"All of them at once?"

Maureen nodded thoughtfully. "Good point."

"Something's going on here," Sarah said. "And how the bank reacts to some money will tell us something."

"That's not going to change the facts if they're behind. It's a straight line to summary judgment. You know the drill."

Sarah crossed her arms and stared into the empty hallway. "Something tells me there are some kinks in that line."

Surprised by the sound of his voice, both Sarah and Maureen turned to face Stanley when he said, "You're doing it again."

Glancing at Maureen, then back at Stanley, Sarah asked, "Doing what?"

"Windmills." Looking at the two empty desks where the two young lawyers had worked their six months and were now gone, he said, "That's a lot of time and effort that could be better spent on cases where we can actually help. Foreclosures are a formality. Read through them to make sure they're in order." He held up his index finger. "Once. Then write a letter explaining the hearings they'll have to attend. Then mail that to each of them. And that's it."

Sarah followed Stanley's gaze and studied the empty desks for a moment. Her mouth slightly agape, Sarah squinted at Maureen. "I thought you said you had candidates lined up around the block."

Maureen cast her eyes down. "That was just to get you to settle down." Looking back up at Sarah, she said, "Truth is, nobody wants to do this kind of work these days."

"Why not?" Sarah asked.

"They don't see it making much of a difference," Maureen said. "So they don't bother with it. Just move on to the associate slots, all gunning for a partnership, billing a hundred hours a week."

Sarah narrowed her gaze and took a step closer to Maureen. "So, the only reason I have a job is because I'm the only one willing to do it?"

"That's right," Stanley said. "So do as I say."

"Stanley, that's not fair," Maureen said. "She's learning and she means it."

"And I have people to answer to. Hand-holding deadbeats who can't make a house payment is not the business we're in. That's not what brings in the grant money."

"Then what does?" Sarah asked.

Stanley glanced at Maureen, who looked away. Settling his gaze on Sarah, Stanley said, "Doing what I tell you to do."

## *TOO CLOSE FOR COMFORT*

Sitting in the reception area at Haley National, Sarah tugged at the belt of her skirt. Earlier that morning, looking through her meager selection of skirts - three from Ross and one fancy skirt from JCPenney - she had wanted to land somewhere between lawyer and harlot. The result was the navy blue skirt from Penney's that tapered just a little too much and made her vaguely self-conscious of her back side. The blouse was strictly office wear, buttoned all the way to the collar. The matching navy blue blazer had only one button, which she fiddled with for what seemed like the hundredth time to make sure it was still fastened as she waited for the Vice President of Haley National to give her the time of day. She had to stop herself from tugging at the button so it wouldn't come off completely.

The receptionist sat hunkered down behind a semi-circular affair that seemed more fortress than desk, answering the phone and occasionally glancing at Sarah with a catty smile to remind Sarah that she was a subject of the small fiefdom that was the waiting area. She held up a finger, spoke a few words into the phone and then turned to Sarah. "He'll see you now."

Sarah stood up, grimaced at the snug feeling of the skirt against her back side and let out a quick breath. "Thank you."

A young associate opened the door flanking the desk and said, "This way please." He briskly led Sarah to a conference room with a mahogany table and leather-backed chairs. The room was completely walled by glass, so everyone would see her talking to the Vice President of Haley National. Sarah wasn't sure why he hadn't chosen a more private room. He probably thought putting her on display would subdue her efforts.

The associate pointed to a chair at one end of the table and said, "Please have a seat. Mr. Haley will be with you shortly."

Sarah looked at him blankly. *Of course he will.* She didn't want to sit down, but the associate insisted. "Please," he said, gesturing again at the chair. Frowning, Sarah sat down, dropped her courier bag on the table and crossed her arms. The associate smiled, left and closed the door behind him.

Refusing to look out the broad windows to see if he was on his way, Sarah tried to ignore her annoyance at the Vice President's clumsy announcement of his power by showing up late.

A few moments later, the door opened and a tall man stepped in. He stepped half-way through the door and then stopped without saying a word. Sarah's breath caught when she saw his face. She stood up to find herself staring at the man that she had spilled coffee on after her first hearing. She could feel her cheeks warming as she remembered hot coffee soaking into his expensive-looking shirt after her soapbox lecture to the disinterested patrons. Too many of her bold moments inevitably aged to become humiliating memories that she could never seem to let go. She would remember the coffee encounter at inopportune times on her own. She didn't need to face it in the flesh. Now, all she wanted was for a hole to open up in the floor so she could drop into a dark place very far away.

But she had clients to take care of. So she grimaced as the memory steeped her mind in humiliation.

His face lit up with a bright smile that creased the corners of his eyes. He stepped all the way into the room and held out his hand. "Nathan Haley."

Sarah moved her mouth, but no words came out. Sarah took his hand and managed to say, "I think we've met?"

The man gripped her hand firmly, but not powerfully. Just enough to hold hers in place while they shook hands for a moment or two longer than she felt comfortable. "Yes, I suppose we have."

Sarah pinched her nose and put her other hand on her hip. "Look," she said, "I'm sorry about that. It's just that I was having a bad day and seeing you step out of line to-" She stopped when he winced at her words. "Well, anyway," she said, "Sorry."

"No, not at all." She thought the memory made him as uncomfortable as it did her, but something deeper whispered to her that wasn't the reason behind the pained look on his face. She expected to find satisfaction in that revelation, but instead she felt a vague heaviness in her chest as she remembered the same worried look he had on his face as hot coffee soaked into his shirt. It was the oddest thing, but now he looked like a man who didn't deserve that. Then his expression softened. "What public service attorney worth her salt wouldn't fight for the people's right to a cup of coffee?"

Sarah forced a meager laugh. "Right." She unzipped her courier bag and took out her pocketbook. "How much is it?" she asked.

It was then that she noticed he hadn't moved. There were only two feet between them and she was uncomfortably aware of how close he was. Surely they weren't going to conduct their entire conversation this way?

"The cleaning bill," she said.

He laughed a little too loudly, tilting his head back. "Oh that. Don't worry about it. I didn't get it cleaned."

"why not?" Sarah immediately looked away and stared at the floor with a grimace. *You're not on a date. What are you doing?*

"I had been meaning to buy a nice working shirt anyway. Now I have one."

Still staring at the floor as she tried to regain her composure, Sarah put her pocket book away. She took a step back, looked back up and said, "Shall we?"

"Oh, right," he said, and sat down in the chair right next to hers so they were sharing a rounded corner of the table. It was customary to sit on opposite sides, but he was once again just two feet away from her. Sarah wanted to move away to put some formal distance between them, but she sensed that he would take that as some kind of rebuke and she didn't want him to clam up. So she endured the uncomfortable intimacy of the table corner.

"What can I do for you?" he asked. He smiled at her with an unexpected warmth that she tried to believe was disingenuous.

"Well," she said, reaching into her courier bag to take out a file, "it's about these foreclosures."

His eyes dimmed and then he looked away as he seemed to realize just then that they had business to discuss. The tone of his voice dropped and his words came out flat. "Yes. Sunfield Farms."

"I have in here a motion for injunctive relief, a request for declaration, a restraining order and a motion for discovery." She patted the file gently.

Nathan smiled sheepishly. "That sounds like a lot of legal things happening at once."

"That's because I feel there is more than meets the eye here. An entire subdivision foreclosed at the same time? That seems odd to me."

His face tightened and Sarah couldn't escape the bizarre notion that he looked like she had just refused his invitation to the prom.

Holding his palms open, Nathan said, "Look, my hands are pretty tied here -"

Not letting him say anything more, Sarah cut in. "Oh, of course." She leaned forward slightly, clasping her hands. "Why is it that men of power are powerless except when they're trampling the rights of their victims? But when it comes time to help, you're so hopeless and helpless. Really?"

Now the man looked as if she had squarely kicked him in the groin. "What do you think is really going on here, Ms. Thomas?"

The question took Sarah aback because it opened a door to inquiry which people in his position usually liked to keep closed.

Patting the file again, she said, "This TRO, injunction, declaration and motion all center on one simple idea." She stopped, still puzzled by the pained look in his expression.

"And what is that, Ms. Thomas?"

"Predatory lending."

Nathan closed his eyes and rubbed his chin.

Sarah studied him carefully, trying to discern if his discomfort was genuine or just a show for her benefit. "And if I can prove that, then I can have the court suspend the mortgages while we work out a restructuring deal."

"Well, if they can't pay anyway, what difference would that make?" Nathan narrowed his gaze and lightly drummed his fingers on the table.

Sarah stood up. Sliding her courier bag across the table, she said, "I'm sorry, but -" She stepped around the table and sat down across from him so there were now several feet of table between them. "It's just customary," she said.

His eyes drooped and his lips parted as he watched her sit back down. Sarah smiled politely and said, "To answer your question, the difference is you can't sell dead paper."

Nathan blinked a few times, looked down at the table and adjusted his tie. When he looked back up, his expression was, for the first time, executorial. Whatever his personal feelings were, his expression hid all of that now. "What are you proposing so we can avoid all -" Nathan waved dismissively at the file. -"that?"

Sarah hoped she was hiding her feelings just as well because, to her surprise, she missed the man who had been sitting next to her just moments before. But this was the way it was supposed to be. He was the bank executive throwing her clients out on the street. And she was their lawyer. Everything else -. Sarah tightened her fist and quietly thumped it against her thigh. There was no *everything else*. There couldn't be. She opened the file, pulled out a cashier's check for $38,001.48 and slid it across the table.

Nathan picked up the check and studied it. "In exchange for-?"

Sarah took a deep breath. She waited until the silence compelled him to put the check down and look at her. "Six month abatement and a restructuring plan that makes sense for everybody."

There it was - that smug look of amusement when the powerful are asked to do the right thing and know they don't have to. "I'm sorry Ms. Thomas, but like I said, my hands are tied."

"Have you seen the credit scores?" she asked.

"I have."

"Then you know I have a strong case." When he didn't respond, she pushed on. "Look, if I make this motion for discovery, everything is going to come out. Everything. I'm willing to set that aside if you will just work with me here. I don't think I'm asking too much under the circumstances." She waited for him to respond, but as the moments dragged on to build a wall of silence between them, she realized she was going to have to go to court. Which was fine by her except that it made things harder for her clients, who would sit in limbo wondering if and when they were going to lose their homes, quietly hoping that somehow she would save them. She had a strong case. But there were no guarantees. A deal would have been better.

"You're not asking too much, Ms. Thomas. But you're asking more than I can give."

Sarah shook her head. She put the check back in the file, the file back in her courier bag. "It's here if you change your mind," she said. Nathan just nodded. She stood up and shouldered her courier bag. On a whim, she asked, "What would you do if you were me?"

Nathan narrowed his gaze and leaned forward a few inches. "I would file that paperwork."

Sarah couldn't believe what he was saying. If it was hubris, then he was grossly underestimating the damage she could do. Her mind drifted back to the beginning of their meeting, when his expression ran across his face like a silent movie. She couldn't help wondering if his answer wasn't hubris. If it was something more - personal.

Now, Nathan stood up and just as he did, the door opened and her escort stepped into the conference room.

Sarah stepped around the table and towards the door. "I'm sorry we couldn't work something out."

Nathan let out a sigh, put one hand on his hip and stroked his chin. "There's something you should know," he said.

Sarah sensed he was on the fence. He seemed like a deer in a forest, ready to run at the slightest provocation. Sarah almost held her breath as she waited for him to continue.

"Sunfield Farms was the first tract my father funded. He applied for every community improvement grant and loan he could find. He drove hundreds of miles a week to tell prospective backers his story of a ruined town looking for redemption. And then one day, it all came together. And he was terrified. Because it was his only shot. All or nothing on one roll of the dice. The town and its people would either step up or they wouldn't. He would either be a hero or he would face the humility of selling a deal he couldn't make work." He paused, then took her hand and cupped his other one over hers. "So don't be sorry."

Studying his face one last time, Sarah couldn't shake the feeling that he was trapped somehow. She couldn't see him as the powerful man she wanted so much to hate. She didn't feel sorry for him, either. Just as he had at the beginning of their meeting, Nathan Haley just seemed oddly vulnerable.

He let go of her hand and, as if on cue, the associate gestured towards the open door and said, "right this way, ma'am."

Sarah took one more look at Nathan Haley, suddenly wishing she could give him back that cup of coffee.

As she followed the associate leading her down the hallway, that radar that all women have told her that Nathan was watching her. Now the fact that her skirt tapered a little too snugly against her backside for good taste made her feel undeniably self-conscious. She tugged at the belt and reminded herself that she really did need to get to a gym.

Nathan stood inside the conference room, watching Sarah through glass as she walked away.

He placed his fingertips on the window, longing to touch this woman who was everything in the world that he could never have. He watched her step through the door and into the reception area, hoping she might look back at him one last time. But she simply walked through the door and was gone.

Haunted by the emptiness of her touch forever out of reach, Nathan stepped out of the conference room and traipsed down the hall back to his office.

## *STANDOFF*

Sitting comfortably in front of Gavin's desk, Nathan couldn't help seeing the faces of people Gavin was going to fire. Later, Nathan would shake the hand of every one of those people and hand them a letter of recommendation as they left the building. Gavin, of course, would know nothing about that. Nathan wondered what Gavin would do if he did.

Thumbing through a file, Gavin said, "Three years. Time to go." He closed the file and handed it to his private secretary, who already had three folders clutched against her chest.

Imagining those three faces looking back at him as they sulked out of the building, Nathan said, "We don't have to do this every year."

Glancing up at Nathan for a moment, Gavin asked, "Why not?"

"It's bad for morale. People start worrying more about protecting their jobs and less about actually doing their jobs."

Gavin smiled and grunted. He closed the folder on his desk, handed it to his secretary and said, "That will be all." Without a word, she slipped out of the office, leaving the two men alone.

"Folks shouldn't spend more than two years at any one place. They get too comfortable."

"You've been here for five years."

Gavin smiled. "It's different at my level."

Nathan took note that Gavin said *my level*, not *our level*. "Have I become too comfortable?"

"Maybe." Gavin leaned comfortably to one side and massaged his shoulder. "So what's going on with Sarah Thomas?"

Nathan had thought about that question ever since he'd watched her walk away from the conference room. He did have a fiduciary responsibility to crush her efforts. Not for Gavin. For the bank. He had lost sleep over trying to figure out the difference between the two. Any institution was at least in some part a reflection of the current captain at its helm. But Gavin hadn't yet infested the deeper roots Nathan and his father had anchored in their community.

Nathan had decided that fiduciary responsibility was just a fancy way of letting himself off the hook for not doing the right thing. He could claim a higher loyalty to propriety. He could do that and live with himself. But he was less sure he could live with the casualties. Gavin's secretary wouldn't be holding a few files to her chest. She would be hauling them out on a cart.

Nathan realized Gavin was tapping his fingers, waiting for an answer. "She's going to keep Calhoun busy. Lot of paperwork. Something about discovery."

Gavin leaned forward. "Discovery? For what?"

"She's making a case for predatory lending."

Gavin stared at the wall behind Nathan for a moment. Then a soft smile eased his expression. He grunted and said, "Yeah, we talked about that." Gavin looked to the side for a moment and then patted his desk. "Yeah, I think we'll go with that."

"What do you go with it?

Gavin waved off Nathan's question. "Did she mention anything else?"

"No, just the predatory lending thing."

Gavin chuckled. "And thanks to you, I won't be on hook for contempt when I can't produce the original applications." He jutted his chin out. "But you might be."

Nathan didn't respond and simply stared at Gavin with what he hoped was a convincing poker face. But he couldn't shrug off the slight tremor in his left hand as he thought about prison. It wasn't the thought of prison so much - that was just kind of depressing because of the audacious unjustness of such an outcome. It was his family's name. He was all that was left of it and he couldn't face the thought of it dying in shame. People would ask whatever happened to that bank where everybody got their home loan. *Oh yeah, the son wound up in prison because of some mortgage scam. People like that just can't help themselves, can they?*

"You'll realize sooner or later, Nathan, that it's best to just come on over and help us run the bank."

"I don't like the way you run the bank."

Gavin sighed a little too theatrically and shook his head. "See, this. This right here is what I'm talking about. There's a difference between thinking about how things should be done and actually doing them. Are you starting to get it? Are you starting to understand that your father sold it to me because he knew you weren't ready?"

Nathan decided to change the subject. He would never know for sure why his father sold the bank instead of leaving it to him, but he wasn't going to let the weasel sitting across from him cower him into surrendering those applications. "What's our next step?" he asked.

"Your bleeding-heart public service attorney has side-tracked herself away from the main event and we're going to help her stay on that track."

"What do you mean side-track? What is the main event?" Nathan was worried enough about a possible predatory lending scheme - a scheme he was determined to figure out and shut down. But now Gavin was telling him that whatever they were planning was even worse. He tried to think of what it could possibly be, but all he could do was watch his thumb twitch nervously when he drew a blank.

Gavin showed a pandering smile. "That's above your pay grade, lad."

"I have a legal right to know."

"No you don't. You're in violation of corporate policy. That's insubordination and that gives me the right to fire you." Gavin showed a thin smile and tilted his head. "Honestly, Nathan, as a corporate officer, you should bet setting a better example."

"I've read the contract, too, Gavin. The only thing you can fire me for is gross negligence. Insubordination is not gross negligence. It's just annoying." The two men sat in silence for a few moments. When Gavin didn't show any indication that the meeting was over, Nathan decided to just go ahead and ask the question hanging in the air. "Why don't you fire me then?"

Gavin leaned forward, clasping his hands on his desk. His face hardened and he spoke in a soft baritone. "You think those applications are protecting you. But they're not enough. Not even close. Soon enough, you'll realize what you're really up against here. What *we're* up against. And you'll wish I'd fired you. I know that you think you're doing the right thing. But it's dangerous, Nathan. For everybody."

## *CONSPIRACY*

The Diner was way down deep in a part of town where most folks didn't go. Especially people like Nathan, or at least people dressed like him. It had been around since before he was born and everybody there knew who he was because most of them lived in modest but sturdy tract houses purchased with money borrowed from Haley National.

The Diner did not advertise. It didn't have to. Word of mouth kept business flowing and its location kept anyone from buying it up and turning it into a chain franchise. Here, you could buy a meal of delights that you couldn't get anywhere else. And for a lot less.

Nathan thumbed a hefty tip to his Uber driver, took a few steps along the cracked sidewalk with weeds growing through it and opened the grease-smudged glass door.

Inside, the Diner was hot, noisy and crowded. Waitresses glided along the yellow Linoleum floor, their arms stacked with plates four deep and a coffee pot in their hands. Both the skinny fry cook from Thailand and his not-so-skinny partner from Alabama worked the grill as if they were playing piano, their hands constantly in motion, not a single move wasted as they drew plates from the shelf over the grill, heaped sausage and hash browns onto them and cracked fresh eggs on the grill in a single fluid motion. Listening to the thick sizzle of fresh bacon on the grill, Nathan breathed in deep the smell of bacon, eggs, grease, butter, pancakes and syrup.

The hostess smiled and plucked a menu from the wooden holder. Nathan held up two fingers. "Two."

Picking up a second menu, she led him to the only empty booth - which he had reserved an hour before - and said, "It's been a while, Nathan."

"A little too long," he said.

They passed an older black man sitting with his grandchildren. The man boomed out the words that took Nathan back to a different world that had somehow slipped away. "Give a working man a break and you'll have a customer for life." Nathan's face lit up at hearing the old slogan from the days when he and his father ran the bank.

Nathan stopped to shake the man's hand. "How's the house working out?"

The man gripped Nathan's hand firmly and affectionately, as if they were old friends even though Nathan had never met the man. "Paid up and tripled up. But I wouldn't sell it in a million years."

Nathan smiled and said, "We appreciate the business. Stop by if there's anything we can do for you." It's what his father always said back when the bank was just a savings and loan in an outlet mall and stopping by meant walking in to see both he and his father working in plain view. He wasn't sure how that would work out going downtown, riding the elevator to the 10th floor and asking for Gavin.

He was in a parallel universe where time stopped and let him remember what his life had once been. Mulling his plan over in his head, he couldn't help wonder if he might get at least a part of that life back. If he could capture just a moment of it when he looked in Sarah's eyes and brushed her cheek so she would know that she wasn't alone with her pain. Even if she was a lawyer who had to sit on the other side of the table.

As he sat down in his booth, the hostess laid down the menus and said, "Best not be bringing somebody in to talk business. Would be better if it was a girl this time. You need to get out more."

"A little of both, actually." Nathan checked his watch and looked at the front door. "Hopefully."

"Alright then. Maxine will take care of you today." Within thirty seconds, a young and stout woman with a bright cherubic smile was at his table filling his coffee cup and placing a metal pitcher of real cream on the table. Just by the way the hostess had placed the menus on the table, Maxine knew to let him spend time with the menu instead of rushing to take his order.

Nathan liked to peruse the menu, looking at all of the pictures of eggs, hash browns, bacon, sausage, three kinds of toast, pancakes, steaks and chops. There was an homage to healthy eating on the back of the menu with salads and lean-cut chicken sandwiches with light mayonnaise.

Although he enjoyed perusing the menu, Nathan already knew what he wanted. The Banshee was the crown jewel of The Diner, a four-egg omelet with three different kinds of cheese, an unidentifiable gravy and an equally unidentifiable meat cut up into small squares. Nobody knew exactly what went into the Banshee. And nobody asked. Because it was the only place in the whole world where you could get one.

Sarah sat in the back of the Uber, staring through a light mist at a crooked-looking building with a black and white sign perched above the greasy window that declared it was “The Diner.”

It was starting to get dark and a low thick-lensed yellow light hummed to life. The neighborhood was reasonably clean and nothing looked all that run-down but Sarah didn’t want to get out. She couldn’t put her finger on what was wrong. It didn’t seem particularly dangerous, just - old. She looked at her smart phone to check the message Nathan had sent her. “Are you sure this is the place?” she asked.

“It’s the only The Diner in town, lady. It’s the right place. Don’t let the neighborhood fool you. Good folks around here.”

“Alright.” Sarah thumbed the Uber a tip, opened the door and gingerly stepped out onto the cracked sidewalk in front of The Diner.

Watching the Uber pull away, Sarah suddenly felt trapped, wondering what she would do if she had to leave in a hurry. She tugged at the belt of her skirt and opened the door.

Her nose was assaulted with the smell of grease and fried things and the noise was so loud she could barely hear the hostess ask her, “Are you Sarah Thomas?”

“Yes, that’s me,” Sarah yelled.

“I can hear you fine, honey.” The hostess smiled and led Sarah to Nathan’s booth. Along the way, they had to stand sideways to let a waitress through with plates stacked up both arms. Sarah watched in fascination as the waitress dealt the plates like cards on to a table and then whirled around to fill coffee cups at the next table.

“Right here, honey.” Sarah turned to see the waitress pointing at the empty booth across from Nathan. He was looking at her and beaming, as if they were long-lost friends. Which they most certainly were not.

Sarah slid into the booth and set her purse down. Looking around, she asked, “What is this place?”

“It’s The Diner,” he said, then laughed. “Isn’t it great?”

Sarah shrugged. He looked like a kid in a candy store, but she had to tell him, “Sure, if you like clogged arteries.”

His smile vanished and Nathan suddenly look wounded. Sarah felt a shallow ache as she realized she had hurt his feelings. She blinked a few times as the thought of reaching across the table to touch his hand came to mind. Then she wondered why she should care about Nathan Haley’s feelings. She had come expecting to talk about the case, not look across the table at his sad puppy-dog eyes because she didn't like his favorite restaurant.

Nathan looked down at the table for a moment. When he raised his head back up, his eyes were warm, as if he had never heard what she said. He smiled and asked, "What was that thing you did out there?"

Looking over her shoulder, Sarah asked, "What? I walked into The Diner?"

Nathan blinked slowly, once, and said, "With your skirt."

Sarah's mouth fell open at such a rude question. *Touché*. She had struck a nerve. Now he was striking back. That was fair. But she really didn't have the time or patience for his little game.

"OK, I'm sorry about what I said. Obviously this place means something to you. I can appreciate that." She mulled it over and added, "I can respect that."

Nathan folded his hands in front of his face, as if he were praying. Peering over them, he asked, "Why did you do it?"

"I'm brash. I'm a lawyer. I like to pick a fight. I dunno' pick one."

Nathan shook his head. "No, the skirt thing. Why did you do that?"

"Look, I said I'm sorry." She waved her hands impatiently. "I was just reminding myself I need to get to the gym, OK?" She leaned back and studied him for a moment. His eyes didn't waver as he stared at her over his steepled hands. She couldn't decide if he was being tactical, trying to throw her off balance, or if there was something more behind his stern gaze. "Why am I here, Mr. Haley?"

"Let me tell you something," he said. Nathan weaved his head back and forth a couple times. "It's going to sound weird, maybe even a little creepy, but it's true."

Sarah didn't respond, knowing that nothing she could say was going to stop him.

"In Renaissance Italy," he said, "you would have been considered underweight."

Sarah looked at him dumbfounded. She couldn't imagine a more insanely inappropriate remark between a defendant and plaintiff's counsel. Not to mention between a man and a woman he barely knew. If this was Nathan Haley's idea of a first date, he really needed to work on his routine.

"And the only reason you should go to the gym is for your cardiovascular health. Not your dress size."

Nathan placed his hands down on the table and smiled. Then it hit her. Every image of him looking at her starting from that first day in the coffee shop. It was always the same smile, as if he were glad to see her.

Because he was.

Sarah closed her eyes and shook her head. "No no no no." Then she opened her eyes and asked, "Why are you telling me this?"

Nathan tapped the picture of the Banshee on the menu. "Because you need to try one of these."

Sarah looked at the picture than back at him, incredulous at his audacity. She scoffed. "No. I'm not going to eat a side of deep-fried cow or whatever."

"It's an omelet."

"Whatever." She slapped the menu with the back of her hand and laid it back on the table. "Why am I here?"

"It's called the Banshee and all I'm asking is that you take one bite." He arched a brow. "Just one."

"Why?"

"Because the only way for us to have any kind of productive relationship going forward is for you to take just one bite of a Banshee. I insist."

Sarah let out an exasperated laugh. Her mouth agape, she shook her head and held up her hand, trying to think of what to say to get him to explain the real reason for their meeting. But watching him stare at her with that boyish grin, she knew he wasn't going to let it go. "Fine. One bite."

Nathan looked across the room to catch Maxine's eye. He held up two fingers, then pumped his fist twice. Maxine grinned and nodded. A few voices rose up from the booths around them. "Banshee!"

Wondering what she had gotten herself into, Sarah glanced around the room. The ripped and taped booths. The tables with Formica faux wood worn to the white. The industrial steel rafters strewn beneath a concrete ceiling. Without realizing it, Sarah let a faint smile ease her expression as the most curious thought entered her mind: This was not the kind of place the rich and powerful came to. Everyone was dressed in blue jeans, Dockers, polo shirts, t-shirts and short-sleeved button-downs. Feet were covered in boots and sneakers. Everybody was working class. Except for Nathan. And yet he didn't look out of place. He just looked pleased with himself for convincing a woman who was too self-conscious about her weight to order an omelet.

A while later, Sarah was sopping up the last of the gravy from her Banshee with a piece of toast. She took the last bite from her fork, closed her eyes and hummed as she savored the taste of it.

She looked down at her plate, disappointed that it was now empty.

Glancing at Nathan, she could see him gloating.

"See? Isn't it good?"

Sarah glared at him, wishing she could wipe the smile from his face. The Banshee was hands-down the best thing she had ever eaten in her life. And that included her grandmother's cinnamon apple pie, the recipe for which was still a subject of speculation at the annual county fair.

And even though she had to reject the way Nathan was looking at her, she couldn't help wonder if it was such a bad thing that this man looked at her with affection. And looking at him just then, even if he wasn't exactly handsome, there was a sturdy reassurance about the way he looked at her. In that moment, Nathan looked like a man who would die before letting down anybody he had made a promise to.

But they couldn't be friends. He had to know that.

When Maxine arrived to pre-bus the table, Sarah sighed and said, "As much as I enjoyed that, I think it's time for us to get down to business. What do you have for me?"

"Of course." Nathan adjusted his position in the booth and she could see his eyes dim and his smile fade as he tried to change gears. "You said something about discovery at our last meeting. What does that mean?" he asked.

"Discovery means a party to suit has to disclose all information and evidence pertaining to the issue at bar."

"Um, I'm just a banker. Can you translate that for me?"

Sara smiled at his boyish humility. Even if it wasn't sincere, it was cute. "It means you have to show me all your records."

"All of them?"

Now he wrinkled his brow and seemed to stop breathing. The warm glow that had descended on her evaporated as she realized that he was once again the defendant sitting across the table from her.

"Well, not all, but close enough. Your lawyers will provide the necessary guidance for you to know what to disclose. They usually provide more than is actually required just to avoid trouble."

"And if we miss something?"

"If it comes to light that you withheld relevant evidence, you could be found in contempt. Usually that just means you have to fork it over, but it could lead to actual jail time. Jail, not prison. The judge could also rule the evidence exists as presumed or exclude evidence favorable to your case. Like I said, your lawyers will know what to do."

He was staring at her intently, trying to soak it all in. He was trying to understand, certainly, but there was something more going on in that mind of his.

"Why do you ask?"

Nathan ran his hand over his face. He held his hand lightly against his throat for a moment. Sarah sat very still, as if she were once again watching a deer that was trying to decide if it needed to bolt away. “Well, when I mentioned predatory lending, Gavin said the oddest thing.”

Sarah waited for him to continue, then realized he was waiting for her to prod him. “What?” she asked, hearing the annoyance in her own voice.

“He said that he was going with it, as if he had already made a decision.” Sarah held her breath now, waiting to see if he was going to say anything more. “As if it was acceptable some how.”

“You got all that just from him saying he was going with it?”

“Well, that and the tone in his voice. The way he said it. You know how it is.” He let that sink in and then asked, “Why would he sound like the predatory lending might be something that could help him?”

Nathan waited for Sarah to answer, but she was drawing a blank. Predatory lending was no joke. It could lead to the bank losing its accreditation. Gavin and the man sitting across from him would probably never work in the financial sector again. It was a civil liability, not criminal. There were worse things to get in trouble for.

There were worse things to get in trouble for.

Her gaze shot to Nathan’s eyes and she said, “Because there’s something more.”

Nathan nodded slowly. “Because there’s something more.”

They sat in silence for a moment, savoring the mutual pleasure of their discovery. Then Nathan said, “Look, there are some things I can’t get to, but there’s a lot I can. Just give me a list of what you need and I’ll make sure you get it. Or tell you if I can’t, but you’ll at least know what should be coming your way.”

Sarah studied him for a moment, not knowing whether to trust him. Handling evidence properly could be tricky business and some judges were very finicky about that sort of thing. “I can give you a list of what I’m looking for and you can tell me if you have it. But you should transfer that actual evidence under cover of subpoena.”

“What happens if I just give it to you?”

“Well, it would be a violation of your fiduciary obligations as a corporate officer and could, at the very least, get you fired. Probably sued. And the evidence would be no good to me after that because it was improperly obtained.”

“OK, I get it. I’ll check your list.”

She had to ask because she was far from convinced that she could trust him. “What do you think it might be?”

“I don’t know.” Nathan held up his hands and sat back in his booth. “I was hoping you might be able to find out.”

# *INTERFERENCE*

Returning from a hearing, Sarah stopped short when she walked into the clinic. Stanley, Maureen and a rugged man in his mid-sixties were all standing in the middle of the room looking at her.

The older man asked, “Is that her?”

Stanley replied, “Yes sir.”

Maureen spoke next. “Sarah come over here and meet Mr. Emmerson.”

Sarah’s mind raced as she tried to think what she could possibly have done to draw the attention of the foundation chairman.

She stepped towards the man as he smiled and held out his hand. He was an intense individual, the type of man who filled the room with the expression on his face. Sarah sensed he was not a man that heard the word ‘no’ very often.

“Wyatt Emmerson,” he said. “Pleasure to meet you.”

Sarah shook his hand. “Sarah Thomas.” When she pulled away, he insisted on holding her hand a moment longer.

“At last,” he said, and finally let her hand go.

Hoping nobody noticed her wiping her hand against her skirt, Sarah asked, “So, what brings the chairman to our humble clinic?”

He frowned sympathetically. “Humble?”

“Yes sir,” Sarah said, pointing at the light over her desk. “You’ll hear it at some point I’m sure.”

Emmerson eyed her carefully. “I’m sorry we can’t give you better accommodations, dear. We have a lot of responsibilities. The clinic here is only one of them. No less important, but everybody has to share the burden.”

Understanding the standard power broker playbook which required putting the victim off balance at the earliest possible moment, Sarah nevertheless felt disappointed. She was hoping Emmerson, being a philanthropist, would be different.

"No," she said, "Um, the office is fine." As she was gathering her thoughts for what to say next, everybody noticeably ignored the light over Sarah's desk starting to buzz. Sarah smiled as if she were a flight attendant greeting a passenger. "I just meant, what can I do for you?"

"Well, I'm no lawyer, but I had a thought about this case with Haley National."

Sarah felt herself flinch. It wasn't so much that the chairman had suddenly taken a personal interest in her case. It was that such an obvious power broker in the community had taken an interest. He was here to make sure things went a certain way. And she had no trouble guessing what direction that was. She was sure of it: they were circling the wagons. It didn't occur to her to take pride in the fact that it was because of her.

With a knowing smile, Sarah said, "Well, we're always open to suggestions." She glanced at Stanley, who nodded vigorously. Of course he did. "What's on your mind sir?"

By the way he shifted his stance, his pervasive grin and his piercing gaze, Sarah knew immediately that he could see right through her.

"I was thinking that maybe it sounded like predatory lending." He looked at each of them, soliciting agreement with his proposal.

Before anybody could speak, Sarah asked, "Who told you that was a good idea?"

Emmerson looked down at Sarah with kind eyes, but she knew they didn't match the thoughts spinning through his mind. They couldn't because, as he said, he was not a lawyer. He was a power broker.

"Nobody, Ms. Thomas. It was just something that came to mind. When you deal with as many business leaders as I do, you hear things. Sometimes they come to you like a Post-It note reminding you of something."

"Something you came up with?" Sarah took a step closer and stared straight into his eyes. She could see it back there now, the desire to reach out and slap her across the face. Put her in her place. But she knew he wouldn't. No, he would withdraw, plan his revenge, marshal his resources and, when she least expected it, reach into her life and crush her with one swift stroke, just like any good power broker would.

Shifting his gaze to Stanley, Emmerson let out a forced laugh and said, "Wow, quite the go-getter you have here Stanley."

Stanley shot Maureen a stern glance and said, "Yes, Ms. Thomas has been making the rounds at the courthouse, putting your money to good work." He paused and shifted his gaze to Sarah. "Even if she does get carried away sometimes."

Sarah felt Maureen's hand on her shoulder. Still looking up at Emmerson, she said, "No offense."

Knowing he had won the round, he showed that pandering grin that said, *why did you even try?* "None taken. Keep up the good work."

Maureen whispered in Sarah's ear. "Come on honey, we need to go."

Refusing to look away from Emmerson, Sarah took a step backwards. Sarah winced and looked down to see Maureen's hand squeezing her shoulder a little too hard. She looked at Maureen, who arched a brow and nodded her head towards her desk. "Let's go over there and talk about your strategy."

When they reached Maureen's desk, she looked at Emmerson and Stanley to make sure they were still talking. Then she leaned down to Sarah and said in a harsh whisper, "You don't bite the hand that feeds you."

Sarah pursed her lips and folded her arms. "Yeah, well I don't like the sound of his bark."

## *DIVERSION*

After Emmerson left, Stanley retreated to his office. Maureen checked her watch. Sarah started to ask what was going on, but Maureen put her finger to her lips. She checked her watch again and said, “Go on in. He wants to talk to you.”

“About what?”

Maureen’s expression was stone cold. “About the case.”

Sarah threw up her hands and strode over to Stanley’s office. She knocked once, opened the steel door and stepped inside to stand in front of his desk.

Stanley’s speech was a little slurred and Sarah could detect the scent of the whiskey that he kept in his lower left-hand desk drawer.

“Why am I letting you handle this case?” he asked.

“Because I’m the only lawyer on staff?”

“That’s right. Besides, I’m too old for this sort of thing.” He pulled a folder from his middle desk drawer and laid it on the desk. Patting the folder, he said, “Maureen and I have already done a lot of the preliminary research and we’ve written up what we think is a good legal theory.”

They had made it all too easy. Like a barker at a carnival, ushering her into the tent to see the bearded lady. Step right this way boys and girls. Everybody, including the defendant, was pushing her towards predatory lending. And now, she was less inclined to trust Nathan. He could just as easily be asking her for a list of things so he could hide them. His tactics were unusual, but they led to the same outcome: her doing his bidding. But there was one possibility he had brought to her attention that she thought was worth pursuing.

“I appreciate this.” She picked up the file, flipped through a few pages and set it back on the desk. “You know, I was thinking -“

Before she could finish, Stanley put up a hand and said, “Let me stop you right there.” Sarah waved her hand slowly through the air. *Go ahead.* “You will refrain from making this case out to be more than it is. It’s going to cost a significant portion of the foundation’s budget to run through all these hearings and serve process. We need you to stay focused and win this thing as efficiently as possible.” Stanley leaned back and clasped his hands behind his head. “Besides, it’s pretty much cut and dried. Just follow the procedures we’ve outlined for you there.” He waved casually at the file.

Stanley looked at her blankly, his hands still clasped behind his head. She had waited for him to finish his little speech, but he had to know she wouldn’t give up that easily. “What if there’s more to it?” she asked.

“More to what?”

“What if there’s more to what’s going on at Haley National? What if this thing goes deeper than just predatory lending?”

Stanley leaned forward. Glaring at Sarah, he asked, “What business are we in?”

“Serving our client’s best interests.”

“That’s right.” He ran a hand over his bald head. “We are not private investigators. We are not class action attorneys. We are not personal injury lawyers. We can’t go digging. We can only work with what our clients bring to us.” He stopped talking and Sarah could see the question on his face. Was she listening? “And it’s all right there in front of you. They’ll have six worry-free months to find a place to live and get on with their lives instead of worrying about a debt they have no hope of paying.”

Sarah squinted at him. “Wait. What six months? Where did that come from?”

He beckoned for her to come closer. Sarah leaned over the desk and braced for what she knew was coming. Instead, Stanley spoke in a low, calm voice, almost a whisper. “You won’t win. They won’t let you.” He arched a brow and his expression softened, as if he were talking to his granddaughter. “One thing you’ll learn in this business - It’s better to do some good than no good at all.”

## *NEEDLE AND THREAD*

Sarah's used business phone rang just once before she picked up the handset. "Sarah Thomas."

Whoever was on the other end didn't speak for a moment, then she heard Nathan's voice. "Hi Sarah, this is Nathan Haley."

She didn't want to talk to him. But she knew she had to. "What can I do for you Mr. Haley?"

"Do you have my list?" At least he got right to the point this time.

"Yes."

"And?"

"And, you'll get the list of requested evidence along with the complaint, just like everybody else."

She heard Nathan sigh. "It would be better if you sent it to me now. I'm telling you, if there's anything on there they don't like, they'll get rid of it."

"As I told you, withholding evidence can lead to contempt charges, among other things." She propped one elbow on her desk and leaned forward. "So I would caution you not to do that."

Sarah listened to the faint background hiss as she waited for him to respond. She could almost see the hurt look in his eyes. Finally, Nathan asked, "Do you think I would do that?"

Sarah waited for a moment before responding. It was one thing to think about what she was going to say. It was harder to actually say it. Although it shouldn't have been any problem at all to engage the opposing party. But telling Nathan what she had to say was more difficult because she knew it would hurt him, even though she knew that shouldn't matter.

"I don't know if you would or not. But if everybody is served at the same time, you can preclude the others from doing anything improper." She closed her eyes. "And they can do the same for you."

"If they destroy anything, I'll never see it. I don't know everything that is going on around here. Gavin has made sure of that. But if you tell me what you're looking for, especially what might hurt them the most, I can try to track it down and keep it safe."

"They?" Sarah asked. "Don't you mean 'we'?"

"No. *They* have too much to lose. *They* are the ones who can be hurt the most. *They* are the ones who would have no regret committing a felony as long as they can get away with it. Me, I'm just a Vice President *they* have cut out of the loop who is trying to save what his father spent a lifetime building."

Sarah deliberately ignored the theatrics, extracting the testimony from his statements. She had nothing to compare that to. And since she couldn't verify what he was saying, she filed it away as something she heard but was unverified and thus probably meaningless.

When she didn't respond, Nathan said, "Are they pushing you to charge predatory lending?"

Sarah bit her lip, unable to dismiss this question as irrelevant. "Yes."

"I told you. And while you're distracted by that, they'll make sure to protect whatever else they're up to."

"And what exactly is that, Mr. Haley?"

Sarah heard another sigh from the other end. "I don't know. If you tell me the evidence that can hurt them the most, I bet the smoke will kick up if I go after it. That might give us something we can use to find out more."

"Us?"

Sarah could feel the boyish grin on his face. She wanted to reach across the line and slap it off his face.

"You and me, counselor. Us."

Was he trying to seduce her? For real, James Bond no-kidding seduction? That possibility and the fact that he kept insisting she tell him about evidence prior to proper service made the decision for her.

"There is no us, Mr. Haley." With that, Sarah hung up.

Standing in line at the clerk's office, Sarah nervously thumbed the folder she held in her hand.

She had them dead to rights. The case was open and shut. Cut and dried. Over and out. Served up on a silver platter with a big fat red 'win' button.

As she stepped up to the counter, she seemed to see it in the clerk's eyes. *Oh, got an easy one here. Well, good for you. Way to lawyer up and all that.* The clerk was smiling, but it faded quickly and Sarah realized she was scowling at the clerk.

She handed over the folder which contained the complaint, the filing forms and other attendant paperwork. The clerk flipped through the pages. "Everything seems in order." She took the check from the folder and clunked down on the complaint with a heavy metal stamp. She handed the folder back to Sarah and said, “Have a nice day.”

Sarah stepped to the side and wandered into the hallway, staring at the floor. She opened the folder and stared at the stamp. Cut and dried. And she wondered if she really had been bought off by a civil case that would give them time to hide something more insidious. Was she helping them do the very thing she had sworn to fight? Was she already one of those lawyers who had abandoned her mother?

Reaching into her courier bag, Sarah whispered, “Goddammit.” She pulled out a scrap of paper and looked around for the remote office. Hidden in the corner beneath a dingy sign that read ‘computer’, Sarah found a PC with a single monitor, a printer, and one of those archaic devices that nobody used anymore. Unless they wanted to make sure nobody saw what they were sending.

She put the motion for discovery in the feed tray of the fax machine and tapped out the numbers on the scrap of paper. She pushed the send button and waited for what seemed like an eternity as each page crawled through the rollers. After the machine beeped, Sarah put the papers back in their folder and ripped a blank page from the legal pad she carried in her courier bag. She scribbled a note and tapped out the numbers again.

The note read, *Don’t make me regret this*.

Nathan pulled the pages from his fax machine and started to read through them. Before he got to the end of the first page, he froze, staring at the words that jumped off the page and punched him straight in the gut. *Original Applications.*

He scanned the rest of the pages showing nothing but mundane and easy-to-get information that Gavin would have no reason to hide. Account balances. Mortgage statements. Sarah had already seen one of the switched applications, so he was sure Gavin had corrected all of them to reflect the borrowers’ true credit scores. So handing those over didn’t lead to any kind of smoking gun. They were just another part of the predatory lending red herring that Sarah was chasing.

No, the only person that had anything to hide from this list was himself. He wanted to ask her how much of a difference it made to her case if she didn’t have them. But he didn’t want to expose himself to the nuclear logic grenades she would pepper him with to quickly isolate the truth.

And then they would toss him out on the street. And he couldn’t help her if he wasn’t Vice President of Haley National, could he?

## *THE OTHER SHOE*

In preparation for his meeting with Gavin, Stanley poured another drink from the bottle of bourbon he kept in his lower left desk drawer and slugged it back.

He was already feeling dazed, but it wasn't enough to contend with the implications of meeting with two bigwigs in one week. They wanted the clinic to not do its job. And if he wanted the grant money to keep flowing, he had to make sure it didn't.

He heard a knock at his office door. Outside, Maureen waited for exactly how much time it took Stanley to down his drink and stash the bottle before she opened the door.

She poked her head inside and said, "Gavin's here to see you."

Stanley nodded and Maureen ushered Gavin into the office.

Beaming, Gavin lumbered forward, holding his hand out. "Stanley, you old warhorse, how the hell are you?"

Stanley stood up, pasted a grin on his face and shook the man's hand, half not caring if he smelled the liquor on his breath. "Just fine, Gavin, and you?"

Gavin looked around the room but could only find two plastic chairs.

"We're just a clinic here," Stanley said, gesturing towards one of the chairs.

"Right," Gavin said, laughing nervously and adjusting his tie as he pulled one of the chairs up to the desk and sat down.

"What can I do for you?" Stanley asked, sitting back down.

"Well, first thing -" Gavin looked down at his tie as he fiddled with it. "-Calhoun doesn't need to know about this meeting." He glanced at Stanley, as if he had to wait for Stanley to agree. As if Stanley had anything to say about it.

“That’s um -“ Stanly steepled his fingers and tapped the tip of his nose. “-That would be unorthodox.”

“You mean unethical?” Gavin asked.

“No, but it could make his job harder. And he won’t like it when he finds out you talked to me without his counsel.”

“Well, like I said, he doesn’t need to know about this meeting.”

“I won’t say anything unless he asks.”

“Close enough.” Gavin flipped his tie down and tried to disarm Stanly with a nervous laugh. “So, it looks like you have us quite across a barrel here.” He held his hands out, as if he were asking for help.

Stanley eyed him coolly, wishing he’d never met the man. But he knew that wouldn’t matter. The players changed. The game did not.

“Oh, I don’t know about all that. It’s a strong case. We caught you with your hand in the cookie jar. But you have good lawyers.”

Gavin winced at Stanley’s candid summary of the naked truth. “Well I was thinking maybe we could come to some kind of agreement.” He went back to looking at his tie as he fiddled with it. “You could tell Calhoun you were open to a settlement.” He flipped the tie down and looked at Stanley, not smiling this time. “You could do that, couldn’t you?”

“I’d have to talk to Sarah. It’s up to her.”

“Ms. Thomas?” Gavin again laughed nervously and said, “Well, she works for you, right? Couldn’t you just tell her to take a settlement?”

“I could, but I can’t guarantee she would abide. She’s a young crusader with a fire in her belly. Not all that receptive to compromise.”

Stanley glanced down as Gavin rested his hand on the desk, quietly invading his space. “You know, I could take this to Emmerson.”

Stanley held a hand up. “I get it. You want a settlement. You’re making me a deal I can’t refuse.”

Gavin stood up. Nodding, he said, “Something like that. Just, you know, push this thing in the right direction.”

He put his hand out, but Stanley didn’t take it. With a blank stare, Stanley said, “I’ll take care of it.”

Gavin scowled at Stanley’s rebuke. “See that you do.”

## *REALITY CHECK*

Sitting next to Stanley on a bench in front of the headquarters of Foley Crane and Winkler, Sarah watched autumn leaves chasing down the sidewalk. They were prettier when they were still on the trees.

Looking straight ahead at the building in front of them, Stanley said, "I know what you're thinking."

"And what would that be?" Sarah asked.

"You're thinking that it's your job to do the right thing."

"According to Maureen, my job is to serve my client's best interest. If that means sailing in harm's way to do the right thing, then so be it."

"Look at me."

Sarah turned to see a man who couldn't let go of the pain that came from a past he didn't want to admit. But now he was going to.

"Old, wrinkled, dried-up and forgotten. That's me. And while that's why I drink, I'm not telling you this so you'll feel sorry for me. I'm trying to warn you. This is what happens to somebody when they do the right thing instead of the correct thing. There is a reason I'm not a partner somewhere."

Sarah was tempted to ask if it was because of his drinking. But she recognized the look in his eye - that distant stare that stills against the winds of time when somebody remembers what wounded them. "I'm listening"

Stanley nodded somberly. "My last case, a case I won, came with some strings attached. There was a conflict of interest that I wasn't aware of. That I couldn't be aware of because these guys couldn't tell me." He pointed at the building in front of them.

"You used to work for Foley?"

Stanley held a finger against his mouth. *Shhhh.*

"I was told to withdraw from the case. That it was going to be handled by another law firm who could better represent the client. I was close and I knew I had a good chance with the judge. I knew that letting the case slide while it moved to another firm would kill it. I had the right combination of events at exactly the right moment."

"So what did you do?"

"I did the right thing."

Sarah could see he didn't want to tell her what that was. But if he was going to force her do things his way, he was going to have to tell her why. "What was the case?"

Stanley shook his head. "You're going to make me do this the hard way?"

"Are you going to let me handle this case my way?"

Stanley let out a sigh. "My client was a woman, about your age." He looked up at the sky, the pain of the memory flooding through him. "She had a son with no father, so her reputation around town was irreparable. Things were different back then. And she had to take the only job she could find."

Sarah felt a chill run down her spine.

"Her boss knew this and he found her quite comely." He stopped and looked at Sarah with sorrow in his eyes. "Are you sure you want to hear this?"

Sarah couldn't speak as the memories from her own childhood formed like dark clouds in her mind. She reached out and squeezed his hand, managing a single nod.

"He gave her a respectable title, a nice salary. A job that gave her a place in the community even if she was known as a harlot. She had a life." His jaw clenched in anger as he thought back to that day. "But it came with a price." Stanley held his breath for a moment. "Most nights, she had to work late to take care of 'special business' with her boss. This went on for years, mind you."

Sarah sat transfixed, nearly blinded by the memory of her mother coming home late, looking exhausted, disheveled and ashamed. She asked him the same question she had wanted to as her mother a hundred times. "Why didn't she say something sooner?"

"If she lost that job, she most likely wouldn't have found another one. And if she lost her job, she would lose the only thing she cared about."

Sarah's voice quivered as she spoke in a near whisper. "Her son."

Stanley nodded. "Her son." He looked back up at the sky. "Anyway, at some point, her boss made the one mistake that could send her over the edge." Stanley took a deep breath. "She wasn't proud of how she took care of 'special business' for her boss, but it had become something she tolerated. As long as nobody ever found out. One night, he brought a friend.

And she was mortified about what would happen if that friend talked. Men like that tend to boast."

"What did she do?"

"She taped one of their sessions. And then she called me."

"What did you tell her?"

Stanley let out an ironic laugh. "I told her blackmail was illegal. Then I told her about a new concept that was making the rounds. Sexual harassment. Nobody had really done much with it yet, but I thought I could make it work."

"Did you win? Did you settle? What?"

Stanley grunted. "Neither. I was arrested on charges of distributing pornography with unlicensed models." He grunted. "How obscure is that? How they found out about her tape I'll never know, but I was naïve enough to entrust it to the privacy of my lower left desk drawer. But that all came later. I went in that day and I put her on the stand to tell her story. And because of that, other women who had been through the same thing started to come forward. Her boss settled quickly and quietly. She wouldn't have to work another day in her life, as long as she kept quiet. And then I was arrested. The judge dismissed the case when the firm conveniently misplaced the tape. They just wanted to get my attention. But I did go on their blacklist when they fired me. And that's a list that is known throughout the republic."

Sarah took Stanley's hand in both of hers, squeezing hard. "Thank you."

Stanley smiled warmly. "My goodness, you really are a bleeding heart, aren't you?"

"No," Sarah said, sniffling. "You don't understand."

"What is it?"

"Your client, whoever she was, that's what happened to my mother. Except she didn't have an attorney with the courage to do what you did. They told her there was nothing they could do and so she could either put up with it or lose her job. If I had known, I would have run away because the only reason she had to endure such abuse was to take care of me."

"Oh my God." Stanley took his other hand and placed in top of hers. "Now you listen to me. You're not to blame for any of that."

Sarah smiled at Stanley's compassion - something she didn't think he had in him. "I know that. I found out on my eighteenth birthday. She wanted me to know once I was old enough. So the same thing wouldn't happen to me. She had written a letter where she told me to do the one thing that she didn't."

Sarah trembled as she thought back to the day her grandmother sat her down and told her the story of her mother.

"What was that?" Stanley asked.

"Fight."

Stanley nodded somberly. "What happened to her?"

"I was spending the day with my grandmother when the sheriff came by. They wouldn't let me know what they were talking about, but I knew something was wrong. The other thing I did when I turned 18 was get a copy of the police report. My mother drank an entire bottle of bourbon and then slit her wrists in the bathtub."

Stanley's face sagged in agony. "Oh god."

Sarah clenched her jaw, refusing to allow the tears welling up in her eyes to escape. "So that's why I'm here."

Stanley put his hand over his mouth and studied her for a long moment. Letting his hand down, he said, "I understand. And you're going to despise what I'm going to tell you next, but you need to listen to me." He waited for Sarah to nod in agreement. "Your mother is gone and you're fighting in her honor. I get that. But you have a decision to make."

"What decision could I possibly have to make when the right thing is so obvious?"

"Obvious to you," he said. "I don't mean to sound cruel, but your perspective is not the only one that matters here."

"What are you saying?"

"I'm saying that Calhoun is going to say something in court today and you need to listen to it very carefully if you want to stay in a position where you can keep fighting." He stroked his chin, let out a sigh and leaned forward. "Sometimes there is a difference between doing the right thing and doing what you can to help. And we *can* help, just not in the way you want."

Sarah watched him for a long time, watching the leaves tumbling down the sidewalk from the corner of her eye. "Are you saying you're going to fire me if I don't do this your way?"

"I'm not the one saying it."

"Then who is?"

## *A PLANTING OF FLAGS*

Sarah stood behind the plaintiff's table, watching the same judge from her very first hearing talk to the bailiff and leaf hurriedly through a file. He looked at his watch, then at her. He immediately scowled when he saw her. Justice on a clock, which meant she had to get it right the first time, something she was getting better at with practice.

Calhoun looked her way and smiled cordially. Sarah nodded without smiling back. She had come to tolerate the man when she realized that he was doing exactly what he was supposed to: work hard for his client's interests. But she couldn't help resenting the simple fact that the type of clients he took care of had those rights in the first place. It was a childish thought, but she couldn't help it.

The judge banged his gavel once, looked at Sarah and asked, "Alright, what do we have here?"

Still standing behind the plaintiff's table, Sarah said, "Motion for contempt, you honor. My client has provided everything on my list except one piece of evidence that is critical to my case."

"And what would that be, counselor?"

"The original signed mortgage applications."

Looking more bored than impatient, the judge said, "I see." Glancing at Calhoun, he asked, "What about it? Are you guys holding out?"

Calhoun smiled, trying his best to disarm the room with his charm, which Sarah had learned meant she had to brace for a curve ball. Calhoun stepped out from behind the defendant's table and said, "Your honor, I think we can wrap this up right here and now." Looking at Sarah, he said, "I think we've come to a settlement."

"Oh, well good," the judge said. He picked up his gavel. Preempting his tendency for premature rulings was something else Sarah had learned with practice. "Hold on," she said, raising her hand.

"Dammit, what is it this time?" the judge asked.

"Let me see it," Sarah said, holding her hand out towards Calhoun.

"Wait," the judge said. "Haven't you already seen it?"

Sarah glared at Calhoun because he had put her in the position of having to lie to the judge, which she wouldn't do. But she didn't want him to rule against the settlement on procedure just in case it was a good deal, so she had to let Calhoun off the hook, which really pissed her off. It wasn't a lie, but she still didn't like saying it. She was going to twist the words like any good lawyer would. "I don't have my copy," she said. "I want to confirm some details."

The judge waved his hand dismissively. "Hurry up."

Sarah walked over to Calhoun and held her hand out. With a sigh, he picked a folder up from the table and put it in her hand.

Thumbing through the pages, she froze when she saw the phrase, strangely familiar. *Six months*. Without admitting any liability, the bank was offering to waive all costs and fees expended on the foreclosures and pay each plaintiff enough money to sustain their current expenditures for six months. It then went into some elaborate formula using their bills from the past year and the national poverty level. It didn't matter. She wasn't going to take the time to figure all that out.

"No deal," she said, closing the folder and handing it back to Calhoun. The judge eyed her as she walked back to the plaintiff's table. She didn't care. She wanted him to be annoyed. He should be annoyed.

Back behind the plaintiff's table, she said, "Your honor, this settlement does not contain the provisions we require."

"Well now, hold on," the judge said. "It sounds quite reasonable to me. I mean six months of free living is nothing to sneeze at."

There it was again. *Six months*. How did he know? Sarah narrowed her gaze and said, "Begging your pardon sir, but it sounds as if you've seen this deal ex parté and now you're advocating defendant's interests." She let that sink in and then said, "My clients are not interested in being paid to give up their homes. We want a restructured note." She turned her head towards Calhoun, "Of which my esteemed colleague is aware." Calhoun smiled sheepishly, but she could tell he wanted to reach over and strangle her.

The judge glared at her because he was used to hustling most lawyers through his courtroom. Sarah figured he must have forgotten that she was the one lawyer in his cadre of court officers that wouldn't let him get away with it.

Scowling, the judge shook his head, then held out his hand. "Alright, let's see that motion counselor."

She handed the folder to the judge. He put on the reading glasses hanging around his neck and read through it briefly. Still looking at the paperwork, he asked, "What about it, counselor, can we get these documents over to Ms. Thomas here?"

"Your honor, we've asked Ms. Thomas to stipulate that those documents are no longer available due to factors reasonably beyond our control. If she's willing to do so, we'd be willing to reconsider the restructuring settlement."

She glared at Calhoun with a wicked grin. Not only was he lying, but he was putting her on the spot in front of the judge once again, who snapped at settlement offers like a Doberman snaps at steak. "Come now, Robert," she said. "This isn't the first day of school anymore. I'm not going to give you the chance to have all this dismissed on appeal for lack of evidence." She tilted her head slightly. "We can't afford it."

"Alright, that's enough," the judge said. "Mr. Calhoun, you have thirty days to find whatever's missing on this list." He slammed down his gavel and nearly shouted, "Next case."

## *A FRIEND IN NEED*

Elaine's invitation to Bernards couldn't have come at a better time. Sarah knew she had just put her job on the line and she was no closer to getting her clients relief. And she knew the bank was holding out on the evidence to stall her case. She could only hope that the threat of contempt would smoke them out. But there was no way she could know for certain.

So she twirled her drink with a twizzle stick at the bar in Bernards. She had ordered a big girl drink this time, a Kamikaze. Watching the ice merry-go-round in her glass, Sarah said, "It must be nice to have clients you can bill."

Sipping primly at her Tom Collins, Elaine asked, "What do you mean?"

"I mean money, sister." Sarah realized that while not drunk, the drinks were having an affect. She had to be careful. "Money to do things. Hire research assistants. Hire detectives. Get at the heart of things. See what's really going on."

Amused by her friend's half-drunken musings, Elaine asked, "Is that what you think we do? Get at the heart of it all?"

"Well don't you?" she asked. "I mean, that's why you win, isn't it?" She thought about it for a moment and asked, "You do win, right?"

"Sure," Elaine said. "Mostly."

Sarah slapped her hand against the bar. Elaine glanced around, seeing if anybody had noticed. "I mean, goddammit," Sarah said, "I have them right by the balls, you know?"

"You do?"

"You betcha. Except they can afford a law firm that bills by the hour." Sarah went back to stirring her Kamikaze. "So they don't have to follow the rules. They just ride it out and hide behind the corporate veil." She let out a clumsy laugh. "I mean, what is the judge gonna' do, put their building in jail?" Sarah picked up her glass and drank.

"It doesn't have to be like this," Elaine said.

"What do you mean? Like what?"

"Like always one step behind, never enough time to prepare a case properly. Lawyers throwing land mine settlements at you." She paused for a moment. Sarah felt suddenly self conscious as her friend studied her. "Not being able to conduct your case the way you want to."

Sarah scoffed. "Like you can do it your way where you work. I'm pretty sure you guys employ the common legal concept of Billibus Maximus."

"Not always," Elaine said softly.

Sarah reached out and grabbed Elaine's forearm and shook it. "You know what I like about you?" she said, smiling from behind her slight stupor.

"What?"

"You're the only person around here I can actually trust." Sarah took her hand away, drained the rest of her drink and said, "Yep, the only one." She waved her glass in a toast, started to take a drink and laughed when she realized it was empty. "Well, and maybe that Nathan guy."

Elaine stopped mid-drink and put her glass down.

"What?"

"You know, the banker. The suit-wearing, client-screwing, probably-secretary-screwing, screw-everybody guy over there at the bank. Nathan." The bartender quietly placed another drink in front of Sarah. Elaine caught his eye and nodded once. *Put it on my tab.*

Sarah stirred her drink, transfixed by the ice scraping along the side of the glass. "But damn he's cute." Sarah smiled as she allowed herself to imagine him standing in front of her with that never-let-you-down smile of his. For just this once, she looked at him in her mind's eye and let him be the man she hoped was behind that smile. Just this once.

"What's this?", Elaine asked. "Sleeping with the enemy?"

Still staring at the ice, Sarah whispered, "I wish." Just this once.

Elaine looked amused with her prim little smile on her Merle Norman face. "It's alright to like somebody. So long as you don't act on it. So, what is it about this guy?"

"Well, he is cute. Not hot. Just a nice, sturdy look about him. The kind of guy who would reach out to keep you from falling if you slipped on the ice. And he said I'm not fat."

Elaine's eyes widened. "Wait, what? He said that to you? That's horrible."

"Well, he didn't just come right out and say it. He did it in a kind of funny way. It was cute."

Sarah took a long drink and turned to Elaine, her smile fading. She imagined Nathan standing next to Elaine, listening. “Plus I think he might be trying to help me.”

Elaine put down her drink, fixed her eyes on Sarah and leaned in. “What do you mean?”

“I don’t know. He could just be playing me. But I wonder if maybe he really is trying to help.”

Elaine studied her for a moment, then quietly said, “Tell me everything.”

## *A CIRCLING OF WAGONS*

As he liked to do every evening when he left work, Stanley took a walk around a circuit that took him past the Foley building and then down to the park where he had sat on the same bench for the past ten years to watch the sun go down.

Mesmerized by the glistening rays flooding out from the horizon, he didn't notice the man who had sat down next to him. He flinched when he heard Gavin's voice.

"So this is where you go to get away from it all."

Still watching the sun, Stanley said, "This isn't the place, Gavin. If you have business to discuss, come to my office tomorrow. My door is always open." He turned to face Gavin and said, "I guess it's always open for you now, isn't it?"

"It's easy to find you at your office," Gavin said. "It wasn't so easy finding you out here."

Stanley looked around, wondering if somebody had been following him.

Turning back to watch the sun, Stanley said, "I can't help it if she won't listen."

Stanley winced at the pain when Gavin placed a hand on his shoulder and squeezed. Hard. "Then you need to get her out of the way."

"She's the attorney on record. Ultimately, the legal decisions are hers to make."

"Oh really?" Gavin tilted his head and looked at Stanley as if he were studying an insect. "Is that really the best you can do?" He stayed like that for a moment, his gaze locked on Stanley. "Really?"

"Look, Gavin," Stanley said. "I know you're somebody in this town -" He gave Gavin the once over, hoping the man saw the disdain in his eyes. - "somehow. But I work for Emmerson. This sort of thing really needs to go through the foundation." He thought for a moment and added, "It's for our mutual protection."

Gavin smiled dismissively and scoffed. "He's not involved anymore."

"I work for him. He's involved."

"Yeah, well, somebody else is involved now."

"Alright, who?"

"Somebody you don't want to meet. Somebody who also has a, what did you call it? Oh, yeah. Mutual interest."

"You've made a mistake, Gavin."

Gavin feigned shock. "Oh, really?"

"I may subvert my clinic at the behest of Mr. Emmerson." He pulled his shoulder away. "But I don't respond well to coercion."

"How do you know? Have you ever been subject to coercion?"

"Isn't that what this is?"

Gavin laughed. "This? No. This is not coercion. This is more like -" he glanced to the side, then looked back at Stanley. "-persuasion."

"I don't need to listen to this." Stanley started to stand up but Gavin pulled him back down.

"Now is not the time to get sanctimonious. You're already bought and paid for."

Stanley dropped his chin to his chest and studied his shoes. "That was uncalled for."

"You were about to forget your place, old man."

Lifting his head back up, Stanley said, "I don't work for you. I'm going to Emmerson."

Holding Stanley fast by the shoulder, Gavin took out his smart phone with his other hand and thumbed the entry. He put it on speaker. After a few rings, they both heard the answer.

"This is Wyatt."

Gavin said, "Good evening Mr. Emmerson, how are we doing?"

Stanley didn't like how resigned Emmerson sounded. "Fine. What's the score, Gavin?"

"I have Stanley with me. I think there's something you want to say to him." Gavin held the phone close to Stanley's ear.

Wyatt's voice was flat and tinny, but unmistakable. "Do what he says, Stanley. That's it." The line went dead.

Blinking at Gavin, Stanley felt his heart sink as he realized just how out of control the situation had become. Emmerson had always expected to have a certain influence over the clinic. Business was business, after all. But he never expected the man to get involved in *this* kind of business. More distressing, he knew that Emmerson couldn't protect him this time.

Stanley let out a sigh. His shoulders slumped. “What do you want then?”

Putting the smart phone away, Gavin said, “I don’t care who is on record for what. You find a way to get this bitch out of my face.”

Stanley waited for Gavin to follow up with a threat. When Gavin didn’t say anything for several moments, Stanley asked, “Or what?”

Stanley braced himself for whatever Gavin was going to promise would happen to him or his home or his dog or whatever. But then Gavin said something that scared him even more. “Or I won’t be able to protect you any longer.”

## *OFF THE FIELD*

Sarah stood in front of Stanley's desk. Maureen was standing next to her and Sarah shrugged the question: *what's going on.* Maureen shrugged back and shook her head. Sarah turned back to Stanley, watching him stare at her in silence from behind steepled fingers.

"Do you know why you're in here, Ms. Thomas?" Stanley asked.

Sarah glanced at Maureen, who was obviously there to witness the event. Sarah closed her eyes and nodded. "You're firing me."

"No. It's not going to be that easy for you. There are reasons to keep you on."

"What reasons?"

Stanley narrowed his gaze. "Reasons. But I am taking you off the case."

Sarah smiled and said, "You can't do that. Only my clients can do that."

"Are you sure you represent their best interests?"

"Look, I get it. Maureen explained that to me. But you can't drag that out and beat me with it every time I do something you don't like."

"No, I'm serious," Stanley said. "Are you?"

"Six months? Are you kidding? All that's going to do is postpone the inevitable and make them look like deadbeats. That's not in their interest. A restructured note, that's public record. That says something. That not only helps my clients, but sends a message to the rest of the community."

He seemed fascinated by her tirade, but still hid behind the steeple. "Which is?"

"Which is to stay clear of Haley National because they're a predatory lender."

"Haley built this community one home loan at a time. When we lost the industrials to overseas markets, he made sure people could come to town and find an affordable place to live while its business leaders built a new core industry from scratch."

"So I've heard," Sarah said. "But that was before Gavin Neilsen took over. Now it's just another financial institution screwing its customers because people like you will let them get away with it."

Maureen gently squeezed Sarah's arm. "Sarah."

Stanley unsteepled his fingers and both Sarah and Maureen flinched when he slammed his hand on the desk. "And there it is," he bellowed.

"There's what?" Sarah asked.

"The windmills. You and the goddamn windmills. Every time." He stood up and pointed at her. "What you're describing is a crusade, not representation of client interests. You need to be honest with yourself. Are you here to help people or do you just have an axe to grind?"

Sarah mulled his words over. He had a point, but Sarah knew there was more to it than that. She knew, down in her gut, that the bank was just trying to buy her off so they could hide what was really going on. Something so bad that they were willing to pay her clients to walk away from their homes.

"Fine," she said. "Sometimes there's more at stake than just the client's interests."

"Like what?" Stanley asked. He jutted his chin out and tilted his head to the side. "Tell me, you, the windmill fighter who's been practicing law for five minutes, tell me what is more important."

"Justice."

"Do you know what Haley National is?" Stanley asked.

"Yeah, the bank that's trying to screw my clients out of a just settlement."

Stanley sat down, let out a huff and spoke in a calmer voice. "Haley National is the financial engine of this town. It keeps the money flowing to the right places so the community continues to function, thrive and grow. We all know what kind of man Gavin Neilsen is, and the right people have let him know that he made a mistake. Bringing down the bank just to get to him is going to hurt a lot more people than just the hundred or so they've evicted."

Maureen stepped in now and said, "Remember what I told you. We move the needle to the right. We can't save the world. All we can really do is help people cope with the reality that they have brought on themselves. This is not the worst settlement. They'll find affordable housing. They won't be on the street. They'll come out of this in one piece."

Glaring at Maureen, Sarah said, "That's the best you can do?" She waved her hand around the room. "The two of you, that's the best you can do?" When neither of them responded, she said, "I'm sorry, but that's just not good enough for my clients."

"Yes it is," Stanley said.

"That's not your call. It's mine."

"No it's not."

"Goddammit, I'm the attorney on record. Why are we even having this conversation?"

"No, you're not."

Incredulous at how obtusely he kept coming at her, Sarah scoffed and flicked her hand in his direction.

Stanley opened his center desk drawer and pulled out a folder. Handing it to Sarah, he said, "Read this."

Sarah opened the folder and started reading through the 42 signatures on a filing for substitution of counsel in the case of Wainwright et al vs. Haley National Bank. Her mouth fell open and she felt her shoulders slump. "What's this?" she whispered.

"It's a class quorum," Stanley said. "And it's enough to pull you from the case."

Sarah turned to Maureen, holding her hands out. Maureen spoke in a gentle tone. "I'm sorry, Sarah."

Disgusted at her suddenly realizing just how powerless she was, Sarah knew that she couldn't do any good at all from the sidelines. "Fine," she said. "I'll take the settlement."

"Yeah, well," Stanley said. "That's what you should have said at the hearing."

Sarah looked between them.

Maureen gently wrapped her hand around Sarah's arm and said, "We filed the substitution this morning."

Sarah stared at her as she gulped in shallow gasps of air.  Her forearm tingled and she could feel her shoulders tensing up.

"This is just for the predatory lending counter-suit," he said. "You're still on with the foreclosures. So don't screw that up."

Sarah bowed her head, not knowing what to do. While related, the two complaints were separate cases. Her counter-suit for predatory lending had derived from the foreclosure proceedings, but with the settlement she knew they were going to take, it had no effect on the foreclosures. They would get their money. And then, at the summary judgment hearing for the foreclosures, the judge would bang his gavel and say, "so ordered."

And then the sheriff would start showing up to kick people out of their own homes.

It was all going to work out just as they had planned. And all she could do now was watch.

## *LOCKOUT*

Sarah sat in the courtroom gallery with her arms folded as she waited for Stanley, Calhoun and the judge to close out her lost dream of extracting justice from Haley National Bank.

She stared at the bar, feeling wounded that she was no longer allowed to walk past it for this case. Later, when they gathered for the final blow in the foreclosures case, she would be allowed past the bar just so she could listen to the judge throw her clients out on the street.

Sarah could hardly stand to watch as Stanley stood up and said, "Your honor, if it please the court, the parties have agreed to a settlement."

The judge nodded and held out his hand. Stanley handed him a folder and waited while the judge thumbed through the pages. "Mr. Calhoun, you agree to all of this?"

Calhoun stood up behind the defendant's table. "Yes sir."

Sarah flushed when the judge looked directly at her even as he spoke to Calhoun. "Well come on up here and take a look."

Calhoun stepped up to the dais and took the folder from the judge. Giving its contents a cursory review, he said, "Yes sir, this is the deal." He handed it back to the judge.

"There being no objection, the agreement is hereby ordered into effect and this case is dismissed with prejudice." He slammed down his gavel.

Without even thinking about it, Sarah jumped to her feet and cried, "Objection."

A few laughs and then a murmur floated through the gallery. A few people pointed at her while leaning over to whisper to each other.

The judge bellowed across the room. "You are no longer the attorney on record for this case, Ms. Thomas. Sit down."

She pointed at Calhoun and said, “Your honor, you can’t dismiss with prejudice, there is still evidence pending which could have influenced the outcome.”

“The parties have come to terms. Those terms are equitable. Those terms are now in force. Now if I hear one more peep from the gallery, I’m going to send the bailiff to escort you from my courtroom.”

Sarah blinked at him, but knew there was nothing she could do. It didn’t matter if her arguments were cogent, correct, legally viable or customary as a matter of common law.

She had no say in the matter.

Because all these people had worked so hard to maneuver her out of position so they could push through the settlement.

Why? What were they afraid she might find?

And now the one man she could never bring herself to trust was the only person left who could help her.

Or would Nathan shake Stanley’s hand and stand by while Emmerson congratulated him for a job well done as he handed over another grant check? Would Nathan then turn his head to look at her with a gleam in his eye because he had fooled her into doing exactly what he wanted her to do?

## *PEOPLE'S CHOICE*

Sarah stood up when she heard a group of people shuffle into the clinic's waiting area. They all quietly crowded in front of the clapboard, their faces slack and shoulders slumped as they watched Sarah walk towards them. A middle-aged black woman wearing a red knit cap stood at the front and eyed Sarah directly. *We need to talk to you.*

Sarah approached the crowd slowly, her mouth thin as she imagined them all signing the paperwork to throw her off their case. But they were the clients. So she stopped at the clapboard and asked, "What did I do wrong?"

"We didn't know."

"You could have asked me."

Maureen now stood up from her desk and stepped up to the crowd. The leader eyed her coolly and said, "We're consulting with our attorney."

Maureen was polite with her tone as she stepped between Sarah and the crowd. "Ms. Thomas doesn't represent you anymore."

"We've looked into it and as best as we can determine, we took her off the predatory lending case."

"That's right," Maureen said.

"But that doesn't affect the foreclosure case. She's still our attorney as far as that goes." The leader leaned to the side to look at Sarah now standing behind Maureen. "Right?"

Maureen squinted and looked to the side for a moment. Then, she admitted, "That's right, but you're not going to get any more deals like the settlement you got for the predatory lending case."

"Yeah, well, we thought that deal included us keeping our homes."

"Oh," Maureen's eyes widened a bit and she pursed her lips. "Well, somebody should have explained it to you."

"Well, somebody didn't." The leader held out a piece of paper. "Here is a copy of the complaint we filed on Mr. Arthur." Maureen stood still and didn't reach out to take the stack of pages. But when the leader stared her down and refused to take it back, Maureen huffed out a sigh and took the complaint from her hand.

"That really wasn't necessary," Maureen said.

Sarah looked at her feet, trying to suppress the smile on her face.

"Yes it was," the leader said. "Mr. Arthur told us a great many things that led us to believe Ms. Thomas wasn't the right girl for the job." The woman took a step forward, leaned against the clapboard and pointed at Maureen. "And I'll tell you another thing - he led us to believe that the bank would take back the foreclosures."

"I'm sure he didn't," Maureen said.

"Are you calling me a liar?"

Maureen's eyes flared and Sarah wondered if she was going jump over the clapboard and slap the woman. Instead, Maureen pasted on her most disarming smile and said, "Of course not, ma'am. What I meant is that I'm sure Stanley did not intend to mislead you."

The leader didn't look satisfied, but she let it go. "Then we all got to talking about it," she said. "And as best as we can tell, Ms. Thomas here did a fine job explaining things to us." She paused to lean to the side again and acknowledge Sarah with a nod. "And then you all came in and tried to tell us that she wasn't experienced enough and was more interested in her own agenda than our rights."

Sarah felt her shoulders tense. She stepped up now and shot a glance at Maureen, who shrugged and shook her head. Sarah turned her attention to the leader as she continued. "And now, looking back, we realized that was about the same time we stopped understanding just what the hell was going on."

"I'm sorry, Ms. -" Maureen started to say.

"Ma'am is good enough for you," the woman said.

"I'm sorry, ma'am. These things can be complicated sometimes and we do our best but it isn't always clear what's going to happen in court, not even to us. All we can do is try to look out for you to make sure the system does its job."

Turning her head, the leader looked askance at Maureen and said, "Well, that makes a mighty fine pamphlet their Ms. Henderson, but if it's all the same to you, we'd like to keep Ms. Thomas here for the remainder of our ordeal."

Sarah looked at her shoes, stifling another smile. She knew it wasn't fair to Maureen, but it was the first time she had heard anybody say something nice about her since she had started at the clinic. She looked at Maureen and ached her brow. *Well?*

Maureen threw up her hands and said, "That's your prerogative, of course." The leader nodded in affirmation. "But this case, as I'm sure Ms. Thomas will tell you, is very different than the predatory lending case. Foreclosure proceedings are really just a formality."

The woman said, "Let me ask my attorney about that." She turned to Sarah and said, "Ms. Thomas?"

Sarah was staring through them, her gaze inspecting the pattern of the cinder-block wall across the hall. Lost in thought, she barely heard the woman's voice. When she realized they were waiting on her to say something, she asked Maureen, "3501.3, do you know it?"

Maureen knit her brow and held up a finger as she walked over to Sarah's book case and took one of the books from the shelf. Thumbing through the pages, she found the statute.

She looked up and asked, "Fraud?"

"And negation," Sarah said. Her voice laced with excitement, she continued, "And reversion of rights by possession and -" She looked at Maureen, her mind racing. "Is it possible?"

Maureen shelved the book and studied the thread-worn carpet.. "Hard to prove."

"Not if I can get the originals."

Maureen looked up. "Which they wouldn't let you have the first time."

"Well, that was then, this is now."

"Excuse me," the leader said, "but what are you all talking about?"

Sarah stepped to the clapboard and placed both hands on it, palms down. She surveyed the gathering and said, "I think I can make it so you can keep your house."

The leader tilted her head and scowled. "Now, hold on. The last thing we need is more false promises. Are you sure?"

Beaming, Sarah said, "Yes!" Then she turned her palms up. "I mean, I can't promise anything, but there is a chance. There's something I can try. And it will stand up in court in court if I do it right."

The woman's eyes glistened. She squeezed Sarah's hand and said, "Are you sure or are you just telling us what you think we want to hear?"

Sarah looked around the room, then back at the woman. "Well, we could use some more resources. This isn't something that's going to be easy." She surveyed the other clients. They all seemed to be holding their breath, their eyes drying out from not blinking as they waited for her to say something that would let them believe. "But I'll give it everything I've got."

The leader nodded slowly. “Just don’t let us down.” She jutted her chin out and eyed Maureen. “We’ve had enough of that around here.”

“I won’t,” Sarah said.

The clients shuffled out of the waiting area. When they were a safe distance down the hall, Sarah turned to Maureen and said, “I’m going to need those originals.”

“Yes you are.”

“This doesn’t work without them.

Maureen shook her head. “No, it does not.”

## *JUST THIS ONCE*

Sitting at a table cloaked by the dim lighting of the ballroom, Sarah tugged at the belt of her skirt as she glanced around the room. Her gaze settled on Maureen, who was sitting across from her. Maureen mouthed the word, *Relax*. Sitting between them, Stanley nursed a nearly empty rocks glass as he looked around for a waiter to wave over for a refill.

Stanley wore a tuxedo. Maureen wore a single-piece silver dress with sequins along the neckline, offset by her faux diamond earrings. Her hair swept up in a gracious wave to reveal her usually-prim face softened by an enchanting smile.

Sarah, on the other hand, wore the same skirt that she had worn to her meeting with Nathan. It wasn't the least business-like attire she owned, but it was far from elegant. And it still felt uncomfortably tight against her backside. She gave Maureen a sheepish smile, wondering if they had failed to tell her it was a black tie event on purpose. All they had said was, "Just some people Emmerson is bringing together for a meeting."

As it turned out, they had dragged her to the annual Emmerson Foundation Charity Ball. Its name bold and bland at the same time, there was no mistake that it was an event where the city's powerfully rich and social elite came together to celebrate their superiority over the masses dependent on them for everything from jobs to charity. Looking around the room, Sarah realized that had they told her the truth, she probably wouldn't have come. Stanley probably would have been embarrassed, so they made it sound like a mandatory business meeting. Which maybe is really all it was after all, just with sequined dresses and bowties.

Sarah frowned as she watched those very people mingling near the dance floor with champagne flutes in their hands, laughing at each others' tasteless jokes and pawing each others' lapels in admiration.

Everybody who was anybody was there. She had already spotted Nathan at a table on the other side of the room and hoped he hadn't noticed her.

And she had endured Emmerson's opening remarks about how a city is a reflection of its people and how proud he was of the work that the Emmerson Foundation had done to lift up the less fortunate and help more people than ever find a place in their thriving community. With the gracious help of all the attendees, of course. Stanley had glared at her when he caught her rolling her eyes.

Dinner had been served, consumed and taken away and Sarah was feeling stuffed from the generous steak with trimmings and a side of cocktail shrimp. All she wanted to do was go home and work on her case.

Instead, she flinched when she felt Emmerson's hand on her shoulder. "Whoa," he said, holding his hands up. "It's just me."

Not knowing exactly what to do, Sarah stood up and offered her hand. Emmerson smiled gently, took her hand and kissed it once on the back. Wishing she could wipe it on her skirt after he let it go, she said, "Wonderful speech."

"Oh, you know. Have to feed the egos and keep the checks coming in."

*Including yours*, she thought.

Taking her hand again and gesturing towards the dance floor with the other, he grinned and said, "Shall we?"

Sarah knew she looked like a deer caught in the headlights. Her entire body stiffened at the thought of trying to move in any way that resembled coordinated with the Chairman of the Board of the Emmerson Foundation. Feeling the blood draining from her face, she tried to demur. "I wasn't really expecting -"

Still grinning, he said, "Don't worry about it." He leaned in close to whisper in her ear, "It's just for PR." He cast his gaze at the bored-looking news crew huddled over video and audio equipment in a corner off the dance floor.

Staring at the news crew, Sarah tried to pull her hand away. Trying to dance in front of the city's elite was one thing. There was no way she could let her humiliation find its way onto the airwaves and, even worse, the Internet. She could only imagine some girl in Thailand pointing and laughing at Sarah strutting like a wounded chicken on the dance floor.

But she couldn't pull her hand from Emmerson's vice-like grip. His jaw tightened and his gaze dimmed as he glared at her, waiting for her to acquiesce.

With a gasp, Sarah stumbled behind Emmerson as he dragged her to the dance floor. Sarah glared at Emmerson as the band struck up a waltz. He still wouldn't let go of her hand, but at least she could do a waltz. All you had to do was count to three. But Sarah decided just then, that she had had enough. She was about the make it very clear to the Chairman of the Board that she didn't care to dance, thank you. But before she could say anything, she caught Stanley's gaze. His mouth was slack and his brow wrinkled over sullen eyes.

As she realized that Stanley was all but pleading with her to just endure the moment, Emmerson slipped one hand around her waist and hoisted her other hand up into the air as if she were holding a torch. Oddly, the image of her holding a sword flashed through her mind. A sword she would have gladly let Emmerson fall on at that moment.

He was a superb dancer. But not a good dance partner. Emmerson swept gracefully to the rhythm of the waltz while Sarah stumbled through the motions of trying to keep up with him as he seemed to change direction with each step.

Then he slowed down. Moving his mouth close to her ear so nobody else could hear, he said, "do you know why these people are here tonight?"

Sarah didn't know if he wanted her to answer him or not.

He twisted her wrist just enough to make it hurt and growled in her ear. "Do you?"

If she could have just put a little space between them, she would have put a knee in the man's crotch. "I don't know, maybe to compare the gas mileage on their limousines?" She tried to glare at him, but his mouth still hovered next to her ear so she couldn't look at him.

He laughed. "You really don't know when to give up, do you?"

"I guess not," she said.

"That's not it." He pushed her through a flurry of spirals and she nearly fell down trying to keep up. "Tribute."

"What do you mean?"

"They're here to pay tribute." He pulled his head back and stared down at her. "To me."

Sarah wanted to look away, but she knew she couldn't. Her entire life, she had wanted to stand toe to toe with a man just like Wyatt Emmerson and tell him he couldn't hurt her anymore. Well, here was her big chance.

"And if people like this," he said, "people with more money and more power than you can even imagine - if they're willing to subordinate themselves to me through this little ritual of ours-" He jerked her closer, putting his mouth next to her ear again. "-What does that say about somebody like you?"

Sarah tried to think of the answer that would finally send him over the edge and make him slap her, right there in front of everybody. In front of the news crew she could still see out of the corner of her eye.

Instead, she gasped when a man's hand slid onto Emmerson's shoulder and pulled him away from her. They both turned to see Nathan's smiling face. His eyes fixed on Emmerson, Nathan nodded at Sarah and said, "Do you mind?"

"Oh I don't know, Nathan." Emmerson eyed the younger man for a moment. "Hasn't she given you enough trouble already?"

Pulling Emmerson even further away from Sarah, Nathan said, "We're all friends here, aren't we Wyatt?"

"Fine." Emmerson clenched his jaw. Staring directly at Sarah, he said, "You don't want to dance with me." It wasn't a question. It was a chilling statement of fact and Sarah felt her knees start to buckle when Nathan stepped in to take Emmerson's place. Nathan guided her gently towards the center of the dance floor and a moment later, they were surrounded by the other dancers twirling around each other to the music. Emmerson was suddenly nowhere to be found.

Nathan didn't smile. He looked at Sarah with gentle eyes that told her she didn't have to hide anymore. Just this once, she let herself hope that her secret was safe with Nathan and she let out a hard breath as her lip trembled. She nearly fell limp in his arms as the shock of Emmerson's threat overwhelmed her and she knew she had no choice but to let Nathan see that. Nathan nodded once and all she could see was the never-let-you-down gaze that she wished she could believe. More importantly, he was dancing in small steps, slightly behind the beat of the waltz, just like she was. With Nathan, it wasn't hard to move to the music, his body seeming to float around hers as if he were a tethered balloon. He laid his hand lightly on her waist, using his fingers to gently signal when they were going to turn, when they were going to go straight. Already, she could feel her strength returning. Her lip stopped trembling. Her knees stiffened. Her breathing subsided.

"You're really good at this," she said.

"It's easy when you have a good partner."

Sarah scoffed and said, "Yeah, well, I didn't want to come out here in the first place. He just kind of dragged me out on the floor."

Nathan's voice grew soft, intimate in a way she hadn't heard before. "Who?"

"You know, Emmerson."

Nathan pulled her a little closer, smiled warmly and said, again, "Who?"

Sarah grunted and then smiled, the burning tension draining from her body as she felt a warmth filling her chest. She felt lighter and in that moment, everything around them faded. The only thing in the entire universe was this gentle man dancing with her in small steps to a simple waltz.

In that moment, Sarah grew tired of the fight. She wanted it all to go away, just for a moment. She wanted to believe in the simple kindness of a man who had come to her rescue at just the right time.

Letting out a sigh, she felt the turmoil of her life swirl out of her mind to dissipate in the night sky. She lay her head on his shoulder. Then she whispered, “Thank you.”

## *JUST IN TIME*

After the dance, they had slipped out of the ball to take an Uber to The Diner. Sarah sat in front of an empty plate. She hadn't indulged in the Banshee this time. But she was famished after her ordeal with Emmerson. She had wolfed down eggs, sausage and hash browns, not caring what it was doing to her waistline. Pushing away the empty plate and taking a sip of water, Sarah said, "God, I needed that."

Pushing away his own plate, Nathan said, "Tell me about it." They both laughed and she enjoyed sharing the post-battle high of victory with him. Or maybe it was just the high of being rescued, something she was definitely not used to, and something she expected to resent. But she didn't, which surprised her. Even more surprising, she realized that she hadn't checked the belt of her skirt since Nathan had tapped on Emmerson's shoulder.

He was looking at her now, just the way he had when they were dancing, waiting for her to show him which way she wanted to go, how bold she was willing to be. Slow or fast, it didn't matter. As long as they were dancing.

She put her hands together and leaned on them with her chin. "So, what's the deal with you and this bank?"

Nathan looked at the table, fiddling with the spoon next to his coffee mug. "Well, that," he said.

And that was all he said for several moments. Sarah remained silent, letting him figure out if he wanted to tell her.

"I'm sorry, if it's too personal -"

"We built this town." He looked at her now with glistening eyes and his mouth slack, letting her see a part of him that she knew most people had never seen.

"All by yourself?"

"Well, yeah. Mostly." Nathan planted his elbow on the table, slumped in his booth and half covered his face with his hand. "My Dad was a worker in one of the steel mills. We had some textiles and auto parts factories, too. A solid blue collar industrial town."

"And then that all went overseas."

Nathan nodded. "That's right. We had already lost a lot of it and the writing was on the wall. My Dad lost one of the last jobs in town just after I was born."

"So you didn't grow up rich."

"I never thought of it that way, but no, I guess not. That came later." Sarah sat quietly while he gathered his thoughts. "My Dad had an idea. He got some of the other workers together and they lobbied the city council to take a chance on them. And the first tech incubator was born."

"Incubator?"

"Um, it's like a co-op for high-tech startups. Everybody in the same building, sharing the cost of utilities, Internet, phones, that sort of thing. And it's laid out in a way so they can easily get together to help each other out."

"And did that work?"

"Yeah, it did. Next thing we knew, companies were cropping up overnight funded with angel dollars that seemed to come from nowhere. Word got out. We were startup-friendly and a cheap place to live. That's where my Dad came in."

"Haley National."

"No, not at first. Just a savings and loan back then. Companies were building out the commercial spaces and hiring whoever they could find in town. They brought the rest in from all over the country. And my Dad made sure they had a mortgage and a home. As long as they were a good investment. He didn't loan to deadbeats. That part's important."

"Deadbeats like my clients."

"They're not deadbeats." His gaze narrowed and he pressed his lips together as he thought about what to say next. Sarah waited for him to reveal his true colors, because men like him just couldn't help it, could they? Finally, he spoke again. "But they should never have gotten those loans in the first place, Sarah. I think you know that."

"And yet you gave them out anyway."

Nathan lightly tapped the table. Sarah bit her lip, forcing herself to wait for him to continue. "It's complicated." He said, quietly.

"Please, go on."

Nathan squinted at her, nodding slowly, and she wondered if he was retreating from her now. She kept her gaze steady, admonishing herself for putting him on the defensive. While she wanted to think that she couldn't help herself, she was beginning to understand that it wasn't always the best tactic. Sometimes, you had to let the other side say their piece.

"Anyway," Nathan continued, "workers were coming in, Dad was collecting their paychecks and handing them back out as loans to the lowest risk prospects. Then he put money into the town, buying small stakes in a good portion of the startups. For years, he grinded away at this. Brought me into the business when I was twelve, sorting mortgage payments." He looked out the window. "You can walk down just about any street in the suburbs, even out here in the older part of town, and walk through entire neighborhoods built by my Dad." His eyes started to mist over. "He had a saying." Looking at Sarah, he said, "Give a working man a break and you'll have a customer for life."

"That's downright Rockwellian."

"And he meant it. See, that was the secret to his success. He kept it simple. He was there to help. If you were willing to help yourself first. And he was honest. Mostly."

"Mostly?"

Nathan let his hand down and propped an elbow on the table. Moving closer, he said, "Ever since I started working for him when I was twelve, he told me that it would all be mine some day. While other kids were growing up, I learned how to run a bank."

"But he didn't leave it to you."

"No."

He went silent and Sarah said, "I understand if you don't want to tell me, but how did he -"

"Leukemia." Nathan's chin trembled slightly as he said it.

Sarah thought of her mother and for a moment she felt as if she were looking in a mirror. "I know what that feels like," she said.

"I can see that."

After another moment of silence, she said, "Go on."

"He knew his time was up. One night while I was visiting him in the hospital, he told me that he had sold the bank to 'a man who understands what it means to survive in the real world.'"

Sarah heard an edge of bitterness in his voice.

"I couldn't say anything because it was a dying man's wish, but I was devastated. I had sacrificed everything to take up the family business and now he was leaving me out in the cold." Nathan lightly thumped the table with his fist. "He said, 'You're not ready,' and that Gavin would hand over the reigns 'when the time was right.'"

"God, that must have been awful."

"It was. I mean, I was too angry to see it then, but I know now that he was trying to look out for me. He thought there was more I needed to learn and he knew he wasn't going to be here to teach it to me. So he did what he thought was the right thing."

"How could he not tell what kind of man Gavin is?"

Nathan studied the table for a moment, then said, "You make decisions faster when you're dying."

Sarah looked at his hand resting on the table. She wanted to reach out and take it in hers. Resisting the simple desire to touch him, she closed her eyes for a moment and tilted her head away as she quietly took her smart phone from her purse and held it in her lap where he couldn't see it.

"That explains a lot." She opened her eyes and studied him for a moment before glancing at her smart phone as she quietly thumbed in the instructions.

Sarah understood he was done talking about his past when he stood up and held out his hand to help her from the booth. He threw some cash on the table and headed for the door, Sarah trailing behind.

He opened the door for her and then they were standing just outside, facing each other. He looked down at her with the gentle eyes that she was beginning to understand had been there since their first meeting at Starbucks, in what seemed another lifetime. She reached out and brushed his lapel. Studying the nap of the fabric, she said, "Thank you. Again."

"For what?"

"Oh I don't know." She stopped brushing the fabric and lay her hand still on his lapel. Looking into his eyes, she said, "You're just not what I expected."

"Who am I supposed to be?"

She took her hand down and bowed her head. Still looking into his eyes, she said, "I'm not sure I want to tell you, Nathan." She closed her eyes, shook her head and held her breath for a moment. She couldn't give in to the urge to touch him. But she could give him something that she no longer tried to hold back. She could give him the truth. "You know," she said, "Emmerson."

Nathan's smile faded and he looked away. Looking across the road, as if he were trying to see back in time, he said, "We're not all like that, Sarah."

He turned back to her and she brushed his lapel again. "Sorry," she whispered. He took a step closer. She could see it in his eyes. He was putting himself out there, hoping she would be there to catch him as he closed the distance between them. He stopped short, waiting for her to come the last few inches. She put her hand on his cheek and wished she could stare at him like that forever. Because she knew this was as close as they would ever come.

Just then, her Uber arrived. As Sarah stepped slowly away from him, he asked, "When did you call that?"

Sarah kept stepping back until her hand floated away from his cheek. She felt a heavy ache in her chest as she fought to hold back her tears, wishing she could let him see her cry.

Her breath hitched when she said, "Just in time." Then she turned away, opened the door and disappeared inside. Sarah closed her eyes as tight as she could, but there in the darkness of a stranger's car, a tear seeped out and trickled down her cheek.

The Uber drove away, leaving Nathan standing in the doorway with nothing but the memory of a kiss he couldn't stop hoping for. As the car receded into the darkness, Nathan reached out with his hand and whispered, "See me."

## *BURDEN OF LOYALTY*

Gavin parked the car next to the curb and pointed at the two SUVs from the sheriff's office parked in front of the house across the street.

"That's the first foreclosure, the one your lawyer friend brought to you."

Watching from the front passenger seat as the sheriff's deputies hauled a couch to the curb, Nathan said, "That was fast."

Gavin turned off the car's engine. Looking out the side window as a woman tugged at one of the deputies, her mouth gyrating in some silent plea for mercy, he said, "This is the nature of it."

Nathan's mouth fell agape as he watched the woman start to sob as the deputy evaded her grasp. "Nature of what?"

Turning to Nathan, Gavin said, "This. The banking business. At the end of the day, it is all about one thing." He turned to Devorah, who was sitting in the back seat. "Money."

Nathan watched Devorah as she looked out the rear passenger window. "Is that what this is about?" he asked. But she didn't answer. She just kept staring out the window. "Devorah?"

She turned away from the window. Glancing at Gavin, she said, "Yes." She turned to face Nathan. "Yes, it is." Her gaze was distant and her mouth slack. For the first time since Nathan had met her, Devorah didn't look like she was plotting three steps ahead. She looked lost.

Still looking at Devorah, Nathan asked, "What about building a community?"

Gavin looked back out his window, scoffed and shook his head. "Workers for startups funded by angel financing who expect a return on investment. And those workers paying for their house three times over in interest on their mortgages." He turned to Nathan as he drummed his fingers on the steering wheel. "Money." He paused for a moment and said, "Your father knew this about you."

Nathan bit his tongue at the mention of his father and then asked, "Knew what?"

Gavin glanced at Devorah. As if on cue, she said, "That you really thought it was all about the community. The people. That you were living in Bedford Falls." She looked at Nathan with a deadpan expression and her words came out flat, as if they had been recorded. Then she looked back outside as the sobbing woman sat down on the curb next to her belongings. Nathan studied Devorah as she watched the woman sitting on the curb hang her head and pull a smart phone out of her purse to call somebody.

Turning to Gavin, Nathan said, "You didn't know my father in the early days, when he and his friends were left with a house payment and family to support while their jobs packed up and went to China and Vietnam."

"Oh, I imagine that's about the time he realized he was living in the real world."

"Or maybe that was when he decided to make the world a place he would want to live in."

Gavin's eyes narrowed as a thin smile crept onto his face. "So here's what's going to happen." Gavin swept his hand through the air. "You're in charge of making sure this all goes smoothly." Pointing at the woman sitting on the curb, he said, "That sort of thing there just slows things down and makes this unnecessarily difficult for everyone involved. Especially the sheriff, who has better things to do." He leaned forward a little, his smile growing broader. "You're good with people. So you will personally accompany the sheriff to each house and ensure that things go-" He weaved his head back and forth, as if he were searching for just the right word. "-smoothly."

"I don't think so, sir."

"How could you possibly think that you can go up against me and win, Nathan? It's not just me." Gavin leaned even closer, his smile disappearing. In a low voice, he said, "These associates of mine, you have no idea what they're capable of. And they want this to go smoothly and quietly."

Nathan felt Devorah's hand slide onto his shoulder. He looked at her sideways, not wanting to face her. She wrinkled her brow and came closer. Speaking in a near whisper, she said, "Believe it or not, I don't want you to get hurt, Nathan." For just a moment, Nathan believed her.

His gaze still fixed on Gavin, Nathan asked, "So what do you do then, Gavin? If I refuse to front this crime of yours? You fire me?"

"That's right." Gavin cast his gaze aside. "And that's when things get really bad for you."

Nathan scoffed. “Why? Because I’ll be out of a job? Because you’ll destroy what’s left of my reputation? Because you’ll tear down the last remnants of my father’s good name?”

“No.” Gavin looked back up, his face now a complete blank. “Because I won’t be able to protect you.”

## *OLIVES AND THORNS*

Nathan sat behind his easel, his hand on his chin, a brush hanging from his fingertips. He was trying to figure out how to paint something that looked convincingly metallic. Normally, he would experiment until he figured it out. But he had the sense he was running out of time. So he had to get it right the first time.

He set his palette and brush on the table and walked over to the door. He opened it to see the dark interior of his gallery with only a few track lights splashing dim pools of pale yellow on the floor.

This was his favorite time to be in the gallery - when it was just him and the paintings. With nobody around, he didn't have to pretend to understand the experts who told everybody what they were supposed to appreciate about the art hanging on the walls. And he didn't have to try and understand what patrons were trying to express in their own way what the paintings meant to them. He could just look at a painting and let the artist's vision teach him. Whether he actually understood that vision wasn't important. So long as it was meaningful to him. It was even better with the unknown artists because nobody was talking about them. They stood on their own, daring the world to form an opinion.

It was well after hours, so he froze and held his breath when he saw a figure moving through the shadows between pools of light.

While he did have a few paintings that were worth something, he didn't expect anybody would try to rob his modest collection. He was insured in any case. But the figure wasn't moving quietly. They weren't taking pictures off the walls. Whoever it was moved slowly and deliberately. Deliberately towards *him,* he realized.

He winced when he saw Devorah's face emerge into the pool of light just in front of him. Her black hair swept down straight in front of her shoulders with bangs clipped just above her brow. She wore thick makeup and dark red lipstick. She smiled softly as she looked at him with some amusement, seemingly delighted at surprising him in the one place she knew he felt safe.

"What do you want, Devorah?"

"Aren't you glad to see me? Maybe I'm here to finish what we started the other night."

Nathan didn't want to draw her attention to his studio, but he desperately wanted to look over his shoulder to see if he had closed the door. But he couldn't risk it. He could only hope that he hadn't left it wide open for her to find the one secret that could destroy him.

"Or maybe you had something in mind with your new girlfriend."

Nathan took a step back, hoping she couldn't see his eyes too well in the dim light. "What -"

"Sarah Thomas," Devorah said sharply. She stepped forward, closing back in.

Nathan held both palms up. "What the hell are you talking about?"

Devorah looked as if she were admonishing a young boy. "Oh, Nathan, that idiot Gavin may not see what's going on here, but I do."

Nathan forced himself not to avert his gaze, wondering just how much she could know. But, by the way she knit her brow, the way her mouth tightened, the way her chin jutted towards him, he could tell this wasn't about the bank. This really was about Sarah.

"If you think there's anything going on between us that is outside the scope of the case, you're barking up the wrong tree. There's nothing going on there." Not that he didn't wish there was.

Devorah scoffed. "I believe you, Nathan. I believe that you think there isn't. But let me explain something to you about men that I've learned over the years. They don't take an interest in a woman unless they want her, even if they don't see it."

"Well, that would explain why I have an interest in spending as little time with you as possible."

Devorah put on a mock pout. His words probably did sting but Nathan knew she wouldn't let him see that. "Are you willing to go to prison for her, Nathan?"

"One thing I can tell you, I sure as hell am not willing to go to prison for *you.*"

Nathan could see by the faint wince of pain in her face that he had scored a hit. But he wasn't sure that was the best idea.

A resigned tone in her voice, Devorah asked, "Are you, Nathan? Are you willing to go to prison for her?"

He shook his head and said, "No, I'm not interested in going down with the ship."

Devorah cocked her head to the side. "Then we would all be more comfortable if the applications were back in the vault where they belong."

A pained smile stretched his mouth. "I'm sure you would. But that's not going to happen."

In a low voice, she said, "I know." She took another step towards him and now he could smell the exotic perfume that was supposed to entice him into her web. Her expression was soft, her eyes open and glistening. "Because you're a good man, Nathan." She looked at him in silence for a moment. "The only good man I know, really."

Nathan wanted to say something. He could see the pain emerging from her soul and he wanted to say something to keep that from happening. He didn't want to look into her eyes and wish he could take that pain away.

"I know what you see when you look at me," she said. "The woman who slept her way to the top. The woman who uses her body and her smile to persuade men to give her what she wants."

"Devorah, I think that's the most honest thing you've ever said to me."

"You are so quick to judge what it's like for somebody like me to make her way in a world controlled by all the right people when I'm not one of them."

Nathan knit his brow. "What do you mean?"

"I mean my degree isn't from Harvard and I didn't grow up knowing all the blue bloods. I'm just a girl from Texas whose ambition exceeds her grasp. Because, no matter how you slice it, men like you see girls like me as a threat. It's still an all-boys club Nathan."

For a moment, Nathan felt a swell of compassion for her and he couldn't push it away. He could hear the tinge of anguish in her voice. He could sense the shadow of truth woven between her words. And then he closed his eyes and let out a sigh.

"You know what your problem is, Devorah?"

She shrugged and held up her hands. "Why won't you help me, Nathan?"

"Because, right at this exact second I can't tell if you're trusting me with your version of the truth of if you're just trying to play me. Again." He frowned and arched his brow. "I just can't tell."

She stepped up to him and slid her hand onto his shoulder. She studied his chest for a moment, then tilted her head up to look into his eyes. "Are you sure, Nathan? Are you sure you can't tell?"

Nathan stared into her eyes. A part of him wanted to believe her. Not so he could reciprocate. But so he could believe that a part of Devorah Harlow was at least a shadow of a good woman. So he could see the remnants left behind after letting the world break her because she couldn't believe in herself. Nathan almost wanted to take that pain away.

Almost.

"No, Devorah, I can't."

Devorah nodded slowly, as if she had made a decision. She lowered her hand and let it rest on his chest. Her smile faded. Her eyes narrowed. Whatever part of herself that she had shown him for just that moment slipped away and he knew he would never see it again.

"Just remember," she said, "I came to you first."

## *OUT OF THE GAME*

For the second time in a week, Emmerson stood in the law clinic, waiting for Maureen to knock on Stanley's door and discretely give him time to put away his bottle before she told him the chairman was waiting to see him.

Expecting to be invited into the steel box that was Stanley's office, Emmerson cocked a brow when Stanley emerged from his office and walked across the room with a slightly unsteady gait.

Emmerson shook his head and let out a soft sigh. Some people just couldn't adapt to knowing their place in the world.

Emmerson held out his hand. Stanley responded with a limp handshake and then looked at Emmerson with half-closed eyes. "What do you need this time?"

Emmerson's smile faded and he worked his jaw for a moment, trying to decide which way to handle things. "It would be better if you knew," he said.

"Knew what?"

"It would be better if you knew why I was here and just agreed to get it done." He tilted his head and arched a brow.

"I'm a lawyer, Mr. Emmerson. I don't guess at what people have to say."

Emmerson pressed his mouth into a thin line, then said, "Fine." He took a deep breath and let out a sigh. "Look, I didn't want this. Nobody did. But I have no other choice at this point. You need to let Ms. Thomas go."

Stanley looked over his shoulder, then back at Emmerson. "Do you want my office, too? I mean, if you're going to run the clinic and all." He paused for a moment. Emmerson blinked as a waft of whiskey-soaked breath stung his eyes. "Although I guess you can just phone it in from your downtown office. It's more comfortable, after all."

"Can I count on you, Stanley?"

Stanley looked up at the ceiling, then steadied his gaze on Emmerson. "Why are you all so obsessed with this girl? She's just trying to do the job you pay her for."

"Are you really that obtuse, Stanley?" Emmerson scoffed and swept his hand through the air. "There is way more to all of this than your little clinic here."

Stanley's face was tight now and he spoke with a slight growl. "Oh I know that," he said. "You're all fine with it as long as we provide a good PR service and only go against people who can't hurt you." Stanly nodded, lifting his brow. "But now she's opened a real can of worms, hasn't she?"

"Not yet," Emmerson said. "We derailed her with the predatory lending thing. But then you couldn't keep a leash on her. From what I hear, her clients went around you."

"Something like that. And who is *we*?"

Emmerson took a step closer. "See, that's why I'm doing you the courtesy of speaking plainly today." He casually waved his hand. "Here in this slum of an office where nobody really cares that you're drinking yourself to death."

Stanley clenched his jaw and narrowed his gaze. "That's right," Emmerson said. "I'm not going pretend. I'm going to do you the courtesy of reminding you of your place." He smiled and shook his head. "Come on, we all know the deal here. All you have to do is what you've always done."

Stanley squinted harder, working his jaw even tighter. "Who is this *we*?" he asked again.

"You don't want to know."

"For Christ's sake, Wyatt, what have you gotten us into?"

Emmerson let out a sigh. He wasn't sure if it was best to let Stanley see that he wasn't in control of the situation. But he had orders and he knew that he had to carry them out. He didn't want to put the old man on the street. He really didn't. But the old man had to know his place. And so far he didn't seem to.

"Let me be plain. Unless you want to spend your days sitting on that bench in front of Foley, you'll fire this girl and move on with your life."

Stanley blinked at him, his expression suddenly sober. "You're threatening me?"

"Oh no, Stanley. I'm not. I'm telling you that you'll be out of a job. That's not a threat. Trust me." He took another step closer. "I've heard threats. I know what they sound like. And, unlike you, I do know my place."

"You look scared, Wyatt."

"Maybe I am."

Stanley stared at him now, searching for some deeper truth in Emmerson's stern gaze. Emmerson only hoped that Stanley understood the truth was in plain sight.

The old man must have finally seen that truth because he looked away and said, "Alright, I'll do it. But I need to know why."

"You don't want to know."

"Maybe when this all blows over then."

Wyatt took a step back and hung his head for a moment. Looking back at Stanley, he said, "It never blows over."

## *VOW*

Sarah leaned on the table with her elbow and rested her forehead in her hand. Studying the wood grain of the table, she imagined all the students and lawyers who had sat there doing the same thing she was doing - pouring through thick volumes of statutes, rules of evidence and common law decisions. Ten such volumes were sprawled in a semi-circle around her, all of them open.

She was stitching together the relationship between statutory fraud and corporate negligence when she felt a light tap on her shoulder.

Sarah jerked from her reverie to see a librarian standing behind her, smiling patiently. The lights had dimmed. All the other tables were empty.

"I'm sorry, miss, but it's closing time."

Sarah let out a sigh and shook her head. Of course it was closing time. Because she was in the middle of a very complex analysis that required several more hours of cross-referencing the fortress of volumes on the table around her. She liked it that way. There was a depth and subtlety to manually cross-referencing all of that information that links on a computer screen could never duplicate. Now she could do neither because the building with everything she needed to save her clients was closing. Justice, it seemed, kept banker's hours even thought injustice did not.

Sarah started to close one of the books. "That's alright, I'll take care of that," the librarian said. She gestured towards the door.

Sarah stood up and nodded her surrender. She shouldered her courier bag and traipsed towards the door. As she stepped outside, she looked over her shoulder. She would be back the next day. But she would have to start over. And the summary judgment was only a week away.

Later that night, not only did she lie awake worrying about being ready for her clients, but she lay awake worrying about her rent and utilities. Her career. Even her survival. So she took Benadryl to get to sleep, but woke up the next morning with the fog that always came from taking Benadryl to sleep.

Over her morning coffee, Sarah inspected the scant wrinkled papers that she still had in her possession regarding the case. She had access to the filings, of course, but all the internal notes she had created now belonged to the clinic and Maureen had reluctantly told her she couldn't hand them over. She couldn't even let Sarah through the door.

Now, Sarah bumped her fist lightly against her forehead, trying to remember the serpentine path of logic she had etched out while working the case. But too many of her moments of brilliance were buried in the past, clipped to a particular moment where the light might have been buzzing and her mind wandered seemingly at random to just the right place to uncover an epiphany. This was why she wrote all that down. Because she couldn't duplicate these mental excursions at will.

She had read the papers in front of her over a dozen times, imploring her mind to reconstruct the scaffolding of a legal thesis that could save her clients. She didn't even have her own law books, even though Stanley had assured her the clinic would send them over. She could sue, of course. But how would that look? She could see the words on the ticker that would scroll along the bottom of the screen: *Social justice attorney sues local law clinic for poor over law books.*

She wanted to open a book, feel the heavy press-board cover in her hand and the sensation of riffling the slick pages with her thumb. She wanted to read the law. She checked her watch. The library wouldn't open for another two hours.

All she could do until then was drink coffee and look into the depths of her mind - a dark cavern where she knew there were outcroppings of crystal that led the way to saving her clients. But there was nothing to light them, so she could see nothing.

With nothing to distract her, Sarah's mind wandered to the one place she dreaded most. The last thing she had done before leaving to start her job at the clinic was to visit her mother. She closed her eyes and saw the tombstone and the daisies wafting in the breeze on a cool autumn day. The grass covering her mother's grave. She knelt down, reached out to the tombstone and ran her hand across the rough stone. Her own words echoed from that day. *I promise. I'll never give up. Ever. They'll have to kill me first.*

## *HELPING HAND*

Sarah thumbed her driver a tip as she closed the door to the Uber, stepped out on the busy downtown sidewalk and looked around.

She stared at the blue sign with white lettering. *Lomas Street Station*. Her stomach tightened as she peered down the steps leading into darkness. She could see the aged urban ambiance of The Diner as something quaint. As she hailed from rural farm country, everything in the city had been an expansive experience, really. There was a sizzle to the orchestrated chaos of city streets that she found exhilarating. But the notion of careening through dark tunnels and squealing wheels just made her vaguely nauseous.

She stepped gingerly onto the concrete steps that led into the cavernous station below. Everything about it was old and tired. The steps had shallow grooves worn down by the million heels that had trodden down them. The upper tiles of the wall were blanched by years of sunlight. The lower tiles were dulled by years of grime that had cemented itself to their surface. A faceless throng trudged up and down the stairs and mingled on the platform, oblivious to it all. To Sarah, it was an unexplored dungeon. To everyone else, it seemed to just be the subway.

Reaching the station floor, she stepped aside as riders shuffled by, some of them bumping into her or brushing her elbow, so she didn't notice Nathan right away.

She swiveled her head back and forth, trying to keep track of all the people as they walked past, until she turned and found him standing right next to her.

Nervously, she asked him, "Is there a reason we're meeting in the subway instead of inside somewhere like civilized people?"

"Because we need to take that." He pointed at a string of cars pulling into the station

Sarah winced at the sound of a straining electric hum and hissing brakes.

"What, is your smart phone broken?" she asked.

"It's the only way to get there without anybody noticing."

Frowning as she watched riders spew from the narrow doors and the sea of riders waiting on the platform drain back into them, she asked, "Get where?"

He gently took her by the elbow and ushered her towards the turnstile. "You'll see."

Gripping a strap hanging from the handrail, Sarah struggled to keep her balance as the train veered around corners and bounced over the seams between the rails. Her body swayed from side to side. Occasionally, she had to bend and stomp her foot to regain her balance. Nathan, on the other hand, seemed to bob and weave with each gyration just fine, almost as if he were dancing.

"You ride the subway often?" she asked.

Smiling at her, he said, "I used to."

"Instead of going to the gym," she said, "I could just do this once a day." She rubbed her shoulder, which was starting to ache from the yanking and pulling against the train's attempts to throw her to the floor.

Nathan chuckled. "Gym would be cheaper."

The train slowed as it pulled into a station. "This is our stop," Nathan said.

The doors clunked opened and Sarah stared at the haggard faces of the riders on the platform. They didn't look like people as much as they looked like beings whose sole purpose in the world was to ride the subway.

They seemed to form a wall that wouldn't let her pass, so she didn't move. Before she could protest, Nathan took her hand and dragged her out of the car and towards the stairs, weaving his way through the crowd.

Once they were upstairs, Sarah could see they were in an older part of town. There was something vaguely familiar about it.

"This looks a lot like -"

"It is," Nathan cut in, smiling. He pointed down the street and said, "The Diner is two blocks that way."

"Oh." Looking around to catalog her surroundings, she asked, "Is that where we're going? I could have just met you there."

Nathan stopped in his tracks, turned around and grabbed Sarah by both shoulders. Startled, Sarah stared at him wide-eyed. For a fleeting second, she wondered if he had lured her into a trap from which she would never return. But he wasn't that kind of man. She knew that now. But she still couldn't think of any good reason for him to drag her onto the subway.

"Listen to me," he said.

"Uh-huh."

He blinked a few times, then let go of her and smoothed out the sleeves of her coat. "Look," he said. "You really pissed off the wrong people." Looking around, he continued, "But I know you won't give up. So I found something that I think will help." He wrinkled his forehead and bit his lip. "But you need to be discreet."

She knew that her refusal to toe the line had annoyed a lot of people, including Emmerson himself. But just then, she saw a look in Nathan's eyed that made her shiver.

"What are you talking about?"

Nathan took her hand, gently this time. "Come on," he said. "Let me show you."

Nathan fumbled with the keys to the brown metal door of a small office that looked like it had been left back in 1967. He opened the door and ushered her inside.

"It's dark," Sarah said.

She felt his hand brush her hair as he reached behind her and flipped on the light. Two sets of fluorescent lights flickered to life. But they did not buzz. If fact, they didn't make a sound. Sarah looked at them, mesmerized by the glow of a silent fluorescent light.

A heavy wooden desk sat in the middle of the room, facing the door and the shuttered window next to it. Behind that, a credenza with a tower PC.

"It has Internet," Nathan said. "And phone." He pointed at the black business phone sitting on the desk. "The number is unpublished."

Sarah surveyed the room. It was walled entirely with cheap dark wood paneling. The carpet was blue, but it had no runs and Sarah smiled at the sensation of her foot sinking into the semi-plush piles. She had always assumed she would work in a run-down office like the clinic. Better was something she had never even considered.

He took her into an alcove separated by a half-wall jutting into the room and showed her a book shelf filled top to bottom with her law books.

Sarah gazed at the volumes. Nathan started to say, "I know you prefer the books, so I stopped by the clinic -", but before he could finish his sentence, Sarah wrapped her arms around his neck and her mouth was on his.

Nathan's head swam as the feeling of Sarah's lip-sticked mouth against his sent a shiver down to the tips of his toes. He reeled from the sensation of her lips sliding over his, her hand gently pawing at the back of his neck. He closed his eyes, and knew that if he died at just that moment, he would have lived a full life.

It was more than a peck on the cheek and he could feel Sarah giving herself to him. For a full two seconds. Then, just as quickly as she had lunged at him, she pulled herself away.

He opened his eyes to see a red blush blossoming on her cheeks. Then he looked into the ocean of her green eyes. For the first time since he had met her, Nathan did not see the old familiar pain in those eyes.

"Sorry," she said, stepping back from him. "It's just that -"

"Don't be," he said. Smiling, he swept the room with his hand. "It's not much, but it's probably better than trying to work from your kitchen table."

Sarah stepped over to the desk, leaned on it with both hands and surveyed it from side to side. Then she looked over the credenza. "This will do," she said. She stood up and picked up the phone, listening to the drone of the dial tone. "This will do just fine."

She sat down in the austere office chair, the only piece of new furniture in the place. But it was firm against her back and she knew she would be able to sit in it for the hours it would take her to read statutes, scribble notes and prepare her case.

She looked at Nathan still standing next to the book case. He was beaming.

She shook her head and said, "I don't know what to say."

"Oh," he said, waving towards the desk. "And there's pads and pens and stuff like that you lawyers like – down in those drawers."

Sarah pulled open one of the drawers to see a ream of yellow legal pads peeking out, bidding her fingers to pummel its barren surface with ink.

"What, you banker types don't like pen and paper?" She smiled at him coyly, still embarrassed by the kiss but wanting to make sure he knew she was grateful.

"We prefer spreadsheets."

Sarah let her gaze linger for a moment. His eyes were soft now, his mouth still curled with a smile. She looked away, ran her hand over the desktop, then stood up. She un-shouldered her purse and took off her coat, hanging both on the back of the chair. She sat back down, took in a deep breath and said, "Thank you."

His eyes still dreamy from the kiss, Nathan said, "You're welcome." He nodded and then said, "Welp, I'll leave you to it." He started for the door, stopped mid-step and turned around. Rubbing his chin, he said, "Something else, though."

Sarah slumped in her chair. She knew it was too good to be true. There were always strings attached. Always.

Her voice was sharp, stabbing the air with a single word. What?"

"It's probably best if this stays between you and me." When she didn't respond, he said, "Understand?"

"You mean you don't want anyone to know that you set this up for me? That I'm a kept lawyer?"

"I wouldn't put it exactly like that, but I think you understand that it's better if the world doesn't know that I'm helping you."

He was right, of course. The lawyer in her knew that he was treading on very thin ice and that she, too, had to be careful about their relationship. But the part of her that wanted to check her skirt belt wished that he could just be the one person who dared to stand up for her.

She looked down at the desk, conceding with a nod. "Of course," she said. Looking up, she saw that vague look of hurt in his eyes that she now understood came from her words. There were better words that she knew would ease that pain. But all she could say was, "Seriously, thank you." She pasted a smile on her face, but it wasn't enough. Then Nathan looked down for a moment. When he looked back up, the hurt was gone. All Sarah could see now was the kind of man who would never let her down. She wanted to stand up, walk across the room and cradle his face in her hands. She wanted to tell him that there was more to her than just *thank you.* But he was standing on the other side of her desk now. And she knew it was better that way.

"You're welcome," he said. His face sagged so that he looked like a man drowning at sea, waiting for somebody to throw him a lifeline. Sarah didn't like seeing him that way and she wanted to look away. But she couldn't. They looked at each other in silence, unable to say the words that would obliterate all the tables, desks, rules and suspicions arrayed between them. Then he turned around, left the office and closed the door behind him.

## *WHEN TO QUIT*

Sitting behind the defendant's table, Sarah tried to put the thought out of her mind that it was her last chance. Instead, she tried to focus on the idea that it was her best chance.

Maureen had been right. Foreclosure hearings were formalities in the vast majority of cases. Finding exceptions had been difficult, but she had scraped together enough common law and a few appellate rulings to formulate a legal theory. It was simple enough, even if it was a bit far-fetched. But she had the law to back it up.

If she could prove fraud, Sarah could ask the court to rule the mortgage contracts invalid. The law was clear on that point, so that shouldn't have been too much trouble. At that point, the homeowners would still have their titles and the bank's liens would, at best, be in limbo. Sarah couldn't determine what would happen after that but her best guess was that the bank would go into receivership, throwing the door wide open to renegotiated terms for paying back the loans. Probably at a discount. And certainly with a payment structure her clients could handle.

It was far-fetched. It was hopeful. But she did have the law on her side. She tried not to think about how much that might not matter based on her treatment by the court so far in her fledgling career.

The judge hustled in from his chambers, frowning at Sarah as he stepped up onto the dais and sat down at his bench.

Addressing the well in general, the judge asked, "What are we doing today, more ice fishing or something about the foreclosures for once?"

Sarah looked at him with a deadpan gaze. He glowered back at her. She knew then that he was going to, once again, take control of the debate instead of mediating it. Calhoun started to say something, but the judge cut him off. "You know, counselor," he said, looking directly at Sarah, "It occurs to me that your insistence on dragging this out is a disservice to your clients. In the end, they're going to be out of a home. And I'm not sure your insistence on filling their heads with hopes and dreams is actually just."

His interference this time was shocking, even for him. Sarah couldn't immediately find the words to respond to the judge's highly out-of-order preemption of her right to be heard.

The judge continued, "You don't have something to say? For once?"

Answering his original question, she said, cooly, "We're here about the foreclosures, your honor. I've requested an evidentiary hearing. You know, where I present some thoughts on why plaintiffs are derelict in their duty to this court and to justice."

The judge shook his head. "Watch yourself, counselor. I'm in no mood."

"Are we in session, then?" she asked. The judge stirred uncomfortably in his seat.

Still glowering, he said, "Proceed, counselor."

Stepping out from behind the table with her copy of the case file in her hand, Sarah said, "Your honor, We have twice subpoenaed the original loan applications and plaintiff has still failed to produce these documents in accordance with this court's order."

"Wait," the judge said, "I thought we did all that with the predatory lending suit."

Sarah knew he was not going to like the fact that she went around him, but there was no hiding it at this point. "The magistrate issued a new subpoena for this case, your honor."

"Because she didn't know you had already done that for a case which has now been dismissed and you knew I wouldn't have signed that subpoena."

"Well at least we all know where you stand, judge."

The judge picked up his gavel, spun it a few times and then set it down with a deliberate slowness as he looked down at Sarah with a seething glare.

He opened the case file lying on his bench and pulled out the subpoena. Sarah knew it was in perfect order. It had to be so he couldn't find any excuse to throw it out. She still wasn't sure if going around him was the best idea, but she knew he would never have issued a second subpoena for her. So it had to be perfect.

"What's the point, counselor?"

"I beg your pardon sir, what?"

"What's the point of this subpoena? What is this going to do for us?"

It occurred to Sarah that Calhoun hadn't said a word. He didn't really have to as the judge seemed to have joined him at the defendant's table in all but actual presence.

"Your honor, I have a properly sworn subpoena which compels plaintiff to turn over specific records - all original loan applications submitted by the residents of Sunfield Farms. I want you to explain to the plaintiff that they have a legal obligation to heed the orders of this court."

"Oh, I'm sure you do, Ms. Thomas. But what I'm asking you is why are you trying to introduce evidence into this case that has already been rendered moot by a settlement?"

Sarah's jaw dropped. For the first time since meeting the man, she wondered if the judge was incompetent. She had always chalked up the friction between them to his dislike for her personally, but now he was just being obtuse.

"I already argued that with the magistrate, your honor. I shouldn't have to answer that question twice."

"Indulge me."

Sarah glared at him, then closed her eyes and let out a slow breath. She couldn't believe he was going to actually make her explain herself when everything was right there in front of him. All he had to do was order Calhoun to turn over the applications. How complicated was that?

"This is a hearing, after all," the judge said, smiling. "So talk to me."

Without trying to hide her displeasure, Sarah threw her copy of the case file on the defendant's table and let it slide across its surface and fall on the floor.

"You dropped something there," the judge said, peering at the papers strewn on the floor.

"That's fine. I already know what they say."

"Then by all means, counselor, please proceed."

Out of the corner of her eye, Sarah could see Calhoun giggling. He wasn't even trying to hide it.

"Your honor, we believe that defendant has committed fraud as it is defined for the purposes of 3501.3." Calhoun stopped giggling. "Contracts made under fraudulent circumstances are rendered moot by statute. That is why we are asking for the applications."

"So you can prove fraud?"

"That is correct, your honor."

"Do you have anything else or is this just a theory?"

"The credit scores, your honor. It is clear that the bank had no reasonable expectation of seeing those loans paid back. So why did they issue them in the first place? So they could sell them to an unsuspecting buyer perhaps?" Sarah glanced at Calhoun as she talked, trying to gauge if he showed a reaction to any of her best guesses. "Or securing funds under false pretenses from Fannie Mae or some other clearing house?" Calhoun just looked bored. "Or maybe to cycle the properties through a buyer ready to scoop them up in short sale and make a windfall?"

Calhoun did not look bored now. He didn't look like somebody who had been caught either, though. He looked at Sarah with a puzzled look on his face, as if he too had been looking for the truth behind all the shoddy paperwork.

"Do you have any evidence whatsoever to back up any of these claims?"

"No, your honor. That's why we need those applications. They're foundational. If there is a discrepancy between the originals and the paperwork proffered right here in your court, then we'll all know that there's more than meets the eye here."

The judge nodded solemnly. "Mr. Calhoun?"

Calhoun adjusted his tie, looked at Sarah with that puzzled look again and then stepped out from behind the plaintiff's table.

"Your honor," he said, "my esteemed colleague is on a fishing expedition in the hopes of finding something to assuage her frustration with what she considers to be an inadequate remedy. This isn't about the foreclosures. This is about the settlement for the predatory lending allegations." He looked her square in the eye and she could have sworn that he was sorry. But he had a client to defend. So he had to do his best to throw her under the bus. But Sarah began to wonder if he really felt right about it.

"This subpoena pertains to evidence that has nothing to do with the debtors' responsibility to pay back their obligations. They applied for loans. That is not in dispute. They got the loans. That is not in dispute. They have failed to pay back those loans. That is not in dispute. How we got here is irrelevant." He picked up a folder from the table and brought it over to Sarah for her to see. "These are the originally signed promissory notes for each of Ms. Thomas's clients. They agreed to pay back these loans and have failed to do so. That is not in dispute. What credit scores are attached to the applications has no bearing on the controversy at bar: these people owe the bank money. Digging up original applications isn't going to change that. They have no probative value whatsoever."

Sarah blinked at Calhoun, overwhelmed by the depth of his argument. All he was doing, of course, was trying to make sure that evidence they both knew would hang the bank out of her hands. Seeing the judge nodding, Sarah knew that Calhoun had played right into the man's favor by limiting the scope of the case so he didn't have to get bogged down with mundane matters such as the actual truth.

"That sounds about right, Mr. Calhoun. Thank you." Turning to Sarah, the judge said, "The matter before us is a simple one. Do they owe? If yes - "

"But your honor."

He tapped his gavel against the strike plate and continued. "If yes, then the question is have they paid -"

"You're testifying, sir. I would like to state my rebuttal."

The judge smacked the strike plate harder this time. "And if they have not paid, then can they? I will tell you if they settle the debt in full before summary judgment, I'll be inclined to dismiss."

"Your honor!" Sarah nearly yelled this time. "Mr. Neilsen and his cohort are using this court to steal millions from these homeowners. They're going to sell short and somebody is going to turn around and make a windfall."

The judge banged his gavel three times and then asked her, "And yet you have no evidence of this. Just an axe to grind. Do you think this is the first time I've met you Ms. Thomas? You have been traipsing in and out of my courtroom for the past thirty years. You're looking for the same monsters under the bed as all the young fired up attorneys I've watched come and go in that time. They're not there. They never have been." He tapped his gavel lightly and said, "As for your motion, it is the court's ruling that -"

"Your honor, please." Sarah was almost in tears, not because she was losing but because she wanted justice from a man who blocked her at every turn simply because she wouldn't help him with his fast-food drive-through courtroom.

He glared at her and said, "That will do Ms. Thomas. Not another word. Now, as to my ruling. The evidence you are requesting, while not prejudicial, is nevertheless irrelevant with regards to the merits of plaintiff's case. Your motion is denied."

Just as he smacked the strike plate with his gavel, Sarah took a step closer to the bench and said, "How do you sleep at night?"

"That's enough."

"If these applications were approved under fraudulent circumstances, you know I have a case."

The judge spoke calmly, almost as if he were actually trying to help her. "Then file suit to have the contracts nullified in the face of fraud."

Sarah scoffed. Was he kidding? She worked out of a ramshackle office at the whim of the very man who stood at the center of the controversy. She didn't have enough money to pay her rent, let alone fund a new case that would require more filings and motions, all of which cost court fees that she couldn't afford to pay. She could ask for a mistrial, of course, but that would only delay the inevitable. No, she had to close the door on the case once and for all and the judge was blocking the only way she knew how.

For the first time in her life, Sarah wondered if maybe the law wasn't enough. Maybe Elaine was right. Maybe it was time to surrender and work billable hours for people who could afford to shape and mold justice to suit their own needs.

"No, really. I want to know." She pointed at Calhoun. "How much are these people paying you to ignore the law, to ignore evidence, to ignore justice?" The judge picked up his gavel, raising it high in the air this time. She flung herself at the bench and asked him, "How much are they paying you to ignore me?"

The judge slammed the gavel hard enough to split the strike plate into two neat halves and send them skittering across the floor.

"I will not be admonished in my own courtroom. Bailiff, take Ms. Thomas to the county jail post haste. You, counselor, are in contempt."

## *SMOKE SIGNALS*

Jail sucked. Sarah was thrown into a community lock-up with thirty other women. Those who weren't high or drunk stank. She knew it was customary for a lawyer to get an actual cell for the night, but she didn't know if it was required. While she dreaded the thought of asking one of the deputies to take her to the judge so she could apologize, she didn't think she could make it an hour in that hell-hole, let alone an entire night.

An hour later, she was surprised when a deputy showed up to haul her out of the holding tank and drag her down the hall to her own cell. He didn't explain why. And she didn't ask.

Five minutes later, another deputy told her she had a visitor. Then he asked her how everything was in her cell. "I just got here five minutes ago," she said. "I'll let you know." The deputy just gave her a stern look and hauled her back up the hallway to a visitation room.

If Maureen had come to see her, Sarah was going to have to stand her ground. It wasn't going to be pretty, but she knew she was right and she was tired of everybody telling her to not do her job. If Stanley had come to see her, she was probably going to ask to go back to her cell.

The deputy sat her down in a chair in a bright white room with a stainless steel table. There were no windows, mirrors or cameras. It was a room reserved for suspects to talk to their lawyers.

Sarah was still working out what she would say when the door opened. Her mind stopped cold when she saw Nathan emerge from the doorway. The deputy standing next to him said, "You all have 30 minutes."

Nathan nodded at the deputy. "Thank you." Just as the door closed, he descended on the only other chair in the room and dragged it close to Sarah.

Part of her wanted to run and hide from the humiliation of him seeing her like this. Another part of her wanted to throw herself into his arms and bury her face against his chest.

She cast her gaze down at the table, unable to look at him.

Neither of them said a word for a full five minutes. She let the feeling of his presence drape over her like a blanket. Friend, foe, enemy, lover. Sarah didn't know what Nathan was to her, but in that moment he was her only comfort in a world where everything was falling apart.

Finally, she whispered, "I think you're going to win."

"Not me, Sarah. The bank."

"What's the difference?" She looked at the floor now. "It doesn't matter." Looking up at him for the first time since he had arrived, she said, "Why are you here? I mean why are *you* here? Why are you the only one here. Why is nobody else here?" He wasn't smiling. His face was just steady, looking at her with that never-let-you-down gaze of his.

His voice was gentle, and reassuring, as if he were a doctor talking to a patient. "I don't think anybody knows you're here." He paused for a moment and said, "I could go tell them."

Sarah grunted a faint laugh. "No. This is more than enough humiliation, thank you."

"I won't tell anyone."

Sarah saw it in his eyes. It wasn't a passing remark or a token comfort. It was a promise. Not that it mattered. Everyone would know by morning that she had been thrown in jail for contempt of court.

But they wouldn't hear it from Nathan.

"Why are you here?" she asked again.

"You wouldn't believe me if I told you."

Sarah wanted to ask him what she wouldn't believe. Why wouldn't she believe it? But she knew better than to ask because she was afraid of what the answer might be. And she wasn't ready for it.

"Are you my friend, Nathan?"

He smiled warmly and reached into the inside pocket of his suit jacket. She kept her gaze fixed on his, waiting for an answer.

He pulled out an envelope and said, "I want to show you something."

The last hope of an answer to her question faded away when he placed the envelope on the table and tapped it. "You were right about one thing," he said.

"What's that?"

"There's some kind of fraud going on. There has to be."

She nodded thoughtfully, then asked him, "How did you know I brought that up in court today?"

"You should look in the gallery once in a while," he said, smiling.

Sarah was both grateful and horrified by the thought of Nathan sitting in the gallery, watching her humiliate herself in front of the judge and Calhoun.

Hoping to distract herself from that thought, she asked him, "What's this?"

Nathan unfolded the pages and spread them out on the table.

"What am I looking at?" she asked.

"What do you see?"

Sarah studied the sheets, all of them charts of some kind with the same jagged downward sloping line. "Whatever it is, it looks like it's going down."

"That's right. These are returns on an obscure portfolio called Select Advisory."

Sarah's mind kicked into gear. She squinted at the paper as she tried to anchor the start of a logic tree that would lead to new information, new ideas. A new chance. "That seems like an odd name for an investment portfolio."

"Indeed." Nathan pointed at a column of numbers next to the chart. "And look at these."

All Sarah saw was an increasing balance of dollar amounts running the entire length of the page. "What are these?"

"Those are purchases. Investments. That's people putting more and more money into the portfolio."

Sarah knit her brow. "The portfolio that is going down?"

"That's right. So, ask yourself -"

Sarah cut him off, arriving there on her own. "Why would all these people keep putting money into a losing investment?"

Nathan sat back, smiling. "Exactly."

## *DIALING FOR DOLLARS*

Nathan sat in his studio and did the one thing he swore he'd never do. He conducted bank business in the same room where he painted. All his life, the two had been separate. His studio had been a sanctuary where the world stopped at the door and was never allowed to come in.

It was also the one place where he felt safe. Here, they couldn't see him. They couldn't hear him. They couldn't get at him, even though Devorah had come close. Still, she hadn't found her way inside. Nor would she.

At the bank, they could see him. They could hear every call he made, read every e-mail he sent. Maybe he was just being paranoid, but he knew he had to do this quietly until he had enough information to protect himself.

Sitting in his studio, he knew the land line came in through steel piping that was thirty years old and ended at a terminal box in a locked room in the back of the museum. It would have been risky if he had used his smart phone or even called from his house. But here, he knew that nobody was listening in.

Most of the calls had been fruitless. The last one had been particularly frosty. While the client didn't appreciate the steep rate at which his portfolio was declining, he told Nathan that he had already taken the matter up with Gavin. Then he asked the oddest question. He asked Nathan why he was calling. Nathan responded with the most obvious answer - he was concerned about customer satisfaction and wanted to check in to see if there was anything he could do to help. The client grunted, laughed and then said, "No, you're not." Then he hung up.

Nathan held the handset in his hand, listening to the drone of the dial tone. He clicked the cutoff button and smiled. He was close to finding something. He could feel it.

Nathan picked up the next file and punched in the phone number to make his fifth call, hoping he could find more than just a quiet line and a stern affirmation of disinterest in his involvement.

After a few rings, a man answered. Half on autopilot, Nathan identified himself and asked if he was speaking to the holder of account number 47839923. He had been careful not to use anybody's name after the first call, where the client had asked in a panicked voice where Nathan got his name and then asked to speak to Gavin.

Waiting for a similar reaction from client number five, he wasn't sure what to say when the man responded, "Yes. What can I do for you Mr. Haley?"

When Nathan didn't respond for a few moments, the man said, "Hello?"

Nathan cleared his throat and leaned forward, caught off guard by a simple greeting without the animosity he was expecting.

"Um, right, well, actually, I was wondering if I might be able to do something for you."

The man's voice went flat. "You said you're the Vice President?"

"That's right."

"Then why are you trying to sell me something. Seems like you'd have people who work for you to do that sort of thing."

Nathan chuckled, hoping to put the man at ease. "No, no, nothing like that. I was just calling because I thought you might have some concerns about these returns."

When the man didn't respond, Nathan was already eying file number six, the last of the stack. After that, there wouldn't be anybody left to talk to unless Maggie could find more sheets accidentally discarded and fluttering in the janitor's trash bin.

Finally, the man asked, "Why haven't I heard from you before?"

Nathan leaned in closer to his easel. He thought carefully about his next words now that he had found somebody willing to talk. "Um, well, as you know, this sort of thing is normally handled by our Director of Financial Services."

"Yes, Ms. Harlow. Who hasn't returned my calls."

Nathan fumbled for a pencil and scribbled hastily on a notepad - *Devorah avoiding.*

"Well, I'm listening now. What are your concerns, sir?"

"Why has it taken you this long to get to me?"

"As I said sir, Ms. Harlow normally handles this sort of thing."

"Yes you said that." The man fell silent for a moment. Nathan resisted the urge to encourage him, sensing that the client was already clamming up. "So why are you calling me now?"

"Well," Nathan said. "It's about these returns." Nathan thought about how to lead the man where he needed to him to go. On pure instinct, he decided to jump right into it. "I wouldn't imagine you're too happy with them."

"You're damn right I'm not," the man said. "Gavin never said they would be this steep."

The investor was complaining about the scale, not the direction. Nathan tapped the pencil against his table. Then he asked, "Would you be happier if they weren't declining so much?"

"I would be happier if they lined up the way we agreed."

"Agreed?" Nathan asked. "Did Gavin make you some kind of promise regarding these returns."

"You're damn right he did."

Nathan stared at the cloth draped over his easel. He knew that Gavin wasn't an honest broker, but making promises about returns was, even for him, crossing a line that he couldn't come back from.

"What did he promise?"

"You don't know?"

And there it was. Gavin had come up with something that he had hidden away from him this whole time. Something that had probably been right in front of his nose. Something he didn't see because he had been too busy worrying about covering his own tracks. He couldn't help feeling that didn't matter anymore. But he also couldn't help if he was sitting inside a prison cell.

"No sir, I don't know."

"Listen to me, Mr. Haley. You need to be real sure about this. Because you are either part of this or you're not."

"Part of what?"

Nathan could tell that the man had a choice to make in answering that question. And the easiest choice would be to hang up. All he could do was wait.

"How did you get my portfolio information?"

"I'm the Vice President."

"So this is the first time you've looked?"

"Yeah. I never had a reason to before."

"Why now?"

Nathan let out a slow breath, leery of showing his entire hand. The man was talking a good game, but Nathan didn't if he was just reeling him in for Gavin. At the same time, Nathan sensed that this investor held the key to everything he needed to know.

"What can you tell me?" Nathan asked.

Nathan counted his breathing as he waited for an answer. He held his breath, half expecting to hear a dial tone end the conversation. Finally, the man said, "I can tell you a lot."

"I'm listening."

"Am I the only one with this type of portfolio?"

"No."

"Can you get your hands on the others?"

Nathan tightened his grip on the receiver, pondering whether he should answer or hang up. At this point, he was either walking into a trap or uncovering a snake pit. He had no way of knowing which.

And he'd never find out if he hung up now.

"I have some. I don't know if I can get them all at this point. Especially if Gavin gets wind of our conversation."

"I understand. Can you bring them to me?"

"The portfolios?"

"Yes."

Trap or smoking gun. Nathan knew it had to be one or the other. All he could do was take a chance.

"And what do I get in return?" Nathan asked.

The man waited a moment, then said, "I'll tell you everything I know."

## *RED HANDED*

Nathan sat in a cramped windowless office on the 12th floor of Foley, Crane and Winkler. It wasn't a room for VIPs. In fact, it reminded him of the visitation room at the jail. Except the table was nicer and the chairs were cushioned.

It didn't help that he had been ushered quietly into the room by the fashionable young woman he had met last time who then closed the door without telling him what to expect.

For all Nathan Haley knew, the police were going to burst through the door and arrest him. Although he couldn't imagine what charge they could bring against him.

Nathan had never felt more like a banker than he did in that moment. A money broker who had never gotten so much as a speeding ticket. His was a world of rules, regulations, laws and, above all else, a duty to serve the community he and his father helped build. And now he was surrounded by people who ignored all of that. Nathan shook his head and looked at the ceiling. God, who was he kidding? He was nothing like these people. They had a lifetime of practicing how to bend the rules, bend people and bend the system that purported to protect them all.

It was at that moment that he realized what his father had done. He had sold the bank to Gavin so he could teach Nathan. But it wasn't to teach him how to run a bank in the real world. It was to teach him that the world was full of men like Gavin. And to preserve everything his father had built, he had to learn the one thing his father didn't have time to teach him. How to fight men like Gavin.

The door flew open and Devorah marched in, gave Nathan a stern look and stood with her back against the wall across from him. After that, she didn't look at him, instead casting her gaze at the wall behind him.

Calhoun trundled in after her and closed the door behind him, then sat down across the table from Nathan.

Nathan sat up straight and looked Calhoun in the eye, waiting for him to speak. Instead, he heard Devorah's voice.

"What did you think you were doing, Nathan?"

Calhoun looked over his shoulder. "I'll handle this," he said.

"No, I want to know. Did he think he was going to get away with it?" She finally looked at Nathan. "Am I such a threat to you Nathan, that you feel the need to humiliate me in front of our clients?"

Nathan looked at her, dumbfounded. "Is that what you're worried about?" he asked, "your reputation as a salesperson?"

Devorah stepped away from the wall and jabbed a finger at Nathan. "Screw you, Nathan. You undermined my credibility with some of the most important, if not *the* most important clients at this bank."

"If they're so important, then why are you putting them in whatever generates a negative 14% across the board?"

"Because their friends are bragging about turning over 100% on whatever hot stock they see on CNBC. They complain. They exaggerate."

Nathan suppressed a smirk and eyed her as casually as he could. "Really? So you're saying their portfolios are not losing money?"

"I'm saying they are getting the returns they were told to expect."

Nathan studied her for a moment. Did she know that he had their records? Or was she trying to smoke him out? It all came down to how much the clients who didn't appreciate his call told her. He didn't know. And he sure wasn't going to ask.

Calhoun cleared his throat and said, "Alright, let's get on with this. You two can fight about it later."

"Get on with what?" Nathan asked.

"Well, you've created a bit of a mess here, Nathan."

"By talking to clients?"

"By inquiring into special accounts that are under strict NDA."

"Which means what?"

"Which means you're not entitled -" Calhoun winced at his choice of words and corrected himself. "-which means you're not supposed to know about these."

"I'm the Vice President. I have a right to know what's going on in my own bank." He leaned forward, resting his elbow on the table. "And I'm getting a little tired of people putting fences around me every time I try to do my job."

"It's not your bank, sir," Calhoun said.

"And," Devorah chimed in, "It never was."

Nathan stood up and slapped his hand against the table.

Calhoun waved his hand for Nathan to sit down. "Alright, that's enough. Please, we need to get through this." He turned and looked over his shoulder and said, "And you, Ms. Harlow, your provocations aren't helping."

"I just want Nathan to understand his place," Devorah said.

"Alright, that's enough. Both of you." Calhoun shook his head and opened the file he had brought with him. He pulled out a single sheet of paper and slid it over to Nathan, placing a pen on top. "I need you to sign this," he said.

Nathan looked at the paper without picking it up. Crossing his arms, he said, "What is this?"

"It's me putting out the fire you've started. Although I'm sure that wasn't your intention."

"Looks like an NDA to me."

"That's right. You've heard about things you're not supposed to know about. We can't undo that. But we can keep things from getting worse. We need to be able to tell your clients that their business secrets are safe with Haley National. Which means anybody having knowledge of that business needs to sign an NDA."

"I once asked you who you work for, Calhoun."

"And I told you that you were a distant third."

"Right." Nathan picked up the paper and read it over. Still holding it in his hand, he asked, "And what if I don't sign it?"

"Look," Calhoun said. "Just sign it. It'll make it easier for everyone, including you."

"Is that your legal advice to me?"

"No. I'm not your lawyer in this matter."

"Do I need one?"

Calhoun sighed. "The contract your father signed that stipulated you stay on with the bank isn't bulletproof."

"I'd have to ask my own attorney about that."

"There is a provision in there that you need to be aware of. I can show it to you if you like."

Nathan hung his head. "Provision for what?"

"If you don't sign this document," Calhoun said, tapping the paper, "then you will trigger the demonstrable negligence clause of the contract, allowing Mr. Neilsen to terminate your employment with Haley National."

"I'd like to get a second opinion on this. I'm sure you wouldn't mind if I ran it by my attorney first."

"That's your prerogative, certainly," Calhoun said.

Devorah stepped out from the wall. "But know this," she said. "If you walk out of this room without signing, you'll be unemployed before you get off the elevator in the front lobby."

"Mr. Calhoun, is that true. Can they do that?"

"They can. You can fight it in court, of course. But you may find it more difficult to get your job back than you expect."

Nathan slumped back in his chair, shaking his head at both of them as if they were children who had misbehaved on a playground. "And if I sign it?"

Devorah lit up with a smile and her voice came out in a disarming lilt. "Well then we can all be friends again, Nathan. And you can come to work tomorrow."

Nathan closed his eyes and let out a long sigh. His world had stopped making sense. The only two things he knew for certain were that he wished his father didn't have to throw him in the deep end where he had to learn to survive on his own, and that he couldn't help anybody, especially himself, if he was out on the street.

## *INTO THE BREACH*

Sarah heard the words over and over in her mind as she opened the door to The Diner. *I have something to show you.*

Sarah could only hope it was more than some crumpled investment charts. She appreciated his effort, found it endearing even, but if he didn't have something concrete this time, there wasn't much more she could do. The summary judgment was coming up in a matter of days. Maybe she would give a speech. Maybe she would implore the judge for mercy. But none of that would work. No, she would just stand there and listen to the judge certify the foreclosure complaints and issue an order for the sheriff to enforce them.

With the image of a woman sitting on the curb wondering what had happened to her life in her mind's eye, Sarah opened the door.

She found him sitting alone and she felt disappointed when she saw he only had a cup of coffee in front of him. Sarah was actually hungry and had been looking forward to a Banshee, but there was no way she was going to scarf down an omelet while he sipped his coffee and watched.

She sat down, setting her purse beside her on the booth. Maxine showed up within seconds with a tin pot of hot water, a cup and a plain black tea bag. "You remembered," Sarah said.

Maxine smiled and said, "Let me know when you need more."

Sarah smiled as she poured hot water over the bag and watched the tea steeping into her cup. Without looking up, she said, "What am I doing here, Nathan?" She flashed him a cursory smile.

"Are you sure you don't want something more?" he asked.

"Not if you don't"

He smiled and said, "I'm too wound up to eat right now."

"And coffee is going to help with that?"

"I like being wound up." He took another sip.

She took a sip of her tea, sucked in a quick breath at the sting of hot water on her tongue. “So what’s up?” she asked.

“Before we get to that, I should tell you that I’m violating an NDA by talking to you.”

Sarah set her cup down and frowned. Picking up her purse, she said, “Then you shouldn’t talk to me.”

He put out his hand, gesturing for her to stay. “No, it’s not that,” he said. “Please.” He waited for her to set her purse back down. “I just want you to know that this is important. That it’s serious.”

She studied him for a moment and said, “And that you are taking a risk for me. Is that it?”

Nathan clenched his fist for a moment and glanced at the ceiling. But he didn’t look wounded. “No. That’s not it.” He took another sip of coffee. “I already did that when I set up your new office.”

“I’m sorry,” she said. She took another biting sip of tea. “It’s just that I’ve lost my case and right now, you all look the same to me.”

“And what do we all look like?”

She wanted to say it, she really did. Quietly waiting for her to cut him down to size, he looked at her with a steady relaxed gaze. He didn’t look ready. He didn’t look prepared. He didn’t look like he was working out how he would respond. He was just listening. He was just trying to understand.

“I don’t know,” she said. “What do you see when you look at me?”

“The same thing I saw that first day,” he said. “A wounded soul that won’t know peace until you find the dragon you need to slay.”

“Maybe you’re that dragon.”

Nathan shook his head. “No. I too have a dragon to slay.” He took another sip of coffee and set the cup down slowly and deliberately. “Maybe we’re after the same dragon.”

“If it doesn’t help my clients keep their homes, it doesn’t really matter.”

“If the bank were shown to be engaging in criminal activity, would it help your case?”

“Only to the extent that the bank would probably go into receivership.”

Nathan smiled. “So that would be a ‘yes’.”

Sarah huffed out an impatient sigh. “More or less.”

“Alright then.” He took an envelope from his inside suit pocket and slid it across the table. Sarah opened the envelope, unfolded the pages and said, “I’ve already seen these”

“I know.”

“So, now what?”

“So, I called them up. Asked them how they felt about the performance of their portfolios.”

Sarah nodded as she leafed through the pages looking for any details she might have missed the first time. "And how did that go?"

"You know," he said, "it was the weirdest thing. They all seemed to think I wasn't supposed to know about any of this. That *nobody* was supposed to know about this, actually."

"People with this kind of money don't like anybody looking at them, like the IRS."

"Yeah, I know. And there haven't been any Suspicious Activity Reports sent out on any of this. Hell, if I pulled twenty bucks out of the ATM, they would tell the IRS. But this -" Nathan reached across the table and tapped the envelope. "This, the bank is keeping a secret." He leaned back. "Even from me."

Sarah knit her brow and tapped the pages with her index finger. If Gavin was keeping Nathan in the dark, then maybe he really did have a reason to help her. Or he could be lying. She was growing weary of the mind-numbing parody of Hamlet's dilemma. To believe or not to believe, that was the question.

"You're saying they don't trust you?"

"No. It's more like I'm an outsider." He took a sip of coffee and smiled. "Like you."

Sarah rolled her eyes, picked up her purse and started to get up. "I don't have time for this. You won. Congratulations."

"Are you proud of the burden you carry, Sarah?"

She whirled around, glaring at him, shocked by her own hand raised in the air, ready to slap his face. But he didn't flinch. He didn't even blink. He just looked at her. Listening. Trying to understand.

"Just because I wear a suit doesn't mean I'm your enemy," he said. "What are you going to say to them, Sarah? That you fought against the bad guy with everything you had because it was the right thing to do?" He stared at her for a moment, letting his words sink in. "Are you going to tell them that being right was enough? Is that going to make it right for them to be homeless?"

"What I'm fighting for is important," she whispered. She lowered her hand. "And I don't know if I can trust you."

"Yes it is," Nathan said. "And I know you think you can't trust me." Nathan gestured at the booth. "Please, sit down and try."

Sarah stood with her purse in her hand. She wouldn't sit down, but she hadn't turned to leave, either. "Why?" she asked.

"They all hung up on me," he said, "all but one."

Again, Nathan gestured at the booth. But he didn't say anything more until she sat back down. As Sarah held her purse in her lap, Nathan said, "I have six records, the ones in your hand." Sarah looked down to see her fist crumpling the reports. She had forgotten about them. She put them on the table and tried to straighten them out. "The fifth caller talked to me."

Still trying to smooth out the crumpled sheets, Sarah said, "Sorry." She looked up at him as her hands continued to smooth out the sheets. "But I guess you can print out another copy."

Watching Sarah's slender hands glide across the pages, Nathan said, "Actually, I can't."

Sarah's hand froze in place.

"But maybe we won't need them," he said.

Eying him carefully, Sarah asked, "What do you mean?"

"The fifth client there. He talked to me."

Sarah wanted to ask him, but she couldn't knowingly put him in jeopardy. "What does your NDA say? Do you have it with you?"

Nathan smiled and said, "See, I knew you cared."

"I'm serious. You could get in real trouble if you violate your NDA."

"They could fire me."

"They could potentially do more than that." By the sudden wrinkle in his brow, Sarah could see that he hadn't thought of that.

"It doesn't really matter at this point."

"What do you mean it doesn't matter?" She narrowed her gaze and cocked her head, wondering why she was trying to protect him against legal jeopardy. He wasn't her client, after all. "Why not?"

"Because I need to tell you, Sarah. Because I want you to know."

"Why?"

He scoffed, teased her with a knowing smile and said, "You really can't tell, can you?" He didn't say anything more as he looked into her eyes, waiting for her to understand.

And there it was. That look she had seen since the first day. But now it was as if she were seeing it for the first time. She wanted to look away, but she couldn't escape his piercing gaze this time. That haunting glimmer of desire in his eye. Sarah could feel herself blushing and she closed her eyes. Not because she was afraid he saw the roses blossoming on her cheeks. She closed her eyes because she didn't want it to be true.

"Because," he said, "you and I are fighting the same man. For different reasons, but still the same fight."

Opening her eyes, she asked, "Is that all? Is that the only reason?"

He stared back at her with a soft smile, but didn't respond.

"It would be better if that were the only reason," she said.

Nathan took a sip of coffee but said nothing.

"Tell me, then," she said. "What happened?"

"He wants to meet with me. He says he's going to tell me everything."

"About what?"

"About Gavin," he said. "About the truth I've been looking for. I think this is it, Sarah. I think this is the smoking gun."

Sarah realized there was only one way to force him to show her if he was telling the truth. "Take me with you," she said.

"I don't know about that. I think he wants to keep this between the two of us for now."

"Did he say you couldn't bring somebody?"

"Well no, but I don't think he's expecting it. What would I tell him when he asks who you are?"

Sarah smiled coyly and said, "Tell him I'm your lawyer."

## *IN HARM'S WAY*

Nathan didn't like the beeping, but he knew it meant she was alive. He didn't know what all the different colored lines on the monitor were or what was flowing through the tube stuck in Maggie's vein. But he understood that she had a pulse and it was steady. He understood that she was alive.

They had taken the mask away, at least. When they had first called him, her face had been covered over with a mask with thick tubes pumping oxygen into her intubated lungs. They had thrust a digital pad in front of him and he had faintly heard them saying something about authorization to provide care. All he really remembered was being shocked at learning that Maggie had put him down as her emergency contact. And that she had filed a living will naming him as her attorney in fact in the event she was incapacitated.

That had been several days before. Just after she had texted him, "I got them." He hadn't heard anything after that when they called him and said Maggie was in the hospital with a gunshot wound. They had handed him a Ziploc bag with her personal effects. Digging through her purse, he had found the portfolio printouts. He didn't know how she got them, only that somebody had shot her because of it. They hadn't taken the time to look through her purse. Probably because one did not stick around when one shot somebody, Nathan mused. A chill had run through him when he realized that they also probably thought she was dead. The lone miracle standing like a beacon in the night was the simple fact that although they had shot Maggie, they hadn't taken her purse. He had wondered about that for days. Maybe somebody had noticed and they had to run. Maybe they didn't know she actually had the paperwork but only knew about it. But none of that changed the fact that she was lying in a hospital room barely clinging to her life.

He was back from talking to Sarah now. He had wanted to tell her about it, but couldn't bring himself to do it. Not that he was worried about involving Sarah any further or scaring her off. It was simpler than that. He couldn't tell anybody until Maggie gave him permission. She was the kind of woman who would be embarrassed by the fact that she had gotten herself shot.

A physician's assistant came in to check on her. Watching him tend to the equipment and check her IV, Nathan said, "She's looking better."

"Uh-huh."

He hated to ask, but he had to try. "Is she going to be alright?"

"Doctor will be around in a bit. He'll update you then."

Of course he would. Protocol and rules and procedures all to protect their collective asses from the lawyers. In the meantime, people wondering about their loved ones had to suffer in silence, worrying themselves to death because people who knew things couldn't talk. *What about those people?* Nathan wondered. *What about us*?

Just as the PA was getting ready to leave, they both turned towards Maggie when they heard a soft moan escape her lips. Then she blinked, staring up at the ceiling. Nathan was at her side in an instant, picking up her hand and looking into her eyes. She smiled and spoke in a weak voice. "Nathan."

Patting her hand and trying to look as reassuring as he knew how, he said, "Hey there you."

"Did you get them?" That was Maggie. Never mind that she was in bed with a near-fatal gunshot wound that had put her in a coma for days. She was more worried about him. Nathan squeezed her hand, forcing himself not to squeeze too hard, not to let the anger boiling up in him find its way to his fingertips.

She had been as near to a mother as he had ever known and he swore he would find whoever had done this. Of course, he already knew. The man responsible was on the tenth floor of Haley National and Nathan could walk in to see him any time he wanted. As much as he indulged the image of raising a gun and firing it into Gavin's face, Nathan knew he had to wait until he had calmed down enough to think straight. It had been personal with Gavin tearing down his father's legacy. Now that Gavin had tried to kill the only family he had left, it was *personal*.

It all led back to Gavin. And the forthcoming meeting with client number five was the key to unlock everything. Then, and only then, would he know what to do. And so he forced the image out of his mind.

"Yeah," he said gently. "You did great."

"Did it help?"

"I think so. I'll know more tomorrow."

Nathan could no longer ignore the policeman who stepped up to the PA and asked, "Can she talk now?"

"She really shouldn't," the PA said. "Not until the doctor has cleared her."

Maggie weakly waved her arm at the PA. "No, it's OK. I can talk. We should probably do it now." She lifted her head a few inches of her pillow and then let it fall back down. It was then that Nathan noticed just how pale she looked. "While I can," Maggie said.

The cop looked at Nathan, who nodded once. The PA stepped aside and said, "Keep it real short. She needs rest."

The policeman leaned down and spoke in a gentle voice. "Did you see the shooter?"

Maggie closed her eyes and grimaced. "Yes," she whispered.

The cop took out a notepad and clicked his pen. "Can you remember what they looked like?"

Maggie nodded vigorously, a lone tear welling up from her eye. "She wore -" Maggie grimaced and grunted, her face twisting in pain.

Nathan heard a new sound he hadn't heard before - a steady low droning alarm that sent a chill down to his toes.

"She wore -" Maggie clutched at the PA as he mashed a big blue button on the wall next to her bed.

Nathan glanced at the monitor. The lines were all wrong now. He didn't know how, exactly, they just didn't look right. He backed away from the bed as his head began to spin. The world around him grayed out and all he could hear were the muffled sounds coming at him as if he were in a dream.

He heard a mechanical voice say, "code blue." And he heard somebody yelling "charge" and then "clear."

And then somewhere in the distance, the faint sizzle of electricity and a thump.

Then, again. "Clear."

Thump.

## *FRIENDS OF A FEATHER*

Sitting on the stool at Bernards, Sarah listened to Elaine ask about her case, but there really wasn't much to say.

Swirling the ice around in her glass and waiting for the bartender to come refill it, she said, "I don't know. It's going to summary judgment and that'll be that, I guess."

"But the settlement, that's still going through, right?" Elaine asked.

"Yeah, sure. Six months expenses."

"Well, hey," Elaine said a little too enthusiastically. "That's great." She lifted her glass in a toast. Sarah waved her class in Elaine's general direction, but they didn't clink. "That's a win," Elaine said cheerily.

"If you say so."

Elaine set down her glass. "No, really, it is. Nobody ever gets a break when things get to this point. They won't be out on the street with nowhere to go."

Sneering, Sarah said, "No, they'll get six months to imagine what it's going to be like."

Elaine let out a sigh, set her drink down and turned to face Sarah. "No, you don't understand."

"Understand what?" Sarah asked. She watched the bartender out of the corner of her eye as he refilled her drink.

"In your world," Elaine said, "this really is a victory. You don't get to win like this very often."

"Why are you always doing that?" Sarah asked.

"Doing what?"

"Talking down to me as if I'm your student." Sarah took a drink. "Just because I don't make enough money to dress in three different brand names doesn't mean I'm not your colleague."

Elaine looked at Sarah in a daze, then she chuckled. "I don't mean to imply you're not doing a good job. Or that what you're doing isn't important. You just chose a different path, that's all."

A silence settled between them and then Elaine said, "I just want you to be realistic."

Sarah could feel her hand tighten around her glass. "Yeah, well, have I got something to tell you," she said.

"Oh? What's that?"

Indulging her growing desire to put Elaine in her place and show her friend just how serious and important Sarah's job was, she said, "Something that's going to blow this whole thing wide open."

Elaine cocked her head and her smile faded. "What thing?"

"Haley National."

"Oh, you mean the foreclosures?"

Sarah put on a smug smile, took another drink and said, "No, the bank itself."

"The whole bank? Really?"

There it was, that smug little grin. Sarah half expected her friend to reach over and pat her on the head.

Sarah couldn't help the anger trickling into her voice. "Yes. The whole damn bank."

Elaine scoffed, not even hiding her disdain this time. "They have an army of lawyers, Sarah. They're not going to let you win." Sarah started to respond, but Elaine held up her hand with a stern look on her face. "No, seriously, Pipsqueak. I'm glad go see you being so feisty. You always did need to work on your confidence. But that doesn't mean you can ignore reality."

"Why do you do that?"

"Do what?"

"Always cut me down sideways like that. Tell me that I'm being a brave little girl but then telling me I need to be careful because wolves are roaming through the woods."

"Well, they are. And you're not as equipped to deal with these guys as you think you are. It's a real world, Sarah. They have more money, more time and more lawyers. It's just the way it is." Elaine looked down at the bar and then back at Sarah. She put her hand on Sarah's shoulder and said, "I just don't want to see you get hurt."

"Not this time," Sarah said.

"What?"

"Not this time, goddammit. This time, we have a smoking gun." She tried to stop herself, but Sarah couldn't hold back from telling Elaine everything.

"We have a meeting with one of their clients who has information that will bring the whole thing down."

"The whole thing?" Elaine asked. "Really?"

"Yep."

"Who is this client you're meeting?"

"Brandt something. Something Brandt." Sarah looked away, trying to remember the name, surprised that she hadn't made a better mental note of such an important piece of information. "Yeah, Brandt."

"Are you sure?" Elaine asked, squeezing Sarah's shoulder tighter.

"Yeah. I think so. Well, anyway, they may have money and lawyers, but they're not going to get away from me. Not this time."

"How did you find out?"

Sarah looked at her drink, stirred it a few times. "Nathan."

Elaine grabbed Sarah's wrist. "Nathan Haley? Nathan Haley is taking you to one of his clients?"

"Yeah." Sarah thought about that for a moment as she saw her friend's face go flush. "Yeah, how about that? He's taking me to one of his clients."

"Do you trust him?" Elaine asked.

"I don't know." She studied Elaine a moment longer. "I guess that if I did, I wouldn't be telling you all this." She took another drink. "I guess the real question is if he trusts me." Elaine nodded. Realizing what she had done, Sarah put down her drink and said, "You can't tell anybody."

"I know. This is strictly confidential."

"I don't know why I told you. I really shouldn't have."

"Because we're friends. You can tell me anything. You know that. Nothing's changed just because we graduated from law school."

"Right." Despite her friend's assurances, Sarah couldn't help feeling that something really had changed since law school. And it was simple, actually.

They were lawyers now.

After waving to Sarah as she rode away in an Uber, Elaine waited for Calhoun to pull up in his Infiniti. She opened the door and stepped into the car. Putting on her seatbelt as he pulled away from the curb, she said, "We have a problem."

## *ERASURE*

Carl Brandt went over his notes one last time and tucked them into his pocket. He had been told to watch, listen and report. Meeting with Nathan was his idea. He hadn't reported it yet. And he wouldn't until after he was finished smoking out Nathan. The truth was, he didn't know if or how much the Vice President of Haley National was involved. But he would soon enough.

Walking from his front door to his car, he didn't notice her parked across the street counting his steps.

Parking on the third floor of a garage down town and walking two blocks to the subway, he didn't see her in line behind him as he stepped through the turnstile towards the blue line platform.

Ten minutes later, when he walked out of the subway station and crossed the street to a construction site, he didn't see her leaning against the wall watching him tuck his notes into a lead pipe and walk away.

It was after he ducked under the scaffolding and into the shadows of the first floor under construction that he saw her. It was over before he could even take a breath to ask who she was.

A single shot from her Smith & Wesson Military and Police 9 M2.0 pistol entered through his left eye, then a black sedan pulled up and the trunk popped open. Sixty seconds later, Carl Brandt was gone.

## *JUST THIS TWICE*

Standing next to Nathan in front of the Knife and Palette, Sarah asked, "You told him to meet us here?" She surveyed the chrome trim on granite walls and arching windows tinted so nobody could see in.

"That's right."

"Wouldn't it be better if it were some place a little more private?"

"I think it's more important that it's some place where we know we can keep certain people out."

"And how are you going to do that?" Sarah swept her hand through the air.

Nathan looked her with a coy smile. "Because I own the place."

Sarah's jaw dropped. "You're kidding."

"Does that surprise you?"

Sarah swept her gaze over the building again. "A little."

"Why?"

Sarah took a breath and started to say something, but stopped herself when she saw a look on his face that he had shown her many times, but she only now understood for the first time. His face was placid and his brow arched slightly. His eyes were soft. Sarah realized that he was letting himself be vulnerable to her. And every time he did, she said something that made him look away to hide that part of him from her. So she thought about what she was going to say next.

"I guess it makes sense," she said. "It's probably a good investment."

"Not really," he said. "It costs me more to keep it open that it makes."

"So-" Sarah thought for a moment, not wanting to scare off the part of Nathan that she was beginning to suspect he never showed anyone else. "You're an art connoisseur then?" Sarah smiled, hoping it came across as disarming.

"Not as much as my curator," he said. "But, yeah, there's something fulfilling about giving artists, especially unknown artists, a place to show their work."

Sarah stared at him, her mouth slightly open as she searched his face for any indication that he was still a man she couldn't trust. A man she didn't want to trust. But all she could see was a gentle man who was suddenly more than just a banker. More than just her legal adversary. For the first time since she had met him, Sarah allowed herself to see Nathan Haley as possibly a good man. She pressed her lips together. That was as far as she was willing to let herself go. Possibly. Maybe. Nothing more.

"Do you paint?" she asked.

Nathan smiled sheepishly. "I do."

"Oh." Sarah knit her brow. The line between possibly and a world she wasn't willing to believe existed was fading. "Can I see your work?"

Nathan looked down for a moment, then back at Sarah. "No." He held up his hand. "It's not you. Nobody sees my work."

That was enough for Sarah to reaffirm a wall of doubt between herself and the false narrative that a man like Nathan would use to disarm her. She shook her head and grunted. "I'm sure they don't," she said. She arched a brow and pursed her lips.

It was about then she expected him to look away, pull himself together and look back at her with a harmless expression. But the man he was showing her now would be gone.

But Nathan still looked at her with a warm smile and soft eyes that made it hard for her to believe he was hiding any part of him from her.

"I'm not that good. It's just a way to relax, really. You know, distract my mind from - " He looked to the sky and let out a long breath. "Well, everything."

Sarah blinked at him. She couldn't tell if it was just a story. "Well art isn't meaningful if you don't let people see it."

Nathan let out a laugh. "You sound just like my friend, Jerry."

"Well then why don't you let me see it?"

"I won't even let Jerry see most of it. Sometimes, here and there. And he's the closest thing I have to a best friend."

Sarah knit her brow and stared at him for a moment. Just once, she let herself believe. Just for a moment. She let herself see a man who had to hide from the world because he might get hurt. "Why not?"

Nathan let out a sigh. "Every artist has a pure vision of what a particular piece means to them. The moment the world sees it, people can talk about it, interpret it and jab at its flaws. It's mystique evaporates. It become less of what it once was."

Sarah smiled, amused by the logic she was about to lay on him. "If nobody has ever seen your work, how do you know that will happen?"

"Because I know enough about art to know that I'm not good enough to make something that can endure that kind of scrutiny. Or worse, if it hung in a corner alone and nobody noticed it at all."

"Oh my God," she said. "Nathan Haley, you're afraid of getting your feelings hurt."

Nathan grunted, his smile perking up at the corners. "Something like that."

Looking at his watch for the fifth time, Nathan said, "He was supposed to be here." Back to business. His smile faded and the soft look in his eyes faded. As she watched him turn his attention back to the task at hand, she realized she already missed the look from just a moment before. And that was going to be a problem.

Sarah followed him as he opened the door and stepped into the lobby. "Can't you call him?"

"He told me not to."

"Yeah, well, did he say he was going to be late?"

Nathan stopped and studied her for a moment. She shrugged. *Well?* He worked his jaw and pulled out his smart phone. After several moments, he thumbed it off and put it away. "Voice mail."

Sarah sat down on a small couch against the wall and watched Nathan pace around the lobby for the next ten minutes.

Finally, he sat down next to her, dialed the number again, listened for a moment and hung up. "Voice mail," he whispered.

Nathan hung his head and stared at the floor. Without knowing exactly why, Sarah took his hand and held it on her lap.

Sarah felt his hand in hers. His palms were soft, as she expected. His fingers were slender and nimble as they lay dormant in her hand. Because of that, it didn't occur to Sarah that he might be lying. There was only his hand in hers and the self-conscious glow of affection that came from knowing you were making somebody feel better.

She tried to think of something to say, something to salvage the moment so he didn't have to give up. Instead, she reached out with her other hand and gently rubbed his back. There was nothing else to do because Sarah realized that Nathan Haley had become the one thing she never expected. He was a man who had been defeated.

"I appreciate what you're trying to do," she said.

"You know," he said, still looking at the floor. "That's the kindest thing you've ever said to me."

## *VINDICATION*

They had come to her office - five of them. "It's not much," they had said. But five of her clients handed over a cashier's check for $1000. It wasn't enough, but it was the best Sarah could do after being fired from the clinic. She could charge a lot less than the type of law firm that Elaine worked at. But she wasn't going to be useful to anybody if she was homeless and starving. It would cover her rent, barely.

Still, Sarah decided to take $100 for herself and spend an hour at the mall. It wouldn't buy much, but it gave her an hour away from the case, the judge, Nathan - an hour away from everything, so she could breathe and put her mind on hold. For Sarah, it was a vacation. $100 wasn't much, but she could always look and dream about what it would be like to wear three different high fashion brands as Elaine did. The thought of her trying to look suave or even pompous decked out in such an absurd array made her laugh out loud as she stopped in front of the ATM across the street from the downtown mall. There were pretentious people in the world and then there were people like Sarah. In this regard, she knew exactly who she was. But there might come a day when she had earned it outright, when she wore fancy clothes and lived in a nice downtown apartment because she had earned it. The fantasy always collided with what she knew was her destiny. Public-service lawyers did not become rich. But she enjoyed the fantasy. Because there was a difference between pretentiousness and legitimate reward.

Snow flurried through the air and her fingers were red from the cold as they numbly stabbed the buttons of the ATM. She looked at the paltry sum of cash as she took it from the slot. Maybe she could pick up some public defender's supplementary checks. She laughed at the thought. When there weren't enough public defenders, the court would offer a nominal sum for a lawyer to freelance as a defense attorney in a particular case. If she couldn't keep a job as a public service attorney, she certainly wouldn't cut it as a defense lawyer.

Sarah's eyes drifted to the urban mall across the street. It had been a long time since she had gone shopping. She only had $100. She would only stay for an hour. Then her vacation would be over.

She didn't notice the slender woman with dark hair follow her through the revolving door to the mall. Once inside, she breathed in the scent of caramel popcorn, smiling at the curious arrival of such a simple and delightful smell.

The store windows glowed with display lights. The faux marble floor gleamed with fresh wax from the night before. Parades of shoppers with rope-handled paper bags floated up and down the escalators.

Clutching the woefully inadequate bit of cash in her hand, Sarah ambled through the mall, her head in constant motion as she took in the sights, as if she were a little girl who had never been to a mall before. Her gaze settled on a Ralph Lauren Chilton black satin dress draped over a very life-like mannequin gazing off into space as if she had descended from another planet and was now trapped in the window display. Sarah tilted her head and calculated the dress size to be 2. The nine inches between that and her size 16 navy skirt might as well have been the distance between that mannequin and whatever planet it came from.

That was part of the fantasy, too, of course. It wasn't just that she would earn the privilege of wearing such an expensive dress, but that she would finally go to the gym and work hard to fit into that dress. Because they didn't make it in size 16.

Sarah hadn't noticed the woman who sidled up next to her. She flinched when she heard the woman's voice.

"Lovely, isn't it?"

Sarah looked the woman over. She was easily a size 2, maybe less. Straight black hair with bangs and enough makeup to do a photo shoot for a glamor magazine. Black pencil skirt and kicky red jacket that looked more like clothing for a doll than for a woman.

The woman looked at Sarah with a warm smile and soft eyes. "It's nice to have a dream, isn't it?"

Puzzled by the woman's remark, Sarah took a slight step back. Realizing she felt vaguely insulted, she spoke curtly and turned her attention back to the dress. "Yes."

"It's nice to have a dream," the woman said again. "It gives you a reason to get up in the morning."

Annoyed by this woman who insisted on interrupting Sarah's reverie with barbs echoing from the girl's locker room in high school, Sarah asked her, "I'm sorry, and you are?"

The woman's face lit up with feigned recognition and she said, "Hey, you're that lawyer doing the foreclosures case for Haley, right? I think I've seen you in court."

Sarah's daydream dissipated like the steam from a pot of water thrown in a fireplace. The real world had arrived and she let out a sigh, perturbed that she wasn't being allowed even the solace of some fanciful window shopping. "Is that a fact?" Sarah asked, her voice now in full lawyer mode.

"Yeah, I'm almost sure of it. The one the judge doesn't like very much."

"Alright," Sarah said, raising her voice. "Who the hell are you?"

The woman tilted her head and smiled like a cat who had caught a mouse and was considering whether or not to set it free so it could chase it down again. She offered a remarkably slender hand with bony fingers. "Devorah Harlow."

The name immediately struck a chord. She had seen it somewhere in the paperwork from the bank, although she couldn't quite put her finger on exactly where. "You work for Haley National."

Nodding slowly, Devorah said, "That's right."

"What can I do for you then?" Sarah crossed her arms and tapped her foot, annoyed mostly by the fact that she would not be able to get back to daydreaming about the dress now that Devorah had tainted the fanciful atmosphere of the mall by dragging the real world into it.

"It's about the case."

"You could come by my office in the morning to talk about that. This really isn't the place." Sarah smiled. "If I had one."

Sarah started to turn and walk away but stopped short when Devorah said, "Actually, it's about Nathan."

Sarah's mind started racing. Did she know about their attempted meeting with the informant? What did she know? How much did she know? Who had she told?

"I have nothing to discuss regarding Mr. Haley."

"Oh sure you do."

"Look," Sarah said, "the case is pretty much over anyway. You guys won. There really isn't anything more to discuss."

"Oh now," Devorah said, laying a hand gently on Sarah's forearm. "I'm sure a smart girl like you isn't ready to give up all that easily." She paused and gently tightened her grip. "Even if she should."

Sarah pulled her arm away and massaged it gently. "You said this was about Nathan. What about him?"

"Well, he's a lot like you, isn't he?"

"How do you mean?"

"Out to save the world from people like me who just take what they want and get away with it."

Sarah laughed. "Is that the way you see yourself, Ms. Harlow?"

"Well, it's true, isn't it?"

"I suppose so."

"At least that's what you would like to think about Nathan. Responsible and kind man, if not all that good-looking, but still rugged and dependable. Like a pickup truck."

"I don't really know him all that well."

"Oh, I know. But that's what you'd like to believe, isn't it? That he's a good man?"

"I suppose so."

Devorah closed her eyes and nodded slowly. She took an envelope out from her purse and held it out for Sarah. "Things aren't always what they seem."

Sarah eyed the envelope for a moment and then took it from Devorah's hand. She fished out the pages inside and leafed through them. When she what was written on the last page, her hand froze and she looked up to see Devorah nodding and smiling back at her like the cat batting the mouse. Sarah felt a coldness seeping into her consciousness. The coldness that came with a truth that you didn't want to hear. That you weren't ready to admit but knew you had to.

"Why are you doing this?" Sarah asked.

"Because I want you to know whose fault this really is."

## *OF KNOWING BETTER*

Sarah stood upbehind her desk when the she saw the doorknob on her office door turning. She smoothed out her skirt and adamantly refused to check the belt. She wanted to cross her arms, but she let them hand at her side instead.

Nathan stepped inside, smiled and ambled to her desk. "What's up?" he asked.

Sarah opened her middle desk drawer, pulled out the paperwork Devorah had given her and slammed it down. "What the hell is this?" she asked, nearly yelling.

Nathan looked at her wide-eyed. She could see he was already angry, but she didn't care. She stabbed the paperwork with her finger. "Explain yourself." She crossed her arms and stared at him, waiting for an answer.

Nathan picked up the pages, tapped the edges on the desk to align them and then read the first one.

He closed his eyes, slowly shaking his head. "This isn't what it seems," he said.

Sarah scoffed. "Like hell it isn't. That's your signature at the bottom of a bunch of fraudulent applications." She leaned forward. "And yeah, this is fraud. Go-to-prison, give-me-my-house-back fraud."

The only problem was the she couldn't prove any of that without the originals. But he didn't know that.

"What if it wasn't intentional?"

"What?" She was nearly screaming at him now and couldn't seem to reel herself in.

"What if I didn't do this on purpose?"

"No, Nathan, it doesn't work like that. You're a corporate officer. Could have known. Should have known. If you don't know what you're signing, that's gross negligence at best. You're held to a higher standard, you know that."

But why was she telling him all this? He wasn't her client.

His hands started to tremble. Speaking softly, he said, "I need you to believe me." His never-let-you-down look disappeared. His forehead was wrinkled and his eyes glistened.

"Believe what?"

"That I didn't do this on purpose. I mean, you're a lawyer, I get it. You have to nail me to the wall. But personally, Sarah. Personally, you have to know that I'm not this guy."

"Then prove it," she said.

"How? Anything."

Sarah grunted. "Really?" Leaning closer, she said, "Alright then, bring the originals to the summary judgment."

"You can't expect me to risk going to prison." Slapping the pages with the back of his hand, he said, "This isn't me."

"Then who is it, Nathan? Because all I see is your name."

"You and I want the same thing here, Sarah."

"Yeah, what's that?"

"To bring Gavin to his knees for what he's done to my bank. For what he's done to your clients."

Sarah shook her head. "I don't give a damn about your bank, Nathan. But my clients, you're right about that part." She really wanted to make a deal with him, but she knew that leveraging criminal charges in any way was very risky. Even if she didn't outright threaten him with it, which was illegal, she could put her law career at risk even so. But maybe that's what it meant to look after her clients' best interests. "You want to prove to me you're not that guy, then restructure the notes."

Nathan let out a sigh. "I can't. You know that."

"Again, when it's time to do the right thing, your hands are tied."

Nathan clenched his jaw, then blurted out, "Is the world really that simple from the bleachers there, counselor? It must be nice to tell others what they're supposed to do when you don't have to put yourself at risk. Talk is cheap when you're not the one with their neck on the line."

"Oh, poor you -"

"That's right." Nathan stood up. "You're not the one who might go to prison. This is the real world, Sarah. But not for you, is it? It doesn't matter who gets hurt, as long as you get the chance to save the world from itself, especially if the people you hurt wear a suit and make more than minimum wage."

"Oh my God, look at you. Poor corporate officer who's being forced to screw over a hundred families just so he can still tell people it's his name on the front door."

"Dammit, Sarah, I've done everything I can to help you. A hell of a lot more than I should have. And even if I did own up to these applications, what would that do? Would it really make a difference? Or would it just put me in prison?" Nathan pinched his nose and took a deep breath. "It's not just my career, it's my family's legacy. My father's dream. I can't fix that if I'm not here."

"Then go to all those people you're putting out on the street. Go tell them about your dream. And explain to them how it's going to keep a roof over their heads."

Sarah stepped back from her desk, straightened her blouse and absolutely refused to check the belt of her skirt. Looking him straight in the eye, she said, "You don't get to choose when and where you're going to have to stand up for what you believe in. But you do have to choose whether or not you're going to do it when that time comes."

Nathan looked at her blankly, his mouth agape. But he said nothing. Sarah slung her purse over her shoulder, opened her center desk drawer and took out the key to her office. She stared at it as she turned it in her hand for a moment. Then she tossed it on the desk. Nathan stared at her, still silent. Then Sarah strutted to the coat rack, put on her coat and walked out the door.

Nathan stared at the door after she left. He glanced at the key and decided to leave it where it was. She would come back after she calmed down. Where else was she going to go? And Sarah was a fighter. She needed the office to do her work. She would be back.

But all of that hope evaporated when Nathan stepped around the half-wall and saw the book shelf where her law books had been. Now, the shelves were bare.

## *TEMPTATION*

Sarah wasn't in the mood for drinking, so she had asked Elaine to meet her at Starbucks. Her friend was looking around, seemingly uncomfortable with the relatively pedestrian aesthetics.

Sarah smiled. Amused at Elaine's discomfort, she said, "Do you remember when we thought coming to Starbucks was a real treat?"

"Huh?" Elaine looked at her. "Oh, yeah. I know."

"We always wound up at Grandos, that hole in the wall with boot-leather coffee."

Elaine laughed nervously. "Yeah, but it kept you up for a week."

"That it did." Sarah nursed her triple-shot white chocolate mocha.

"So are you ready for the hearing?" Elaine asked.

"What's there to get ready for?"

"Oh come on now, you still have to put in an appearance and at least try."

"Try what?

"I don't know. To be a lawyer I guess."

"Yeah, well, for all the good that does."

Sarah waited for the inevitable pep talk from her friend about how Sarah was doing what she said she had always wanted to. Instead, Elaine said, "Well, what did you expect?"

"Excuse me?"

"You're the one they come to because nobody else can help them. Are you a good lawyer?"

"What? I guess so."

"Exactly. You're a good lawyer and they come to you for free and still you can't help them. Do you think it would be any better if they paid you?"

"Well, no. The problem is -"

Elaine grabbed Sarah's forearm. "The problem is that the kind of people who come to you are the kind of people that don't know how to take care of themselves in the first place."

Sarah's blood ran cold. "That's the most heartless thing I've ever heard you say."

Elaine looked back with half-closed eyes and her mouth sagged. "Tell me I'm wrong. Tell me that if you had the money to hire a staff and do research and confer depositions that it would make any difference."

Sarah had to think about that for a moment because she couldn't immediately refute her friend's assertion.

"It lets people know that there's a line," she said. "That they can't go too far. That we're watching them."

"You're watching a line?" Elaine scoffed and took a drink of coffee. "That's a far cry from saving the world."

Dejected, Sarah said, "I know."

"Are you beginning to understand?"

"Understand what?"

"Everything I've been trying to tell you. Why I chose to work with a law firm that actually makes money." Elaine looked away. "You should think about coming over to work for us."

And there it was. Sarah had always known that Elaine didn't understand why Sarah chose her path as a lawyer. But she suspected that Elaine always felt morally inferior and now she was hoping to lure Sarah over to her side so she didn't have to face the ugly truth. That the reason people like Sarah's clients didn't get the help they needed is because they were the ones targeted by the more powerful. Because men like Gavin knew they could get away with it. She looked at the table and her heart felt suddenly heavy. Men like Nathan, too, she realized.

"Why would your people want me over there?"

"Because you're a good lawyer."

"A good lawyer would have figured out a way for my clients to keep their homes."

"You got them a good settlement. That doesn't happen very often with foreclosures."

"Stanley got them a good settlement."

"Yeah, well -" Elaine's voice trailed off.

Sarah laughed, that bittersweet laugh that comes when you finally figure something out that would have been obvious all along if you had just paid attention. "You know what?" she said.

"What?"

"I get it now. I know what my job is." Sarah took another drink, gathering her thoughts. "My job is to stand there in court and give credence to the illusion that the law is supposed to provide some kind of equity. So the court can point and say, 'Look, they have representation. They are being treated equally under the law.'" Sarah scoffed. "The problem is the law itself. It's just a system to keep the machine running."

She looked at Elaine, who had the dead-pan look of welcoming Sarah to the world that Elaine had known all along. It wasn't pretty. It wasn't what Sarah expected. But it was real. Nodding her head, Sarah said, "You can do anything to somebody as long as you let them complain about it."

Elaine smiled sadly and slid over her business card. Sarah's breath caught as she read the card. She looked up and stared at Elaine wide-eyed, as if she were seeing her friend for the first time. As somebody she had never really known. She looked back at the card and still couldn't believe it was real.

*Foley Crane and Winkler, attorneys at law.*

## *BROKEN DREAMS*

Nathan sat in front of his easel, holding his brush just in front of his nose and cradling his elbow with his other hand.

Standing on the other side, Jerry asked, "Can I see?" Nathan shot him a glance which was all Jerry needed to hold his hands up and say, "Just kidding."

"Soon enough," Nathan said.

"Well, I'm looking forward to that," Jerry said. "Maybe this one will actually be good."

Nathan was studying the balance between the sun, clouds and steel on the canvas. Not that he had time to do anything about it if it wasn't right. But it was right. Finally, after all these years, Nathan had produced an artistic vision that would inspire in the heart of the viewer exactly what Nathan was feeling.

"This one's going into exhibition," he said quietly.

Jerry took a step back and blinked his eyes as he stared at Nathan. "Are you serious?"

"Yep." Nathan dabbed at the painting and said, "There's more."

"Oh?"

"You can have it. Just bring that cashier's check in tomorrow."

"OK, now you're scaring me."

Nathan dabbed at the painting some more. "I know."

"I'll take it," Jerry said, "but I have to ask, why now? What changed your mind?"

"It's time," Nathan said.

Jerry dragged a chair out from the wall and sat down next to the easel, staying back far enough not to see the painting. "Time for what?"

"You know why my father sold the bank to Gavin? I finally figured it out."

"Because he didn't have time to properly vet him and made a mistake?"

"No. I mean, that makes sense, but that's not the real reason. There's more to it."

"Are you sure about that?" Jerry spoke slowly and deliberately, as if to a child. "I mean, are you sure you want to go there?"

"He wanted to teach me something."

"By selling you out?"

"No. Not selling me out. Forcing me to face the unavoidable. He knew that if the bank was going to survive - the bank he and I built up over the years - he knew that if all of that was going to survive, I would have to figure out on my own how to keep it alive. I either would or I wouldn't. And Gavin was just the man to force that choice."

"And now you're running away? Is that it? Are you giving up, Nathan? Sell the gallery, take my money, make a new start?"

"Isn't that what you told me I should do?"

"Yeah, I did." Jerry hung his head. "But that was only because I knew you would never do it." He looked back up at Nathan. "Right?"

Nathan smiled. "You know, there's one part that took me a long time to figure out. What my Dad did here, it isn't just a bank or even a community. It's a living thing. It breathes and lives and struggles. And it dies if you let it. So it's not about fighting for what you believe in. It's about doing whatever it takes to make sure it doesn't die."

"What the hell are you talking about?"

"I'm talking about a name. Haley National doesn't need to be called Haley National to survive. It can be called anything. As long is it lives. As long as it breathes."

"I'm not sure -"

Nathan waved his hand, cutting him off. "I have some conditions for selling you this gallery."

Jerry looked at Nathan, shaking his head. Nathan could see it in his friend's eyes: *Don't do this.* Jerry wouldn't buy the gallery because he wanted to. He would buy it because Nathan was asking him to. "What are they?" Jerry asked.

"This painting here, the one I'm working on -" He looked at the door leading to the gallery. "It will be put on display in the center exhibition with a light on it 24 hours a day. It is to never be taken down. It is to never be sold. It is to never be left in the dark." He looked at Jerry. "Do you understand?"

"No, but I can do that for you." Jerry smiled sadly. "Just because you asked."

Nathan went back to dabbing at the painting. "Close enough."

"What are the rest?" Jerry asked.

Nathan dabbed at the painting one last time and then put down his brush. He slowly turned his easel so Jerry could see. His friend's mouth fell agape and his gaze wandered across the painting, as if he were walking through it. Catching his breath, Jerry said, "Wow."

Nathan kept quietly as his friend inspected his work. And he knew by Jerry's expression that he had done it right this time.

Jerry finally nodded and then looked up at Nathan. "What are the rest?" he asked. "What other conditions?"

Nathan turned the easel back around. "We'll get to that later," he said. "For now, I want to look at this. While I can."

## *NOWHERE TO RUN*

Sarah poked her head through the door of the Emmerson Foundation Legal Clinic and looked around. The three lawyer's desks were empty. The light over her old desk still buzzed. She couldn't tell if Stanley was in his office, but since it was after 5:00, she was pretty sure he was gone. And, as she was hoping, she saw Maureen sitting at her desk, her head bent over paperwork that she would work on for the next several hours, finally going home with just enough time to microwave a quick meal and grab what was little more than a nap before coming back in the morning.

Sarah called out softly, "Hey."

Maureen looked up and then went back to her paperwork. "Well hello there. What can I do for you counselor?"

Sarah came all the way into the office and walked over to Maureen's desk. "I didn't think Stanley could litigate enough to keep you this busy."

"Never underestimate the power of whiskey and regret."

Sarah laughed nervously.

"Did I say something funny?"

"Well, I thought so."

"I've got a lot of work here, Sarah. What can I do for you?"

"It's about the foreclosures," Sarah said.

"Uh-huh."

Sarah wanted to ask her old mentor to look at her, but she knew better. Even though Stanley had fired her, Sarah couldn't help feeling that Maureen felt betrayed somehow by Sarah's departure.

"I'd like Stanley to take over the case."

Maureen's hand stopped. Then she put down her pen and stared at the paperwork in front of her before taking off her glasses and looking at Sarah. "And why should he do that?"

"Because he was right."

Maureen stared at her for a moment and then got up to walk over to the table with the coffee supplies. She poured hot water and instant coffee into a plastic cup. Blowing gently on her coffee, Maureen leaned against the table and eyed Sarah. "You know, I wasn't always a legal assistant."

"Yeah, I figured."

"You figured that I was a hooker or a gang bitch or maybe even a gang leader myself. Sound about right?"

Sarah felt a blush rising up on her cheeks. "I wouldn't say -"

Maureen held up her hand and strode back to her desk, stirring her coffee. She sat down on the corner of the desk next to Sarah and said, "I was a lawyer."

Sarah looked up, trying to imagine her old mentor standing behind the podium in the well. Surprisingly, the image looked right in her mind.

"And now?" Sarah asked.

"And now I'm not." She gingerly took a sip from her coffee and watched Sarah process what she was hearing.

"OK," Sarah said. "So what happened?"

"What do you mean he was right?" Maureen asked.

Sarah sucked in a slow breath. "Yeah, that. Well, you know. There's nothing left to do, right? It's just a formality. If the only thing we can do is stand there just so they can say they have a lawyer -" She looked at Maureen. "-well, I figure that's something Stanley can do."

"Oh, I see," Maureen said. "So you're above all this now?" She pursed her lips. "Are your six months up?"

"No, no, I didn't mean it like that."

"Yeah, you did."

"Sorry. I'm just -" Sarah let out a sigh. "I don't know."

"I did come from a rough neighborhood. I thought I understood. I thought I could help." Maureen stood up and faced Stanley's office. Her back turned to Sarah, she continued. "I worked for the PD's office back then. And there was plenty of business as displaced workers and their families had nowhere to turn but the streets. If you hadn't committed a felony, the judge sent you home because there weren't enough of them to hear the cases and there wasn't enough room in the jail for them to wait." She took a deep breath through her nose and turned around.

"I'll never forget that kid's face. The way he looked at me and smiled." She took a drink. "As if I were going to save him."

Maureen's forehead wrinkled and her mouth tightened as she stared back in time. Sarah waited, afraid that Maureen might lose her nerve.

"I lived in the same neighborhood back then. I thought it was a good idea to live with the people I knew I was going to defend." Maureen closed her eyes and shook her head. “I couldn’t have been more wrong. They came to my house one night. This kid’s older brother and his cohort. And they made it real clear that accepting the plea bargain in exchange for his testimony against them was not in my best interest.”

“Blackmail?” Sarah asked.

“Something like that.”

“That’s a felony. Why didn’t you say something?”

Maureen eyed Sarah coldly. “What makes you think I didn’t?”

Sarah looked away. “Sorry.”

“It wouldn’t have mattered anyway. The city was on fire with real crime. They didn’t have time to deal with petty crimes like threats to an officer of the court. We just took it in stride. The important cases got attention. The rest were left to work out on their own.”

“That’s not right.”

Maureen chuckled. “You think?” Maureen fell silent. Her fleeting smile faded away. “Anyway, I knew I was on my own, so I refused the deal. The DA tried to go around me, tried to talk directly to my client, but he was smart enough to know that if his brother was threatening me, then he certainly wasn’t going to be safe in prison, where half the population either knew his brother personally or knew of him.”

“So they couldn’t get the deal. That wasn’t your fault. If the client says no, they say no.”

“That’s what I love about you, Sarah. You believe the system really does work as advertised.”

“I don’t know about that,” Sarah said.

“No, we didn’t take the deal. And the judge threw the book at my client. He went to prison for ten years. But nobody ever touched him. He was safe.”

“And that’s why you got out? Why you quit being a lawyer?”

“No, Sarah. I don’t quit that easily.” Maureen sat down behind her desk now. “Even though I went along with the scheme because I didn’t feel like getting killed, his brother still saw me as a threat. He could tell I would find a way. That I wouldn’t quit until I found a way to get to him. He knew. So he did the most obvious thing. He had his brother file a complaint for negligence. Once he told them that I had talked him out of taking the plea bargain, the hearing didn’t last five minutes. Poof. I was no longer a lawyer.”

Maureen put her glasses back on and started perusing her paperwork again. “And they’ll never let me be one again.”

Shaking her head, Sarah said, “That’s not fair.”

“That’s not the point.”

"Then what is?"

Looking up at Sarah, Maureen said, "The point is that you are still a lawyer and you're giving up just because you didn't win. They got me, boo-hoo. You're a child, Sarah. You need to grow up."

Sarah forced herself to ignore the familiar indignation that came with Maureen's insults. "What do you mean grow up?"

"You can walk past the bar. I can't. You don't keep fighting because you want to. You don't keep fighting because it's the right thing to do." Maureen put her elbows on her desk, clasped her hands and leaned forward. "You keep fighting because there's nobody else around who can."

## *FRIEND OR FOE*

Sarah didn't stop herself from checking the belt of her skirt. Twice. She sat nervously in an almost-comfortable chair just outside the DA's office and she didn't care that she looked nervous. She just wondered how much trouble she was in. And why. She knew she hadn't broken the law. What she didn't know was how high the hand of corruption reached in the city's oligarchy. Did Gavin run it all? She felt a slight burn in her chest thinking about it.

The receptionist flitted her hands around her desk, tapped at her keyboard and answered the phone. She seemed obsessed with keeping her hands in motion and Sarah watched with amusement. Then the woman suddenly turned her attention to Sarah and said, "He'll see you now." She gestured at a tall door behind her and went back to her hand ballet.

The woman had already forgotten about her as Sarah walked carefully towards the door and opened it.

The DA sat behind the largest desk she had ever seen in her life. He was a barrel-chested man wearing a suit vest and tie over a white shirt. His suit jacket was hanging from a brass coat rack next to the door. The wall was adorned with various awards, diplomas and photographs of him accompanied by police, other politicians and even a celebrity or two. Everything in the room reminded Sarah that the District Attorney's office was a political appointment, not a legal one.

"Don't just stand there, Ms. Thomas. Come over here and talk to me."

Sarah closed the door and walked softly across the room. She sat down primly, her back straight, feet crossed a the ankle, and tried to look calm as she braced herself for whatever fate lay in wait with the man sitting across from her.

He pulled a folder out of a drawer, opened it, picked up the pictures inside and tossed them in front of Sarah. "Do you know who this is?"

Sarah looked at the gruesome photos of a man who had been shot through the left eye. Thankfully, a cursory glance was enough to tell her that she didn't recognize the man.

"No," she said, averting her eyes.

"Go on and take a look, then," the DA said. "Make sure."

"I'm sure," Sarah said, pushing the photos away.

The DA set them back in the folder and closed it. "Does the name Carl Brandt mean anything to you?"

Sarah's heart skipped a beat. Almost reflexively, she said, "I'm not sure I should answer any questions without counsel present."

"Well, you are a lawyer," he said. "I guess I shouldn't be surprised by that." He leaned back in his chair. "Look," he said. "You're not a suspect in a crime. This isn't an investigation in the usual sense -"

"Is it an investigation in an unusual sense?" Sarah asked.

The DA grunted. "No. But this does pertain to an ongoing investigation. So what you know may be important."

"Related to Haley National?"

The DA eyed her carefully. "Brandt. Do you know who he was?"

"I knew of him. Nathan said we were going to meet him. That he had some information that would lead to bringing Gavin down."

The DA arched a brow. "Really? He said all that?"

"And more," Sarah said.

"How much more?"

"I've given you the gist of it."

The DA stood up and looked out the broad window behind his desk that looked out over the city. "What is Nathan Haley to you, counselor? I don't need any of the details. Just a general idea."

"Nathan is an enigma, sir. Mostly he's a legal adversary over an issue at controversy."

"The foreclosures."

"That's right."

The DA turned around. "Are you guys friends? More?"

Sarah didn't know how to answer because in all honesty, she didn't know. "Not friends, really. Certainly nothing more." A twinge of embarrassment touched the corner of her mouth. "I think he would like it to be more. Maybe. I'm not sure."

"I could pass him a note."

Sarah sat up in her chair and shot him an icy stare. "That was uncalled for, sir."

"I've heard that about you."

"Heard what?"

“You’re feisty.”

“Sir, what does any of this have to do with your investigation?”

“I’m just trying to figure out why one of my confidential informants is dead. That alright with you?”

Sarah felt the blood drain from her face. “Of course, sir. Anything I can do to help.”

“Yeah, we’ve been looking at Haley National for a while. You stirred up a bit of excitement around here. We thought we might be getting a little help from the civil side. Until they benched you.”

“Not my call.”

“I know.” He mulled over his next words for a moment. “Do you know what they were going to talk about at that meeting?”

“Something about portfolio returns. The customer, er, your CI, didn’t like the way the numbers were running.”

“And how were they running?”

“From what I saw, they were all going down.”

“What do you mean from what you saw? If you have anything pertinent to this investigation -“

“Slow down, sir. I was not aware of your investigation, therefore I couldn’t obstruct anything. I’m sorry your guy got shot, but cornering me isn’t going to help.”

“You’re right. What did you see? What do you know?”

“I saw copies of what Nathan said were portfolio returns. All heading down.”

“By the same amount?”

Sarah knit her brow, trying to remember. “I don’t know. Maybe. They were all going down roughly at the same rate, at least.”

The DA nodded. Then he leaned back in his chair and stared at the ceiling for a moment. Sitting back up, he said, “Alright, so now that you know about this, I’m sure you understand that you need to report to me anything interesting you find.”

“About what?”

“Don’t be coy, Ms. Thomas.”

“I’m not. I need to know what I’m looking for so I make sure you get it.”

“Yeah, OK. Anything from the bank that looks like it might be related to money laundering.”

Sarah knit her brow. “I would know nothing about that, sir.”

“Look, just let me know if you come across anything interesting. OK?”

“Alright. Anything else?”

The D.A. took a photo from the same folder and tossed it on the desk. Leaning forward with both elbows on the desk, he said, "You really need to be careful about what you say to people, Sarah. You have no idea who all is listening."

Sarah looked at the photo and gasped when she saw a long-lens shot of her and Elaine at Bernards.

## *AFFIRMATION*

Standing in the lobby of Foley, Crane and Winkler, Sarah found Elaine's name as one of the listed associates on the sixth floor. Fuming, she clenched her fist, whirled around and nearly ran towards the elevator.

She flew out of the elevator on the sixth floor and stopped short at the sight of an ocean of cubicles. She scanned the room, trying to sort out the top of Elaine's head from the rest. Then she spotted her friend standing next to a conference room like a sentry at a gate. Surely this wasn't all she did for that Sak's Fifth wardrobe of hers.

Sarah ran towards her even as people turned their heads to watch her fly between the cubicles towards the conference room.

Elaine didn't even see her coming and shrieked when Sarah grabbed her by the arm, spun her around and threw her against the wall. For the first time in her life, Sarah was thankful for the weight behind her size 16 skirt as she held Elaine fast. She dragged Elaine down the hallway to an empty conference room, opened the door and threw her friend inside.

Closing the door behind her, Sarah grabbed Elaine with both hands and threw her into a chair. "Siddown."

Elaine went pale, stared at Sarah wide-eyed and held her hands in front of her face, trying to protect herself from Sarah's onslaught. In a quivering voice, she said, "They're going to call the police."

"They wouldn't make it past the front door and the lawyers stumbling over each other to ask them for a warrant."

"You can't just come in here -"

"Yeah, I can." When Elaine leapt from her chair and tried to lunge past Sarah to get at the door, Sarah cut her off and threw her back into her chair.

Elaine burst into tears. "What do you want from me?"

Watching her friend splash tears on what was probably a $300 Milano blouse, Sarah realized there was nothing she wanted from Elaine. More precisely, Elaine had nothing left to give Sarah.

"Brandt."

Elaine nodded slowly, her eyes still wide as she looked around the room for a way to escape. "I know."

"Did you know he's dead?"

"Yes."

Sarah pushed herself away from the door and walked over to Elaine, relishing the fact that the woman had to look up at her.

"Do you care?" Sarah asked.

Even after everything that had happened, Elaine managed to look at Sarah with indignation. "Of course I care. I didn't know how deep this went."

"And how deep is that, Elaine?"

"I don't know. Deep enough to get somebody killed."

"And you still came to work this morning."

"These are not the kind of people you want wondering about your loyalty."

"And you wanted me to come work here?" Sarah waved her hand around. "With these 'kind of people'?"

"I didn't know it was this bad. I just thought they were like any other successful law firm. Do what it takes to win." Elaine wiped her nose and sat up. Straightened her blouse. "Besides, we didn't do this. The client did. Or at least that's the theory."

"I trusted you to keep my secrets, Elaine. Not as a lawyer. As my friend."

Elaine shrugged. "I know. And that was your mistake. You knew better. You knew, somewhere down deep, that talking to anybody, even me, was a violation." She looked at the floor. "What did you expect?"

Her voice cracking, Sarah said, "I expected you to be my friend. Why weren't you?"

Elaine lifted her gaze to Sarah. The feeling of vindication was fading now. Sarah had almost grasped the elation of some victory, but all Sarah felt now was the crushing nihilism of disillusionment. There was no meaning, only strategy. No values, just objectives. No ethics, just rules. No victory, just defeat.

Sarah had sworn she wasn't going to cry. She tried to convince herself that Elaine wasn't worth it. And maybe she wasn't, but Sarah couldn't help mourn the sudden death of the only true friendship she had known since she started law school. She felt unsteady now because Elaine had been a pillar. She was smart. She was worldly. She knew things. Sarah had never felt as alone in her life as she did in that moment. And so the tears betrayed her and rolled down her cheek.

"Why?"

Elaine sighed. Her face went blank. There were no more lies left to tell. "Because I'm a lawyer. I was doing my job, just like you. I was looking out for my client's best interests."

Sarah stared at her, unable to believe what she was hearing. Not because Elaine had the audacity to justify her betrayal with client interest. But because she sincerely believed she was right. And maybe she was.

"I've heard about that a lot lately."

"What?" Elaine asked.

"Client's best interests."

"It's more than just words on paper, Sarah. You have to mean it."

Sarah shook her head, wondering if Elaine understood what she had sacrificed. Or maybe their friendship didn't mean that much to her in the first place. But Sarah couldn't believe that. Not after everything they had been through together.

"Some things are more important then being a good lawyer." Elaine just stared at her blankly. *Like what?*

"Being a good lawyer takes sacrifice, Sarah. You'll understand soon enough that we are the same." Sarah wondered if Elaine was actually trying to convince her that they could still be friends. That what had happened was all just part of the game. That it wasn't personal. It was just business.

"I'm not talking about being a lawyer."

"What is it then?"

Sarah studied Elaine for a moment longer. The expensive clothes. The fancy apartment. The money.

The power.

Sarah spoke calmly now, as if she had found the top of a mountain where she didn't have to shout any more. "I'm talking about trust." Sarah leaned her back against the door. "And that I was right." She looked up at the ceiling, willing her eyes to stay dry. Looking back at Elaine, she said, "You *are* all the same. You. Gavin." Sarah huffed out a sigh and her voice cracked when she spoke next. "Nathan." Sarah looked at the floor. "You're all the same." She closed her eyes. "I can't trust any of you."

## *THE SWORD OF JUSTICE*

Sarah sat behind the defendant's table, waiting for the judge to emerge from his chambers. She saw Calhoun out of the corner of her eye, but she didn't acknowledge him. The truth was she was embarrassed. She had gyrated and pontificated and in the end had just made herself look silly. Sarah had come to realize that the system wasn't anything like she had hoped. It wasn't built for crusaders.

She glanced over her shoulder to survey the gallery. She was surprised to see Nathan there. At first, she wondered if he had come to gloat. Then she realized that Calhoun was probably going to call him to the stand to provide false testimony that she couldn't refute because the judge had shut the door on the one piece of evidence that could save her. Curiously, Nathan was looking at her with the never-let-you-down look that even now brought her a sense of comfort. It was an empty gesture, though. Within the next half hour, he would seal the fate of her clients.

Then she noticed the DA sitting in the back row, staring stoically at the well.

The judge emerged from his chambers and trotted up the steps to the bench. He surveyed the room with typical impatience and then he froze. His expression changed. He was surprised and almost looked like he didn't know what he was supposed to do. His eyes were locked in place. Sarah looked over her shoulder and saw the DA nod, just once. For some reason, she took real pleasure in seeing the judge knocked off balance by the unexpected appearance of the DA in the gallery. Her case had just drawn the kind of attention that made things like docket schedules and settlement-peddling suddenly unimportant.

The judge sat down, looked at Calhoun and said, "Counselor, you may begin."

Calhoun stood up and said, “Your honor, plaintiff calls Nathan Haley.” Sarah shook her head, forcing herself to stare at the front of the judge’s bench.

Nathan strode into the well as the bailiff held the bar open for him. He stopped next to Sarah’s table and waited. Unable to stand it any longer, she forced herself to look at him. Just as she caught his eye, his expression morphed into that same look she had come to miss. That faint smile. Those soft eyes. All to say, *You can count on me.* What she didn’t understand was why he bothered. Why was he still lying to her? What sadistic pleasure did he get from that?

They didn’t tell her about this part in law school. The part where you couldn’t trust anybody. The part where you had to harden your heart and forever walk through life shackled by the loneliness of looking out for your client and nothing else. If she could have gotten away with it, she would have slapped him across the face so everybody could see. She tried to tell herself it was because of what he had done to her clients. But deep down she knew there was more to it than that. It was personal, no matter how hard she wished it weren’t.

And he must have seen all this in her face because his expression changed again and she saw a wisp of sadness in his eyes just before he dropped a thick folder on the table. She eyed it carefully, but didn’t open it. Thick black letters were scrawled across the front: *Trust Me*. Sarah scoffed and shook her head. They never gave up, did they?

Nathan solemnly took his oath and sat down at the witness stand. Sarah looked at the judge for a moment, wondering if he could see the question in her eyes. *Why are we here? Why are we wasting our time when everybody, including you, has made up their minds?*

Then she heard Calhoun’s voice, almost as if it were a recording, as if it were simply a narration of the predetermined verdict. “Mr. Haley, could you please state your position at Haley National?”

“I’m the Vice President.”

“And as such, do your responsibilities include oversight of loans and other debt instruments issued by the bank?”

“They do.”

Calhoun picked up a stack of loan agreements and handed them to Nathan. “Are these the mortgage agreements for Sunfield Farms?”

Nathan quickly thumbed through the pages. “Yes.”

“And are any of the debtors behind on their payments?”

“Yes.”

Sarah rolled her eyes. It no longer felt like a formality. It felt like they were just mocking her now. Even though she knew they had to go through it all so they could say her clients had been relieved of their property by due process.

"How many, sir?"

"All of them."

Calhoun picked up another stack of papers. "Are these the foreclosures you filed with this court in response to these defaults?"

Sarah realized she could have objected. Calhoun was drawing a conclusion. But it would have been silly and the judge would have hated her even more than he already did. There was no point, so she remained silent.

"Yes."

"And were these properly served on the debtors?"

"Yes."

Calhoun collected the paperwork from Nathan, shrugged and walked back to his table. He practically threw the words over his shoulder because nobody expected Sarah to do anything. "Your witness."

She looked at Nathan, who was staring back, even now, with his never-let-you-down look. Then he nodded once and pointed at the folder he had put on her table.

Only because she couldn't help her curiosity and she couldn't overlook any possible scrap of evidence, Sarah opened the folder. The room seemed to still to dead silence as she stared at the contents. She had to clear her throat as a bubble of euphoria welled up inside her and then flooded through her body. She whipped her head up, staring at Nathan wide-eyed.

The euphoria dissipated and now Sarah wanted to cry. She really did. She wanted to call a timeout. She wanted to run away and hide in her grandmother's kitchen where she could smell the gingerbread cookies baking in her gas-fired oven.

Mostly, and for reasons she couldn't explain, Sarah wanted to take it all back.

"I don't want to do this," she said. Everybody heard it.

"You have to," Nathan said.

Her lip quivered slightly and she cleared her throat again. "Why?"

Now he smiled with that same look in his eye that had been there from the beginning. "You know why."

"Is there a problem?" she heard the judge ask. Sarah shot him an icy stare, but his face wasn't hard with impatience this time. Realizing that he was self-conscious in the presence of the DA, she eased her expression.

"No your honor."

She picked up the folder and took it over to Calhoun. When he saw the contents, he shook his head and said, "no way." Then, looking at the judge,

Sarah said, “May we approach?” The judge, almost looking embarrassed now, beckoned them to the bench.

“What is it?” he asked quietly. Sarah handed him the folder, amused by the shocked look on the judge’s face when he saw the contents.

“You ruled on this, your honor,” Calhoun said. “This is not admissible.”

“You also said they’re not prejudicial, your honor,” Sarah said. “And now that they’re here, the issue of a fraudulent contract is front and center. 3501.3 has just arrived.”

“You already ruled on this, your honor,” Calhoun said again, clinging to his only hope of saving his case, now lying in ruins on the bench.

“Yeah, I know,” the judge said. “But I don’t have time to deal with this when it comes back at me on appeal.” He actually smiled at Sarah when he said, “And knowing counsel, that’s exactly what will happen. Now that it’s here, I have to admit it. Step back.”

Sarah walked solemnly back to her table. She should have been elated with her victory, but once again noting the DA’s presence in the gallery, Sarah could only feel the growing heaviness in her chest.. Because she knew where this was going now.

She looked at Nathan and then asked the judge, “May I approach the witness, your honor?” It was a formality that wasn’t really necessary, but the trappings of tradition and protocol were the only reassurance she had left to hold on to. And she could only do it once, so she did it by the book to make sure it would stick. Then, too, there was always the chance that he might say no. But she wasn’t so lucky.

“Proceed,” the judge said.

Sarah hung her head and picked up the folder. Sniffing a hard breath, she forced herself to walk over to Nathan and hand him the folder. “Mr. Haley, could you please tell the court what you are holding in your hand there?”

Nathan cleared his throat and stuck out his chin. Looking Sarah in the eye, he said, “These are the original loan applications for the current residents of Sunfield Farms.”

“And who approved these applications? Whose signature is at the bottom there?”

“I did. I signed these.”

She held up her finger and walked quickly over to the plaintiff’s table. Pointing at the stack of loan agreements, she asked Calhoun, “May I?”

Calhoun smiled and let out a feint grunt. “Be my guest.”

Handing the stack to Nathan, she asked, “Can you tell the court what these are?”

“These are copies of the mortgage agreements we submitted to your office in response to a motion for discovery.”

"Is there any difference between these agreements and the original applications you are holding in your hand now?"

"Yes."

Her voice was broken, almost inaudible now. It didn't feel like she was talking. It felt more like somebody else was using her voice, that what she said next was beyond her control. "And please tell the court what that difference is."

Sarah flinched when the judge cut in. "You don't have to answer that, Mr. Haley. You have a right to consult counsel prior to answering that question. Or deciding not to answer it at all."

Looking at the judge, Sarah nodded slowly. For once, they were in agreement. "He's right," she said. She took a step closer to the stand, staring into Nathan's eyes. "You don't have to answer that."

Nathan smiled and his expression softened. Sarah's heart sank because she knew he was going to say it anyway. "The credit scores on the original applications are inflated. They don't correspond to the actual credit scores annotated in the agreements, which are much lower."

Sarah eyed him very carefully now. He had asked her to trust him. She could only hope that he meant it. Because she had to trust him implicitly if she was going to ask her next question. She didn't know the answer. She didn't even know if he knew the answer. All she knew was this was her only chance to get it on record. And it had to be on record.

"And why would you assign fraudulent credit scores to these applications?"

At this, Calhoun jumped up. "Objection, fraud has not been established." Sarah smiled coyly at her opponent, relishing his being on the defensive for a change.

"I'll rephrase. Why would you annotate credit scores that differ from those provided by the credit bureaus?"

"Objection. Speculation."

"Your honor," Sarah said. "Mr. Haley is an expert in matters pertaining to banks, their practices, requirements and regulations. His enumeration of the common causes for such a discrepancy should be considered expert testimony."

The judge almost looked as if he were smiling at her in admiration when he said, "I'll allow it."

She nodded once and turned back to Nathan. "Mr. Haley. Why?"

Nathan shook his head. "I became aware of the bank trying to sell the loans to an unsuspecting buyer. These inflated credit scores would make the deal more attractive."

"What did you do when you learned of this?"

"I warned the buyer. And he walked away from the deal."

"And that's when the bank foreclosed the loans?"

"That's right."

"Why would they do that? It's my understanding that banks don't like short sales."

"Objection. Counsel is testifying."

The judge shot Calhoun an impatient glance. "Sit down, Mr. Calhoun. Overruled."

"Mr. Haley?" Sarah said.

"On that I can only speculate." He paused as they both looked at Calhoun, who just stared at the space in front of him, fuming. "In a situation like this, houses go to auction. Somebody with enough money could pick up a lot of houses at a very cheap price."

"And based on your observation of other anomalies at the bank, what could this type of transaction signify?"

Nathan smiled and narrowed his eyes.

"It would be one way of funneling financial transactions to a creditor in a way that isn't accounted for in the conventional sense."

"What would be a simpler way of putting that, Mr. Haley?"

Nathan looked to the side for a moment, then back at Sarah. "It's one way of laundering money."

Sarah nodded. Turning to the judge, she said, "You're honor, I move immediately for injunctive relief pending issuance of complaints pursuant to 3501.3"

Even before Calhoun had a chance to say anything, the judge said, "So ordered." Then, turning to Nathan, his voice almost apologetic, he said, "You may step down, Mr. Haley."

Before he had even finished standing up, two policemen were marching towards the well. Nathan looked at Sarah with a resigned smile as they stepped past the bar and cuffed his hands. In a futile gesture to minimize his humiliation, they quietly escorted him out of the courtroom in silence. They would read him his rights and the charges against him once they were in the hallway.

She watched them walk through the gallery to the metal door in the rear. All eyes were on Nathan and she couldn't imagine the humiliation he must have felt in that moment. She looked on helplessly, knowing that she had done that. She had beaten a powerful man in a suit who had victimized those who didn't have the power to stand up to him. Except that wasn't really the truth. Because Nathan Haley was also a victim. A hostage, really, to a legacy that he could no longer save.

She caught the DA's eye and he acknowledged her with a nod. She tried to burn it into his consciousness with just the look in her eye. *You better catch the people behind this*.

As Nathan and his escorts disappeared into the hall and the door closed behind them, Sarah turned and looked at the bench. The judge's face was slack and his eyes already looked off into the distance. Sarah waited for the elation at her victory. She waited for the wash of vindication to flow through her. But all that happened was the judge smacking the strike plate with his gavel and saying, "Next case." Justice had been done.

All Sarah felt was an aching emptiness inside as she realized she would never again go to that greasy little diner to see Nathan's steady gaze that told her he would never let her down. Ever. And then he would take a sip of coffee. And this time she would be careful not to say anything that would bring a wounded look to his eye so he had to look down, pull himself together and then look back up as if she hadn't hurt him. She would make sure he didn't have to look away ever again.

Sarah sat down behind the defendant's table, cradled her face in her hands and let the tears weep from her eyes.

Because that day would never come.

## *TO SEE*

Sarah sniffed in a long breath, lifted her head and shook her hands. She stood up, still reeling from the shock of it all. Then felt a tug at her sleeve. She turned to see an amiable man with soft eyes and a polite smile. He seemed to recognize her even though she had no idea who he was.

"Jerry Westland," he said, holding out his hand. Still half in a daze, Sarah shook his hand meekly and asked, "And you are?"

"A friend." She dropped her hand to her side, waiting for him to explain. "I need to show you something," he said. "I can meet you there, if it would make you more comfortable."

"Meet you where?"

"The Knife and Palette."

Sarah nodded slowly. She didn't know who this man was or why he was asking her to come to Nathan's gallery. But she realized the Knife and Palette was the only part of Nathan that she could still touch. They had taken him away, but somewhere in that gallery, she knew she would feel a part of him they couldn't take away.

"That's OK. We can go together," she said

Jerry nodded and then offered his arm to escort Sarah out of the courtroom.

Sarah was surprised to see him having to unlock the door to Nathan's gallery during normal operating hours. She was more surprised to see that the receptionist was not sitting at her desk. When she saw the darkness beyond the inside door leading into the gallery proper, she stopped in her tracks.

"What's going on?" she asked.

Jerry smiled. “He wanted it this way. The gallery is closed today. And it will be closed on this day every year from now on.” He opened the door and gestured inside. “But not to you.”

“You first,” she said, eying him carefully.

“As you wish.”

Sarah followed him inside and the only thing she could see was a lone pool of light splashing against a covered painting and the floor just beneath it.

He stopped, turned to her and said, “You should know, he doesn’t do this.”

“Doesn’t do what?”

“He has never exhibited his work before.”

“Who?”

“Nathan. You knew he paints, yes?”

Staring at the cover over the painting, Sarah spoke in a distant voice. “And he never shows his work.” She stopped and looked at him. “Except to you. Right?”

Jerry smiled, stepped over to the covered painting and said, “It’s his best work. By far.” Then he pulled off the covering.

Sarah gasped and for a moment felt as if she were looking into a mirror.

A woman cloaked in a robe with a frayed hem and wide belt stood on a grass-covered cliff with a throng of faceless people behind her and mountains towering over them all. She held a tattered book in one hand and hoisted a shimmering sword over her head with the other. The woman had fair skin with freckles peppering her nose and flowing red hair bannered by the wind. She wasn’t a slender woman, but rather stood with the subtle sweep of feminine curves beneath her robe that Sarah had never allowed herself to see. She looked out from the painting with a distant forsaken look in her green eyes. Sarah had never noticed it before, but now realized that was how she looked. Forlorn. Wounded. But never broken.

That was what Nathan saw. Not the avenging lawyer fighting the rich and powerful. Not the heavy girl who worried too much about her skirt size. Not the suspicious woman who had spent a lifetime teaching herself not to trust men like Nathan.

Her. He saw *her*.

Sarah’s knees buckled and she slumped to the floor, holding her hand against the painting. She could feel the wind blustering against her face. She could smell the wet granite that descended to the rocky shoreline below. She could see the distant gray horizon across a stormy sea. Facing them all, she stood fast. Because the people behind her had no sword. And she did.

The painting explained everything she was. Everything she had ever done. Everything she would ever do.

And just behind her painted self, apart from the rest, a lone man was walking away.

Sarah wept as she read the inscription on the brass plate beneath the painting and then closed her eyes.

*Pretium non reddere - The price we pay*

# *JUSTICE*

The trial had gone quickly. But it had been moved to another jurisdiction to escape the infamy that had rippled through the town. Sarah hadn't been able to find out where it was, so she hadn't been able to even visit Nathan in jail. Or at whatever undisclosed location he was waiting in after posting bail. He had simply disappeared.

The sentencing had been just as swift: two years. Sarah shrugged, trying to minimize the impact. His career in banking was over, certainly. But two years wasn't the end of the world. A person could get through two years of anything. Law school, even, she thought, laughing to herself. Yeah, two years was bearable.

She still worked in the shabby office that Nathan had rented for her. The only difference now were the letters painted on the window: *Sarah Thomas, Attorney at Law*. She hadn't decided on a specialty yet and instead let her reputation for catering to those who couldn't afford a "real lawyer" bring her business. It was enough business, in fact, that she needed help and she smiled as she watched Maureen pouring over case files and tapping through LexisNexis on her laptop. They never talked about it, but with the exception of court appearances, Sarah let Maureen be a lawyer again.

Sitting at her desk, Sarah splayed her hand over the newspaper - another penchant of hers for tangible words. She recognized the picture of Devorah. That lush Cheshire smile and piercing arrogant gaze beneath the bangs that just touched her brow. The man in the next picture she didn't recognize. The caption identified him as Gavin Neilsen.

Sarah had held on to the newspaper for months because she knew he would want to see this.  And every day, she had looked at it and then put it away because she didn't know if she could bear to see him crushed by the agony of shame that a man like Nathan Haley would have to bear as he sat in prison.  Nor did she know what he would think of her now that the reality of what she had done had set in. He had been brave in the courtroom. But now that he was all but forgotten and his life was all but over, she doubted he would feel the same way about it. He would hate her now. And she didn't know if she could face that.

But she wondered what he thought of what she had done since he'd gone away. He probably already knew. And he probably knew how to send a letter. She had never received one, so he must not have wanted to say anything.

She closed her eyes, acknowledging it all, as she had every day since the trial. She had crushed Nathan Haley and he would never want to see her again.

But she wanted him to know.

She missed him.

She didn't know how he would take it. She didn't know if he was ready. Or if he ever would be. But Sarah had decided that, for once in his life, Nathan Haley needed somebody to look at him the way he had looked her: with a never-let-you-down expression that let him know that no matter what, she would be there. Even if he turned away and never talked to her again. She would be there.

Sarah made up her mind. It was time.

## *COUNT ON ME*

An hour later, Sarah stood rigidly in a windowless room and grimaced as a hand ran up her leg, cold against her bare skin. She glared at the female guard who moved her hand precisely and with formality. Sarah wanted to ask her, *was this really necessary?*

The guard stood up, snapped off the latex glove and did her best to look stern. "You can proceed."

Sarah left the room and waited for a guard to escort her into the labyrinth of the minimum security prison where Nathan had been incarcerated.

They had kept her purse, her phone and her shoes. They had let her take in two items to give to him, nothing more. Sarah resented all of that, but she reminded herself of those words which she learned in her first year of law school. The words that a lot of people overlooked and didn't understand. Due process. If you wrote the law correctly, you could take everything a person had.

The sound of the door opening echoed through a brightly lit room with white cinder block walls and white graphite tiles with black speckles crushed by years of constant waxing and buffing.

He was sitting slumped over a steel table. The guard walked her over to him and let her sit down on the attached circular steel bench. "You have thirty minutes," he said.

"Thank you." The guard stepped back, but she knew he was watching.

She studied Nathan for a while. Dressed in khaki pants, a light brown shirt with no tie and steel-toed work shoes, he sat looking down at his hands clasped on the table.

"Look at me," she said. He let out a sigh and raised his head. Her heart fluttered with a dull ache when she saw his eyes. Her breath caught and she felt her mouth fall open. Those steady, you-can-count-on-me eyes that had never changed from the first day they met.

Until now. That look was gone and all she could see now was the humiliation and shame. Not because of what had happened to his bank. Not because he was in prison. But because he thought he had let her down. She smiled softly and took his hand. He winced at her touch, but didn't pull away.

And now she berated herself for not coming sooner. For making him wait so long.

"I liked the painting," she whispered.

He glanced at her briefly and then looked back down at the table.

She grimaced and felt a sudden urge to slap him and tell him to pull it together. She had come to realize that she was impatient that way - she expected people to be as strong as she was. But then again, she had never been in prison. She might not have been as strong as she liked to believe.

So, she was gentle. "It made me cry, Nathan." She could see the remnants of a smile barely stretch the corners of his mouth. "You're the only person who's ever seen me for who I really am." She gently stroked his hand with her thumb, sighing in relief when he didn't pull away. "Even I didn't know."

Nathan looked up for a moment and nodded. Then he looked back down at the table.

"Did you get the money from Jerry?" he asked. "From the gallery sale?"

Sarah smiled and ducked her head down to look into his eyes. Smiling as gently as she could, she asked, "You want to come up here and talk to me for a minute?"

Nathan lifted his head but he couldn't look at her for more than a second. His gaze wandered around the room as she continued to stroke his hand with her thumb and then reached out so she was now holding his hand with both of hers.

"Yes." She arched a brow. "Do you want to ask me what I did with it?"

Nathan's gaze locked on hers and he tilted his head. He wanted to know. But he couldn't ask.

"I bought them," she said.

His mouth fell open slightly, as if he were going to speak. Then he looked away for a moment. He opened his mouth again. This time, he said, "Bought what?"

"Sunfield Farms."

His eyes locked on hers and she saw the faintest wisp of the Nathan she had known from what seemed like a different lifetime now.

His eyes glistening, he asked in a ragged whisper, "How many?"

Sarah smiled and clutched his hand tighter. "All of them."

His gaze followed her hand as she reached down to the bench and picked up the newspaper she had brought with her. She turned it over and pointed at the story of how the bank had gone into receivership and how she had bought up every tract for ten cents on the dollar. "See?"

Nathan placed his hand on the newspaper, turned it around and started reading. He looked like a little boy who had found a lost dog when he looked at her and asked, "You did this?"

"Yes."

"They're OK?"

"Yes."

"Nobody had to leave?"

"No." She leaned in a little and shrugged playfully. "I make them pay the property taxes, until we can work out a payment plan that makes sense. You know. No deadbeats." From the faint glint in his eye, she understood the words now. What they really meant. Why they were important. "Give a working man a break," she said, "and you'll have a customer for life."

Nathan's eyes welled up now and he closed them. He tried to turn away, but she put her hand on his chin and turned his face towards her.

"Let me see," she said.

Nathan sniffed in hard, but a lone tear squeezed out from his eye to trickle down his cheek. "It lives."

"There's more," she said. She picked up the newspaper, opened it to the other story she wanted to show him and placed it in front of him, tapping Devorah's picture.

Nathan read the story of how both she and Gavin were found in a motel room, each with a bullet through their left eye.

"She didn't deserve that," he whispered.

Sarah grunted. Knitting her brow, she asked, "Are you sure about that?"

Looking up at her, Nathan said, "She wasn't strong like you. All she needed was somebody to tell her she didn't need to be anybody but herself."

Sarah arched a brow. "Sounds like you had a little torch for her maybe?"

She felt a weight lift off her shoulders when he chuckled at her remark. "No," he said. Looking down to watch Sarah gently stroking his hand with her thumb, he said, "There's only one woman who's ever made me feel that way."

Sarah tried her best to look the way he did when he had put himself out there, just to be battered by an unkind word from her. She didn't know if she could take it like he would, but she knew what it meant now to want somebody to understand you. To be kind to you. Because they were the only one you needed.

"But two years is a long time," he said. Sarah felt her heart breaking when he pulled his hand away. She understood now why he had to look down, pull himself together and then try again when she had hurt him. But she wouldn't look away. She knew he could see the hurt in her eyes. And she didn't want to hide it from him.

"Two years isn't so bad," she said.

"It's bad enough."

"Oh come on, now. This place is a country club. You can deal with this for two years."

"Not that," he said. "I can't ask you to wait that long, Sarah." He looked at her with a resolve she had never seen before. A resolve she never wanted to see again. A resolve she knew she had to break. "I don't want you to come back here," he said.

"Why would you say that? Are you embarrassed for me to see you like this?"

"No," he said. "I mean, yes, I'm embarrassed. But that's not why."

"Why then?"

His back stiffened and she heard an edge of frustration in his voice. "Because I don't want this for you. The last thing you need in your life is a convicted felon."

"Lawyers are involved with convicted felons on a daily basis." She hoped he could see the teasing look in her eye. Feel the tenderness of her touch as she reached out to retake his hand. He had seen her before, surely he could see her now.

"It's a real world, Sarah."

"So you've told me."

"Dammit, Sarah, I'm serious."

"Be honest then."

She knew this could be the moment that it would actually end. Because he had to see the truth. He had to face it. And then he had to let it go because it wasn't the truth after all.

"Fine." Looking at her with the expression of a man who had already said goodbye, he said, "Walking away from you was the hardest thing I've ever done in my life. But I came to terms with that." Again, he looked at her thumb gently stroking his hand. "Sooner or later, the reality of all this will hit you. And I don't think I can take the sight of you walking away from me."

Sarah nodded somberly. "Do you still paint?" she asked.

Nathan slowly nodded. She could tell he was frustrated by her refusing to hear him. "Sometimes," he said.

She reached down to the bench and picked up the other item she had been allowed to bring with her.

She laid his rumpled coffee-stained shirt on the table and gently placed his hand on it. “Then here’s something you can wear.”

She tried to smile, but then he pulled his hand away. Her lip trembled as she waited for him to say something. Anything that told her she wasn’t losing him. Anything that told her he could let go of the lie that he was trying to convince himself was the truth.

“Will you think of me when you wear it?”

His breath shuddered and another tear rolled down his face. “You know I will,” he whispered.

“Good,” she said. “Now, look at me.”

She waited for him to look at her. And then she waited some more.

Finally, she asked, “What will you do if I never come back, Nathan? What if this is the last time you ever see me? What if this really is it?” Sarah took a deep breath before she asked her next question, hoping she knew the answer, even if he didn’t. “Is that what you want?”

Finally, he looked at her, his mouth sagging in a frown, his eyes red from the tears. “No. But I know that’s what will happen.”

“You’re right,” she said. “It *is* a real world.” She took his hand again, refusing to let go when he tried to pull it back. “And the man in my life is a convicted felon. In prison.” She pulled his hand closer. “But that’s not what makes him who he is. What makes him who he is is that he’s a man who trusts people. A man who sacrificed his life to build a town. A man who would never let you down. A man who was taken advantage of by people who used all of that against him as a weapon.”

Sarah felt her eyes watering and then a tear splashed over the brim. “A man who deserved better than what I gave him.” She clutched his hand even tighter and bowed her head. “I’m sorry.”

Then she felt his hand on her cheek, brushing her hair back and wiping away the tears. Looking back up at him, she saw that same look she had seen on the very first day. The look of a man who could see into her soul and see her wounds. A man who wished he could take them away.

Didn’t he know? He already had.

“I’ll never leave you, Nathan.”

They were quiet after that. And Sarah let an image fill her mind, like a movie she had seen in a different lifetime. She and Nathan sat on the floor in front of a fireplace while snow fell in an ever-growing blanket of white that covered the roof, hung from the rafters and waited quietly for young feet to tromp through it as giggles and shouts were swallowed up by the muffled winter air.

She hoped he saw the same thing. She hoped he knew that he had to hold on. She hoped he could hold on to her words and her promise.

And then she realized those words weren't enough.

But these were.

"Because I love you too."

~ THE END ~

www.ingramcontent.com/pod-product-compliance
Lightning Source LLC
Chambersburg PA
CBHW060804310726
48980CB00002B/232

* 9 7 9 8 9 9 2 8 7 4 8 0 8 *